From the Darkest Corner

Eric Rountree

Self-published by Faltarego.com
Halifax, Nova Scotia, Canada

From the Darkest Corner is a work of fiction. All names, places, and incidents are either products of the author's imagination or used fictitiously.

Copyright © 2013 by Eric Rountree

Self-published by Faltarego.com
Halifax, Nova Scotia, Canada

www.faltarego.com

ISBN: 978-0-9937528-1-0

Design and layout by Eric Rountree

Cover design by Eric Rountree

For Jen, Arrin, Tanya, and Sam,
who knew what happened,
and welcomed me back;

and for all my theatre friends,
who help keep me sane.

We fill the dark spaces with light.

From the Darkest Corner

Acknowledgements

It's almost become a cliché, but it's true: Writing is a solitary pursuit.

There are ways to make it less so, such as joining a writing group or teaming up with a writing buddy, but in the end, it's you yourself who is responsible for your output, and it's you yourself who has to be happy with the end result before sending it out into the world.

While the writing can be solitary, the production of a book is much less so. For this novel, I've opted to go the self-publishing route, and I've forgone the traditional hiring of an editor and graphic designer, but there are still numerous good and kind folks out there who have helped me get this thing to the state that it's in. I definitely did not do this in a vacuum.

First of all, this story started life as a NaNoWriMo project. That's National Novel Writing Month, for those of you unfamiliar with the nickname. Every November, hundreds of thousands of writers sign up for this month-long event, in which your goal is to write a fifty-thousand-word novel in thirty days. I signed up in 2009 *(What? Four years ago?)* and managed to spew out just over sixty-six-thousand words in twenty-eight days. I was rightly proud of this novel's first draft. And my finger muscles.

My motivation to do the thirty-day challenge came in large part from the fact that I'd just come out of a really bad period, mental-health-wise. I wanted to latch onto something that would show me tangible progress and results so I could reassure myself that, yes, it is possible to come back from the depths and do something grand.

So, my thanks go out to Chris Baty and the organizers of NaNoWriMo. Their annual event has grown into an annual tidal wave of words, and the online writerly community it's engendered can only help to reduce that solitariness I mentioned above.

I want to extend a particular and hearty "Thank You" to some extremely kind folks who helped me shape the text of this story into something better than it was. They are my beta-readers, and they rock.

So, thank you Marc Trottier, Krista Mallory, Lindsay E. Smith, and Ashley Laffin for giving me feedback, suggestions, points to ponder, and typo alerts. Marc in particular gets a double (nay, triple) helping of gratitude and warm fuzzies, as he read this beast about five times and provided me with some excellent ideas to shape the story. I consider Marc more than just a beta reader. Dammit, he's my editor.

Many artists, artisans, and craftspeople have someone in their lives they consider a mentor. Someone who showed them the ropes, pointed them in the right direction, and helped them take their basic skills to the next level. My mentor is a wonderful lady by the name of Amy Friedman. Though she now lives in California, I was fortunate enough to intersect lives with her when we both lived in Kingston, Ontario. Amy was teaching creative writing courses at St. Lawrence College at a time when I had the urge to explore my writing a bit more deeply. I ended up taking three classes from her, and she taught me more about the craft of writing than I'd learned in all the years before. She truly helped shape me into the writer I am today, and for that I am most deeply grateful. Thank you, Amy.

There's another group of people I'd like to mention, an online writing community with whom I wrote both silly and serious stuff, and they too have helped to shape my writing. The site is called Protagonize.com, and its founder, Nick Bouton, has created something truly magical. The ability to write collaborative fiction is unusual in writing sites, and in this case, it's worked wonderfully. What better way to get to know other writers than to add chapters to their stuff and let them add chapters to yours?

I'd like to thank my Protagonize friends Asheyna, Tricia Heighway, Ana Cristina Simon, Ganga Narayanan, Marc Aucoin, Gwen the Irish Pianist, Chris McIntyre, Andrew and Laura Montgomery-Hurrell, Rachel Farrell, Roseanna Cooke, Robyn Brees, Gilchrist Muir, Trevor and Angela Kozma, Charlotte Perry, Jillian Hewitt, April Schoffstall, Megan Little, and Seldom Polis for their support, feedback, friendship, and frequent craziness. My experience on Protagonize has been both fun and formative.

A huge thank-you also to my brother Scott, not only for reading the manuscript and giving me feedback, but for being my brother. We've been through a lot together, we know each other better than most people know each other, and we have a lot of really silly in-jokes that continue to amuse us to this day. Scott is my favorite male person in the known universe. Here's lookin' at you, Bro. Much love.

Finally, I'd like to thank the most supportive, patient, loving, talented, and amazing person in the whole wide world: My wife Vanessa. She's stood by me through thick and thin, supported my creative dreams, and demanded that I be who I am. She also read the manuscript for this novel and gave me feedback and encouragement. There aren't enough words in the Oxford, Webster, and Random House dictionaries combined to sufficiently thank someone for that kind of steadfast love and support. Vanessa is a miracle with a huge heart. Thank you, my love. You're the best.

But wait a minute. There's one more thank-you to be offered here, and that is to you, the person reading these words right now. Thank you for taking a chance on a writer you've probably never heard of before. Thank you for entering this world I've created and going on an adventure with me. I think you'll find it entertaining, and you might even have a laugh or two.

I hope you enjoy it.

Thanks again to all.

—Eric Rountree
(Halifax, Nova Scotia, November 7th, 2013)

From the Darkest Corner

"Darkness cannot drive out darkness: only light can do that. Hate cannot drive out hate: only love can do that."
—Martin Luther King Jr., *A Testament of Hope: The Essential Writings and Speeches*

"We can easily forgive a child who is afraid of the dark; the real tragedy of life is when men are afraid of the light."
—Plato

"Stars, hide your fires; Let not light see my black and deep desires."
—William Shakespeare, *Macbeth*

"Light thinks it travels faster than anything, but it is wrong. No matter how fast light travels, it finds the darkness has always got there first, and is waiting for it."
—Terry Pratchett, *Reaper Man*

"Time takes it all whether you want it to or not, time takes it all. Time bares it away, and in the end there is only darkness. Sometimes we find others in that darkness, and sometimes we lose them there again."
—Stephen King

Prologue

(Friday, 10:14 A.M.)

On the stove, near the front edge, between the two front burners, stood two small glass bowls. Behind them stood a large clear-plastic drinking glass with swirls of orange and yellow on it. In one of the bowls sat ten small orange tablets. In the second bowl were twenty blue gel-caps. The drinking glass held the contents of an entire pint of rum.

The packaging for the pills was nowhere to be seen. Neither was the bottle that had contained the rum. I had already taken all such cardboard and plastic items down the street and deposited them in the garbage can next to the bus shelter. I was now prepared. I was undressed and had turned down the bed. All that remained was to ingest the items that stood before me on the top of the stove.

I picked up a couple of the orange pills. They were Gravol tablets, intended to prevent me from throwing up any of the other materials I was about to consume. I put three of them in my mouth and picked up the tumbler. Not being much of a drinker, I imagined that downing an entire pint of rum was going to be an unpleasant experience. So I braced myself and took a swig to wash down the Gravol. The rum was strong, but reasonably smooth. I knew Captain Morgan wouldn't let me down.

By the time I'd swallowed all ten Gravol tablets, my lips were beginning to feel a bit numb from the ministrations of The Captain. I knew I'd better get cracking on the blue gel-caps before the Gravol started making me groggy. So I grabbed two of them (they were larger than the Gravol tablets) and swallowed them with a swig of the rum. The gel-caps went down easily enough, but the rum was beginning to get a bit worrisome.

So I sped up the process a bit.

By the time I had downed all of the Sleep-Eze-D gel-caps, I couldn't feel my lips anymore. Captain Morgan had trod upon them with his hob-nail boots and was now chuckling on the other side of the room. I'd thought he'd've been nicer to me than that. After all, I did drink an entire pint of his good wares.

So much for brand choice.

As quickly as I could, I rinsed out both bowls and the tumbler in the kitchen sink and placed them in the dish rack. I then moved from the kitchen into the bedroom, where I lay my naked body down upon the bed and proceeded to wait for the effects of the substances to kick in.

I didn't expect to be conscious for too much longer.

As I lay there, staring at the rather ugly light fixture attached to the ceiling, I found myself recollecting some of the things that had gotten me to this point. I'd had thoughts of suicide before, but I'd always managed to avoid acting upon them. I'd even taken myself down to the emergency department a couple of times over the past three years, because I'd felt that I might do something, and a certain percentage of my brain was sensible enough to at least seek out help and prevent the minority members from staging a coup and tipping the whole thing on its end.

Not so this time. The final straw had been placed upon the spine of the dromedary.

Having dealt with depression in one form or another for most of my adult life, I'd long since resigned myself to the necessity of keeping a close eye on myself at all times. I'd always been easily discouraged in my endeavours and regularly felt the weight of the world sinking down upon me. I often wondered how other people could possibly be happy and productive, and I wondered what the point of doing things really was. If I wasn't happy now, and I couldn't foresee myself being happy in the future, then, really, what was the point of pursuing anything?

I'd once read an interesting definition of depression. The author had called it "chronic grief", and I'd always found that description an apt one. *Weltschmerz* was another fine name for it. Those Germans, they've always had a knack for names. This one literally means "world sadness" and is often used to describe the depression that arises from comparing the world as it is to a hypothetical, idealized world. Or a past world. Or a possible future world. Or any world, really. I'd even have taken an alternate dimension at that point.

Good word, *weltschmerz*. Highly applicable in my situation.

I'd never been one to indulge in drugs and alcohol, as they invariably had unfortunate effects on me, so I immersed myself in sex and pop culture to help numb my pain. The sex was occasional, but the pop culture was constant. I also did a fair to decent job of keeping people at arms length through judicious application of sarcasm.

Somewhere amidst all of that, I'd miraculously managed to find myself in a romantic relationship. No one had been more surprised than I. Gillian was a fashion designer who I'd met through Derek Simmons, the drummer from the band in which I had been known to participate. Derek's girlfriend Tina was studying design, and I was introduced to both her and Gillian at a party one frosty winter evening.

I'd found Gillian to be an absolute delight. She was smart, hip, and sharp as a tack. Her wit was quick and biting, and she didn't suffer fools gladly. She was also petite, slim, and gorgeous. We hit it off right from the get-go.

Little had I known what perils awaited me. The emotional sugar-high I experienced from being around Gillian led me to believe that maybe life wasn't so horribly soul-crushing after all, and in an effort to both understand and alleviate my condition, I'd begun to study up on brain chemistry, a pursuit which ultimately led me to purchasing nutritional supplements via the internet. This, in turn, led me to buying into the business and trying to make a buck or two selling them myself.

What I'd failed to realize that was that all sugar-highs come to an end, and they're usually followed by a thundering crash. Gillian was supportive of my endeavours, and my feelings for her hadn't changed, but the old ways were coming back, and I found myself more and more mired in the mind muck that had sabotaged me for so long.

Long and the short of it: I lost a great deal of money, and I eventually lost Gillian as well.

Which brings us back to today, the pills, the rum, and the ugly light fixture on the ceiling.

As I lay there, thinking about the failed business and the failed relationship, I began to feel a chill, so I put my legs under the covers and pulled the sheet up over my stomach. I shifted my position and stared at the ceiling light again for a while.

No drowsiness yet. How long did it take for this stuff to kick in, anyway?

I tried to imagine what my friends and family might think of what I was doing, but then I stopped that train of thought in its tracks, partly because it was depressing, and I was depressed enough as it was, but mostly because thinking about family was almost as bad as thinking about money and relationships. One parent was dead, and the other was com-pletely out to lunch, and I had unresolved issued about both. Letting my thoughts go in that direction was not the wisest of notions.

I decided to focus instead upon the reasons for my taking this dire action, the bitterness I held in my heart towards so many people and things, and that gave me some amount of solace. It gave me the strength to continue in my certainty that this was indeed the only thing I could now do.

Gillian was gone from my life, as was a bunch of my money. It wasn't bad enough that I was a failed writer, a failed musician, and a failed son. I was now able to add to that list failed businessman and failed lover. I was running out of things to fail at, and I figured I might as well cut my losses and move to another country.

The undiscovered country.

As more of a *Star Trek* fan than a Shakespeare fan, I actually man-aged a chuckle at that. I imagined it would be one of the last things I would do.

Chapter One

I regained consciousness in an entirely different type of lighting. When I'd lain down, the sun had been coming in at an angle through the bedroom window. Now there was a different sort of light, much harsher and directly above me. The quality of the air was different as well, and there were noises.

I looked around, confused, even dazed, but I recognized that I was in a hospital.

Someone in pale green stood to my left. She was adjusting something. I glanced to my right and found someone else there. My eyes were not completely focused, but I recognized who it was immediately.

Lydia.

I opened my mouth, but nothing came out.

"Don't try to talk," the pale green woman said.

Lydia squeezed my right hand as I looked at her again. I tried to squeeze back, but my muscles were weak, and I was only able to move my fingers a small amount.

"Thank God," Lydia muttered.

"Can you hear me, Mister Richmond?" the green-clad woman asked.

I nodded and grunted.

"Do you know where you are?"

I looked around. After a moment, I nodded.

"Okay. You rest easy. I'll be back in a few minutes, okay?"

I watched as the woman left the alcove, pulling the curtain closed behind her. I sighed, allowed my neck to relax completely, and plunked my head back down on the pillow. After a moment, I turned to look at Lydia again. She had tears in her eyes and was looking at me like someone who had just been struck in the solar plexus by their best friend.

Well, I supposed that was true, metaphorically.

"You bastard," she spat. "What the fuck did you think you were doing?"

Even in my brain-fogged state, I marvelled at how her English accent made harsh words like "bastard" sound almost musical. I opted not to say that out loud, however, as I possessed sufficient active brain cells to know that she would not react favorably. At least not at this particular moment.

I had no idea *what* to say to her, in fact, or, indeed, if I were physically capable of saying anything at all. I wondered idly if there'd been a tube down my throat. There was an odd burning sensation on the right-hand side whenever I swallowed, so I figured that *something* had been stuck down there.

They'd pumped my stomach, I imagined.

Lydia wiped her eyes with her sleeve and sniffled. "Do you have any idea what it was like for me to find you there like that?"

There was a rumble and a click inside my head as a piece of the jigsaw puzzle settled into place. So *that* was how I'd ended up here. The knowledge was at once confusing, comforting, and annoying. Of course she still had a key to my apartment. She'd always had a key, for as long as I'd known her. Gillian had never been able to understand that. But then, she'd never really understood the kind of relationship that Lydia and I had. In point of fact, I don't think Lydia or I ever really understood it, either. But it was there, it had always been there, and I imagined, now that I was conscious again and mostly aware of the world around me, that it would continue to be there for some time to come.

The curtain flapped, and the pale green woman returned to my left-hand bedside. I imagined that she was a nurse, so I decided to think of her that way, which was a lot less cumbersome than thinking of her as a green-clad person.

"Mister Richmond?" she asked.

I grunted in reply.

"My name's Sophie. I'm one of the nurses here in the ER. How are you feeling?"

I interpreted that question as an invitation to try out my vocal cords. So I did.

"Ummm… groggy… I guess…" I said.

I found my words strangely distant from the thoughts that were supposedly forming them. It almost felt like I was instructing someone else to speak on my behalf. I had the strongest urge to carefully think out each word before uttering it.

She nodded. "That's not surprising. Do you remember what you did?"

I frowned. "Groggy…" I said, "not stupid."

She snorted. I couldn't tell if it was a chuckle, a rebuke, or some combination of the two.

"Well, I think that answers the question of your alertness." She glanced at Lydia with an expression that seemed to combine sympathy with bemusement.

"He's always been like that," Lydia said.

Sophie turned to the monitors at the head of the bed and reached for something I couldn't see. She then checked the tube that was attached to the back of my left hand and absently adjusted the blanket, which was tucked up underneath my armpits.

I began to recognize the smells associated with hospitals, the antiseptic scent that was draped like a shroud over the underlying tang of disease and death. I'd visited so many hospitals in my time, seen so much disease, so much suffering, that my gut began to churn instinctively as the memories associated with the smells cascaded through my brain.

I put my head back again and sighed.

"This wasn't supposed to happen," I said.

♦

I drifted in and out of sleep over the next couple of hours. Lydia continued to hold my hand and curse me under her breath for much of that time, but for the most part, I was blissfully unaware of it. When I woke up fully, she was gone. If she'd told me that she was leaving, I had no recollection of it. This was unsurprising, as I had little recollection of anything that had occurred since I'd found myself in the hospital.

My mind was still a fog bank, and my muscles were still quite weak. I'd obviously taken enough product to render me seriously inert, but not enough to actually extinguish my life force.

I had mixed feelings about that at this particular moment.

As I stared at the ceiling, trying to derive some entertainment value from the sound of my own breathing, the curtain flapped open again, and a doctor walked in. I assumed he was a doctor, at any rate. He had the requisite white lab coat and a stethoscope draped around his neck. That was pretty much all the evidence I needed.

He was tall and dark-skinned. He looked Middle-Eastern, but I wasn't able to narrow it down any further than that. He pulled a chair over and sat down at the left-hand side of my bed.

"I'm Doctor Choudra," he said.

That sounded like an Indian name to me, but I still wasn't one-hundred-percent sure. I wondered idly why it even mattered.

"How are you feeling?" the doctor asked.

I let out a long breath. "Well, let's see," I said. "You can start with stupid. And add a bit of guilty. Um, a little dash of discouraged. A pinch of depressed. And a heaping tablespoon of tired."

His mouth made a funny quivering movement. He might have been trying to suppress a smile, or he might have had something spicy for lunch. It was hard to say.

"You seem to have your faculties about you," the doctor said. "Have you tried sitting up yet?"

"Yes, and with disastrous results," I replied. "I'm not trying that again any time soon."

"What happened?"

"Well, my head began to fall off, for one thing," I said. "And then my stomach tried to get off the bed by itself."

"I understand." He looked at the clipboard on his lap, the one that all physicians everywhere are required by law to carry with them at all times lest they look unofficial, and flipped a couple of pages.

"Can you tell me what your intent was this morning?" he asked.

I stared at him, incredulous. "My intent?" He nodded. "My intent was to kill myself."

"Can you tell me how you set about doing this?"

I described to him my meticulous sequence of steps, how I had gone to two separate drug stores so I wouldn't be seen buying both Gravol and Sleep-Eze-D at the same time. How I'd purchased the rum after getting the Gravol, but before going to the second drugstore for the sleepers. How I had put the pills into bowls and the booze into a glass and had deposited the packaging in the garbage can down the street. How I had pulled back the bedclothes and stripped off my own. It was thorough, and it was done with all deliberation.

"And why did you go to such lengths?" he asked.

"What do you mean?"

"You took the time and trouble to purchase all of these things at separate stores, and then you took all of the packaging and placed it in a garbage can down the street. What was the reason for this?"

"I'm a neat freak."

He made a clucking sound as he jotted something else down. "I don't think you're being honest with me."

"Fine." I put my head back and looked at the ceiling. "I hadn't really thought much about it, truth be told. I guess I just didn't want to leave any garbage behind. I just wanted to be dead, and didn't want to make it any easier to people to figure out how."

This response seemed to appease him, as he now made a much more positive-sounding subvocalization. He flipped through the clipboard pages again, making additional notes, his officialdom veritably filling the alcove with each ripple of the paper. After a moment, he looked back up at me, his expression somber.

"We're looking at this as quite a serious suicide attempt," he said. "And given that, I don't think we're ready to send you home just yet. I'm recommending admitting you to our Short Stay Unit upstairs, where one of our psychiatrists can evaluate your situation more thoroughly."

I let my head slump back again. For a brief moment, I allowed myself to fantasize that I might actually get some help.

"All right," I said.

He stood up. "Good. For now, just rest. Okay?"

"Okay."

He gave me a final quick once-over, then turned away from me, picking up the chair and replacing it in the spot he'd found it. I watched the back of his white coat as he exited the alcove and closed the curtain behind him.

I put my head back on the pillow and tuned in once again to the Breathing Channel. I returned my attention to the ceiling and tried to let my brain simply rest. This was something I'd always found challenging, as my mind had a tendency to run at a gazillion miles an hour, thinking about all manner of things all the time, but in my drug-induced haze, I found it a bit easier to just shut off.

I shifted a bit in the bed to make myself a little more comfortable, then settled back again. As I reached behind me to adjust the pillow, I thought I saw a slight movement out of the corner of my eye. I turned my head to the right and was surprised to see a woman standing there, looking at some piece of equipment or other.

"Hello," I said.

She turned, seemingly startled. She looked at me with wide eyes.

She didn't appear to belong there. She was wearing a long coat that covered her from neck to ankles, and boots of a type that I had never seen before.

"Who are you?" I asked.

She frowned and took a step towards me.

A noise drew my attention back to the alcove's curtain. A man in blue hospital attire entered and stepped over to the equipment at the head of the bed.

"Hello," he said with a nod.

I grunted and nodded, and then turned back to my right to face my strange visitor.

Except she was no longer standing there. She was gone.

I sighed and dropped my head to the pillow again.

Apparently hallucinations were now part of my mental landscape.

Chapter Two

(Friday, 5:09 P.M.)

A short time after my visit from the doctor and my visitation from the oddly-dressed woman, Sophie re-entered the alcove.

"How are you doing, Mister Richmond?" she asked pleasantly.

"Fine," I replied, looking past her to the small space between the curtain and the wall.

She arched an eyebrow. "Is everything all right?"

I nodded and settled myself in the bed again. "Yeah. I'm fine."

She glanced back at the curtain. "Were you expecting to see something out there?"

I shook my head. "No."

She crossed her arms. "I'm not convinced of that."

I sighed. It was my own fault for staring out into the corridor. I should have been more discreet.

"You didn't happen to see a woman in a long coat leave here a few minutes ago, did you?" I asked.

It was worth a shot. I knew there was no way the strange woman could have left without my seeing her, but I didn't trust my brain or my senses much at all at the moment. And the staff probably all thought I was crazy anyway.

Sophie frowned. "No." She shook her head. "I didn't see anyone like that."

I nodded. "Didn't think so."

She narrowed her eyes. "Was someone in here?"

I shrugged. "Could have been."

"Could have been?"

"I might have imagined it."

Sophie moved a step closer and looked intently at me. "Can you tell me what you saw?"

I was beginning to feel foolish now. The more I thought about it, the more certain I was that I had imagined the whole thing. Still, I figured I'd better answer her.

"I saw this strange woman standing over there by the supply cabinet. She looked like something out of the 1940s. It was the damnedest thing. She seemed surprised that I could even see her."

"Did she say anything to you?"

"No. She just stared at me with really wide eyes. She looked absolutely dumbfounded."

"And she left just before I came in?"

"Well, that's the thing. I didn't actually see her leave. I was distracted for a second, because one of your technicians came in to check on the gear here, and when I looked back, she was gone."

Sophie chewed on her lower lip for a moment. "I'll let security know. They'll be able to spot her on the surveillance tapes. If you don't know her, and she obviously isn't staff, then she has no business being in here."

I stared at the curtain and let my eyes unfocus. "Like I said, I probably just imagined it."

She unfolded her arms and let out a breath. "Well, Mister Richmond, if you're doubting your senses, that's a good sign that they're probably working just fine."

I refocused and looked up at her. "Are you a psychologist now too?"

She smiled. "Why, no, Mister Richmond. I'm just a li'l ole ER nurse."

I sighed and let my head slump back on the pillow. "Well, then. Leave the diagnoses to the shrinks, why don't you?"

The corner of her mouth twitched up just a touch. "Did you hear that?"

I let my eyes slide over towards her. "Hear what?"

"That clanking sound."

I frowned at her. "What clanking sound?"

"That was the sound of your armor going back up."

I rolled my eyes. "Very poetic."

"You can protect yourself too much, you know."

"Really."

Sophie nodded. "Some people protect themselves so fiercely and for so long that they forget how to interact with other people."

"I thought we just established that you're not a shrink."

"No, but I'm a keen observer of the human condition."

I rolled my eyes. "Well, then, you should become a writer. Maybe you'll have better luck with it than I've had."

"Maybe you just need to drop your armor when you're observing."

I glared at her. "Back to that again, eh? Well, as it happens, I interact with other people just fine, thank you very much. You can check my report card. It says 'plays well with others.' It's all there in black and white."

"I see."

"You see what?"

"I see that it's going to take a lot to get anywhere with you."

"And where, exactly, do you want to get?"

I winced as I realized how easily that question could have been misinterpreted.

"That sounded really sleazy," I said. "For once in my life, I actually didn't mean it that way."

She cocked an eyebrow and wrung her mouth.

"I'll let it go this one time," she said, a slightly amused tone finding its way to the surface, "and to answer your question, I want to get to the point where I know you're safe to be left alone."

I had no response to that. I was out of steam.

She stepped towards the curtain, pausing for a moment to look back at me. "I'll check on you again in a little while." With another slight smile, she was gone.

If the sleazy part of my brain had been fully awake, I knew that it would be wondering if I could get anywhere with *her*.

But that would be wrong.

♦

After a few more rounds of "Count the Dots on the Ceiling"—interspersed with fits of dozing—the curtain flapped open again. I turned my head to find Lydia returning to my bedside. She moved slowly, almost uncertainly. Her expression was unreadable, her eyes sunken and hooded.

"Somebody's dog die?" I asked.

She paused halfway to the bed, her eyebrows angling towards each other like pieces of a broken rain gutter. She flared her nostrils and then stomped to the far wall, grabbing a chair—perhaps the same one upon which Doctor Choudra and his clipboard had lately sat—and dragging it back to the bed. The legs made a screeching, vibrating sound as they scratched and scraped their way towards me. Finally, she picked the chair

13

up, slammed it onto the floor, and dropped into it.

"What the fuck is your problem?" she said. Her rain-gutter eyebrows and narrow eyes filled in the gaps that her rasping voice missed.

"My problem? I'm in a hospital, I'm bored, and people keep checking on my to see if I'm still alive."

"Yeah? Well, whose fault is that?"

I glared at her. "Shut up."

She closed her eyes and put her head in her hands. "My God, you're even worse now than you were before. Do you know that? Ten times worse."

"Ten times worse than what?"

She raised her head to look at me again. Tears were running down her face now. "Ten times worse than the acerbic, sarcastic, arsehole bastard I used to sleep with two years ago."

I nodded. "Right. Yeah. Make this all about you, why don't we?"

Something stung my cheek. I blinked several times, hard. My eyes were watering, and the left side of my face was burning. I put my hand up to my cheek and looked up at Lydia, who had suddenly shifted from sitting to standing. The whole thing had taken no more than a second.

"What the fuck did you do that for?"

She was nearly panting. "Because you deserve it, you selfish prick. I'm not making this about me. You're making it all about you. You weren't getting just every little thing you wanted in your life, so you decided you'd show the world a thing or two and bloody well kill yourself. And never mind about anyone else who might actually give a goddamn about you. Oh, no, don't give them a thought. Just do the most dramatic thing you can think of, and grab all the attention for yourself while you slide on out the door. You bastard!"

The curtain rustled again, and Sophie stepped in, frown at the ready.

"Is there a problem in here?" she asked.

Lydia looked back at her and let her shoulders slump. "No. No problem." She sat down in the chair again. "No problem."

Sophie's gaze turned towards me, her eyebrows arching nearly to the shape of question marks. I just shook my head.

"All right," she said after a pause. "But I'm going to have to ask you to keep your voices down. And Mister Richmond, you need your rest. I don't want you getting excited. Okay?"

"Yeah. Okay." I nodded.

Sophie retreated, but not without giving us one more disapproving look.

"They can be so territorial," I said to Lydia.

"Jesus. Fuck. There you go again." Her voice was still pitched a bit too high for my liking, and it had also taken on a slightly reedy quality and just a hint of vibrato.

I shrugged. "What?"

"The sarcasm. The meanness. You're a curmudgeon."

"A curmudgeon?"

She shook her head again. "No. Not a curmudgeon. That's not nearly strong enough a word. It's nearly cute. There must be a word that's worse than that."

"I'm sure there is. You've already dusted off 'asshole' and 'bastard'. Doesn't that about cover it?"

"No. Not nearly. Not by half. You're worse than any of those words. I'm going to need a thesaurus when I get home. Because I can't properly describe you right now."

I stared at her for a moment. "Am I really that bad?"

She snorted. "Worse."

I sucked on my bottom lip for a moment and breathed heavily through my nose. She crossed her arms and glared accusingly at me. We stayed like that for several minutes.

Finally, I slumped back down and gazed at the ceiling again.

"You guys still rehearsing?" I asked.

She smirked slightly. "Well, I guess I won *that* round."

"What are you talking about?"

"Changing the subject is the last refuge of the vanquished."

I turned my head to look at her. "That's terribly poetic, but I actually, really want to know. Are you and Derek and Winston still rehearsing?"

She sighed. "How are we supposed to rehearse without our guitarist?"

I waved the comment away. "You don't need me to have a rehearsal. There's a ton of guys you could get to fill in."

"Jesus, Jack. You wrote half the songs. How is anyone else supposed to know them?"

"There's this little concept called sheet music. A lot of musicians can read it."

"You know what I'm talking about."

"Yes, I know what you're talking about. But those songs are crap, and you know it."

"Oh, Christ. Here we go. If you're not coming off all superior, you're putting down your own natural-born talents. What is it with you?"

"I am a riddle, wrapped in a mystery, rolled in peanut butter and icing sugar."

"Can you be serious even for a minute?"

I thought about that for a second. "No. I don't think so."

She crossed her arms and legs and turned half away from me. "I don't know why I put up with you."

"You put up with me because I'm entertaining and I know how to give you a screaming orgasm."

"You shut the fuck up." She looked back at the curtain to make sure no one else was there. "That's way over, Jack. You know damn well that's waaaaay over. Long gone. You understand me?"

"Well, I don't know why else you'd hang around. It's certainly not my sparkling personality."

She stood up. "I'm going home. I don't have to sit here and take this."

I leveled my gaze at her. "No. You're right. You don't."

She took a step closer to the bed and leaned down towards me. "Grow up, Jack. Just fucking grow up."

She straightened, regarded me for a moment, then turned on her heel and stormed out.

♦

The Short Stay Unit that Doctor Choudra had mentioned was full, so they kept me overnight in my emergency room bed. It was narrower than a standard bed, which made turning on my side a bit of a challenge, but I managed to sleep fairly well. The fact that I had filled my body with Gravol and sleeping pills probably didn't hurt either. The place was cold, but I had always found coolness conducive to slumber, and there was a fairly decent blanket covering me, so I didn't freeze.

Within minutes of my awakening, one of the nurses, a tall, burly woman with curly blonde hair, came in to check on me.

"Let's see if you're any steadier on your feet today," she said as she took down the bed's left-hand rail and helped me to a sitting position.

My excursions out of the bed the previous day had been short, comical, and for the express purpose of reaching the toilet, which was in a small, communal bathroom a few feet down the hall outside my curtained alcove. My legs had been shaky at best, wobbly for the most part, and at times completely unable to support my weight. I'd had no idea what over-the-counter drugs were capable of doing to the human body. That gap in my education was now rapidly being filled in, though admittedly I could have found a less life-threatening way of absorbing that knowledge.

This time, things were a bit better. I still wasn't the most sure-footed creature on God's green Earth, but I managed to make my way to the bathroom with a minimum of assistance. Once I was safely tucked inside the closet-shaped space, the nurse—whom I had in a very short time come to think of as Brünnhilde—closed the door and stepped away.

Dealing with a johnny shirt, whose slit is at the back, and pulling down a pair of undershorts whilst trying to sit on a very low toilet and tottering on wobbly legs is an exercise I did not particularly enjoy, and it is one I am not eager to repeat. The sound my buttocks made as they veritably slammed onto the cold plastic of the toilet seat was not unlike the sound effect many motion pictures use when one person punches another in the face. I would have laughed if I hadn't nearly toppled off the toilet with my bad aim.

Finally, dignity more or less intact, I raised myself from the throne of absolute power, hiked my shorts back up to where they belonged, allowed the curtains to close over my backside, and reached for the doorknob.

With the impeccable timing only a highly trained medical professional could possibly possess, Brünnhilde reappeared the moment I opened the bathroom door. In my mind, she wore a helmet and brandished a broadsword, Wagner's *Ride of the Valyries* sounding as she tromped towards me.

"Are you up for a little walk?" she asked.

I was disappointed. It was such an un-warrior-like thing to say.

I sighed. "That's not really a question, is it? Or if it is, I imagine it's of the rhetorical variety."

"Well, Mister Richmond, it appears as if your wit has survived intact. Let's work on the manners now, shall we?"

It occurred to me to wonder if there was anyone in this godforsaken place who didn't have at least a brown belt in verbal sparring. I began to give up hope that I'd ever meet any medical professionals whom I could reduce to tears with my rough and unpleasant demeanour. These people were no fun at all.

She took me firmly by the elbow, turned me around, and began to lead me away from the alcove. I took a dejected glance back. Narrow the bed might have been, but I knew I would miss it.

"Where are we going?" I asked.

"Down to Psychiatric Emergency Services. You'll have a short interview with the team there before being admitted to Short Stay."

"You mean I won't get to harass you any more?"

"No, Mister Richmond. We're just going to have to get used to life without you."

It was at that moment that I noticed the woman in the long, anachronistic coat again. She was standing beside one of the nurses' stations, staring intently at me. She looked just as perplexed as when I had seen her the day before.

I raised my free hand and pointed in her direction. "That's her. The woman who was by my bed yesterday."

The nurse paused. "Where?"

I waggled my pointing hand emphatically. "Right there."

She looked in the direction I was pointing, then back at me, a questioning expression on her face. "I don't see anyone, Mister Richmond."

I glanced incredulously at her. "What do you mean? She's right—" I looked back at the spot.

The woman was nowhere to be seen.

Chapter Three

Brünnhilde escorted me down the hall to a small room with three chairs and a small, low table, all of which were fastened to the floor with strands of steel cable. Except for those few items of furniture and a small surveillance camera in the ceiling, the room was bare.

I sat in one of the chairs and looked around. There was absolutely nothing to see. The walls were painted a very pleasant soft yellow, just a few shades paler than the center of a Cadbury Easter Cream Egg, I thought, but the pleasantness of the hue would serve to amuse my wandering attention for maybe three seconds at best.

As I pondered the strangeness of my environment, it occurred to me why it was so spare. This was an area where they dealt with psychologically troubled individuals, and they probably wanted to minimize the possibility of anyone injuring themselves. I supposed that if I wanted to, I could stand up on one of the chairs and allow myself to crash to the floor, but I imagined that whoever was monitoring the surveillance camera would likely put a kibosh on any such efforts.

I quickly ran out of things to look at in the room, so my mind turned inwards again. I didn't want to rehash the events of the last twenty-four hours, so I decided to ruminate about the strange woman in the long retro coat. So far I had seen her twice, and I still had absolutely no idea who she was or what she wanted. She'd been in my alcove, looking at the equipment, and then she'd been at one of the nurses' stations just outside, staring intently at me.

If it hadn't been for the fact that I'd just tried to kill myself, I probably would have found this disturbing.

The thing that had struck me most about the woman was the way she managed to look completely incongruous. There was nothing about her that fit into the hospital environment. She looked like she ought to be stepping off a trolley car in 1940s San Francisco, not skulking around a hospital in Halifax in 2004.

It was puzzling. But at least it gave me something to think about. Well, for a few minutes, anyway.

I was soon reduced to looking at the pattern on the ceiling and wondering if it held any deeper meaning. Losing patience with that, I tried to figure out how many strands were in the steel cables that held the chairs and table to the floor. Then I imagined what it must look like in the control room where all the images from all the little surveillance cameras appeared on a bank of little security monitors.

For some odd reason, this made me start thinking about The X-Files and how I only needed to buy seasons eight and nine to complete my DVD collection of the series. I was in no hurry, though. The last two seasons were weird, what with David Duchovny leaving the show and Robert Patrick coming on board as Agent Doggett. I could wait.

By the time I began to consider scraping a bit of paint off the wall and tasting it, the door opened and a young woman entered.

"Mister Richmond?" she said. The tentative tone of her voice must have been a reaction to my facial expression, which was itself a reaction to the fact that I'd nearly forgotten that other humans existed.

"Yes. At least I was when I was brought in here."

Her mouth wavered in some kind of half-smile that was aborted in its second trimester. She took one of the remaining chairs and crossed her legs. She had the standard-issue clipboard.

"I'm Doctor Taggart, one of the residents here in the psychiatric emergency department."

"Nice to meet you. I guess what I did would be considered a psychiatric emergency."

She nodded and killed yet another half-smile before it came to term. "It's good to see you still have your sense of humor," she said. "Not everyone in your situation manages that."

"Well, not everyone is the kind of ascerbic asshole that I've recently been told I am."

She frowned slightly, looking at me askance with her head slightly cocked. "I'm not sure that kind of self-reference is going to prove very helpful to you, Mister Richmond."

I shrugged. "Well, it beats moaning and whining by a country mile," I said.

She jotted a couple things down on her clipboard. I suddenly imagined a clipboard factory in India exploding, leaving the medical profession in tatters.

"Doctor Fingle is our staff psychiatrist. He'll be in to speak with you in a few minutes."

"I see. You're just here to prep me, are you? Make sure I'm well basted before he comes in to turn the skewer?"

She drew her mouth into a tight line. "I understand this has been a difficult time for you, Mister Richmond. But I really don't think this constant sarcasm is going to help either you or us. We want to help you, but we can't if you won't let us."

I sighed. "I already had the solution. I think I just miscalculated the dosage."

She nodded. "Yes. Well, I'd hoped you'd think better of that by now."

"Putting me in a small yellow room is not exactly the best way to convince me to go on living."

She looked down at her clipboard and then back up at me again. She regarded me with an expression I couldn't quite read.

After a moment, she stood. "Doctor Fingle will be in to see you in a few minutes."

"Can't wait."

She turned and left the room, closing the door behind her.

I nodded to myself, folded my hands across my abdomen, and awaited my next victim.

♦

Doctor Fingle was a pasty-faced, mealy-mouthed man with about as much charm as a bowl of cold, congealing Cream of Wheat. He entered the room, shook my hand limply, sat down in the chair opposite me, crossed his long, gangly legs, and rubbed his stubbly chin.

"So, Mister Richmond," he said, his voice low and quiet, his syllables long and stretched. "Doctor Taggart tells me you're not adjusting well to your situation."

"And which situation would that be, now?" I asked.

He stared at me a moment, blinking slowly. He reminded me of a frog waiting for a fly to pass by. "I mean," he said at last, "Finding yourself in the hospital, alive."

"Oh," I said. "That."

Fingle blinked at me a few more times. "Yes," he said. "You're not coping well with it."

"Well," I said. "I'm breathing okay. That part's been no problem. The blinking, that's working pretty well, too, though I must say I don't do it with quite the style that you do. The legs are a bit off, but I'm sure that's just the drugs. Hearing, smelling, tasting, all pretty much in working order. All in all, I'd say I'm coping pretty well."

He looked at me again. His eyelids seemed to move even more slowly this time. It was as if I were watching a scene on a DVD and playing it frame by frame. Again, I thought of *The X-Files*.

"I think," Fingle said after a moment, "that admission to the Short Stay Unit is a good idea. I'd like to have Doctor Navarro evaluate your case. We need to break through some of these barriers you're putting up."

I leaned forward and put my elbows on my knees. This would have looked very undignified to anyone standing behind me, because of the opening in the back of the johnny shirt, but fortunately it was just him and me.

"I just want to say," I murmured, leaning even closer to him, "that I don't like you very much at all. I think you're insincere and that you actually hate your job. You come off as someone who regards patients like little products coming along a conveyor belt. And I don't want to be a part of your little brain cell factory. Am I making myself clear?"

He blinked again, but this time he frowned as well. I wondered if anyone had ever spoken to him like that before. He'd probably dealt with violent patients, drugged out patients, hysterical patients, and, well, flat-out crazy patients, but I doubted he'd ever come across anyone quite like me.

But then, delusions of uniqueness had always been part of my mental landscape.

"I'm glad you're able to express yourself so honestly, Mister Richmond."

I slumped back into my chair. Score one for the cold Cream of Wheat.

Damn.

♦

A security guard, who introduced himself as Phil, led me out of the "interrogation room", as I now thought of it, and offered me a seat in the little waiting area just outside. Apparently, my bed up in the Short Stay Unit wasn't ready yet, so I had to cool my heels there. Phil disappeared for a moment, returning with a brown bag breakfast, which he promptly handed to me.

The meal consisted of a slab of scrambled egg on a croissant, a small packet of cheese, an apple juice, and a yogurt. I thought the croissant was a nice touch. It was soggy, but still, at least they'd tried for that international flavor.

"It shouldn't be too long now," Phil said. He was tall and angular with a long jaw and short grey hair. He had a kind face, but his posture and body language spoke of long weariness.

"I think I've seen enough of these yellow walls to last me well into my dotage," I said.

He smiled and nodded. "A lot of waiting goes on in here."

I took a bite of the soggy croissant and nodded back at him. "Yup. I reckon."

Phil stepped back into the corridor and resumed what I took to be his normal post, which consisted of a high bar-style chair with a circular rung about eight inches off the ground for one's feet. It was a most unglamorous office.

I took another bite of the croissant, and as I chewed, I began to notice that my hands were shaking. I put the sandwich down and tried to steady myself. My breathing was shallow, I suddenly realized, and I could feel a thin line of sweat forming on my brow.

"You okay, Mister Richmond?" Phil asked with a slight frown.

I nodded. "Just a bit jumpy, I think."

I looked around at my environment. I knew what was happening, and I was powerless to stop it. My brain and body were beginning to fully realize just what I'd tried to do to myself.

And for that, I blamed the breakfast sandwich.

I'd been surrounded by all things institutional since the moment I'd regained consciousness in the emergency room, but none of those accoutrements had really pierced my veil of self-denial. It was a simple sandwich, handed to me by a security guard, that had flipped the final switch.

Perhaps it was the fact that I was being guarded that had gotten through to me. Or perhaps it was the sogginess of the croissant that had spoken so eloquently of the institution in which I now sat. Either way, I was awakening to the severity of my situation, and I was not taking well to that awakening.

Emotions were now finding their way out from the cracks and crevices in which they'd been hiding, and my body was reacting in a most unpleasant manner. I had the shakes and the sweats, and the knot in the pit of my stomach was threatening to twist itself around my spinal cord.

I balled my fists, hung my head, and tried to breathe normally. It didn't help. I could feel my jaw tightening and my mind racing.

My world had already been falling apart. Now I'd just made it worse.

"Damn it!" I shouted, pounding my fists on the arms of the chair.

The world seemed to slow for a moment as I realized I'd just shouted aloud in a public place and hammered a piece of furniture with my tightly wound hands. As I raised my head to look meekly up at Phil, I could see ripples in the air around me. I frowned and squinted.

I started thinking about scenes from *The Matrix*. Which was one hell of a lot better than thinking about the chunk of my sanity I was now losing.

A woman in blue scrubs was passing by Phil's chair just at that moment, and as the ripples moved out from me, she appeared to lose her balance.

Instantly, my perception of time returned to normal, and the woman tottered right into Phil, nearly knocking him off his perch.

"Whoa. Easy there," he said to her. "You all right?"

The woman regained her equilibrium, and Phil put a hand on her shoulder to steady her.

"I'm so sorry," she said. "It was the weirdest thing. It felt like a gust of wind plowed into me."

He shook his head. "That's not the weirdest thing I've heard today," he said.

She smiled and continued on her way. Phil just shook his head and smiled. He glanced in at me and raised his eyebrows.

He appeared not to have noticed my outburst.

I found that even more unsettling than the ripples.

Chapter Four

A short time later, a nurse arrived with a wheelchair to take me up to the sixth floor, where, I was told, the Short Stay Unit was housed. Why I needed a wheelchair was beyond me. I wasn't in tip top shape, but I was ambulatory and fully capable of walking on my own. I didn't argue, however. Policy was policy, I supposed, and besides, my limbs were still a bit rubbery.

So, I bid Phil a fair *adieu* and was on my way.

I didn't know anything about the Short Stay Unit. I'd never even heard of the place before yesterday, but then, I reasoned, I'd never been in a mental health crisis before. So, it was a whole new world, one about which I would soon be educated.

The elevator doors opened with a sickening ping that only a very aged chime could emit, and the nurse wheeled me aboard. The elevator arrived at the sixth floor to an equally half-hearted musical accompaniment, and my silent companion pushed my carriage over the threshold and down the hall to a security door. She waved her ID badge over a small black unit on the door frame, and the lock opened with a definitive click. She opened the door, wheeled me through, and took me down another hall.

The Short Stay Unit was a large room with a nurse's station and five curtained alcoves, each containing a bed, a bedside table, a wheeled tray table, and a chair. My chauffeur rolled me into the last one on the right, nearest the nurse's station, helped me out of the chair and onto the edge of the bed, and swiftly abandoned me. Almost immediately I was joined by a rather corpulent woman in tan slacks, a pale green blouse, and a white cardigan.

"Mister Richmond?" she intoned cheerily.

"Mmm-hmmm." I was so sick of meeting new staff members that I couldn't even muster a wry retort.

"My name's Norma," she said. "I'm one of the nurses here at Short

Stay. This will be your room for the next few days. Do you have any belongings with you?"

I shook my head. I'd asked for nothing, and Lydia had offered to bring me nothing. I didn't care. I just wanted to lie down.

"Well, there's a phone over by the lounge area if you need to call anyone to bring you anything."

"Okay."

"For starters, you'll only be able to leave the unit for a half hour at a time, and only if you're accompanied by someone. Once we're sure you're not going to try and harm yourself again, you'll be able to go out by yourself, and for a bit longer than half an hour. Any questions about that?"

Harm. Harm myself. What a lovely euphemism that was. What a wonderful way it had of letting you hide from the truth. It almost sounded whimsical.

"No. That sounds fine."

"There are newspapers and magazines on the table in the lounge area. There are also a few games and puzzles on the shelf over there."

I nodded.

"There's also a shower over by the bathroom. This is just a suggestion," she said, "but you'll probably feel a lot more human if you get cleaned up."

"Is that your subtle way of telling me that I smell bad?"

"Believe me," she said. "I've experienced worse."

I allowed myself a slight smile at that, then nodded again.

"Lunch will be coming up at about twelve-thirty. Do you have any special dietary needs?"

I looked up at her. "I just require food," I said.

She smiled. "Well, we have that. Tea or coffee?"

"Coffee," I said. "Black. Strong."

"I'll see what I can do."

With that, she turned and exited, closing the curtain behind her with a swish.

I sat on the bed for a moment, my hands dangling between my knees, and gradually came to the conclusion that Norma was probably right. If I wanted to feel better—which I did—then getting some sense of normalcy back into my day might be a good start.

I stood and stepped towards the curtain. I wasn't thrilled about the notion of moving through the common area, because I had no idea who else was staying in the unit or what their troubles might be.

I took a deep breath, screwed my courage to the sticking place, and ventured forth.

A man who looked to be in his sixties was currently occupying one of the comfy chairs, staring at the television. He was a short, round fellow with a few stray hairs protruding from his otherwise bald head. He appeared unaware of my presence as I moved towards the bathroom.

He was staring vacantly at what I presumed to be a replay of the previous evening's *Tonight Show with Jay Leno*. As I sidled over to the laundry rack to grab a towel and a face cloth, I noted that Jay's guest of the moment was Teri Hatcher. She was talking about her new series, *Desperate Housewives*, which was due to premiere a week from Sunday.

I sighed. To me, geek that I was, she would always be Lois Lane. I swore to myself for the millionth time, that if they ever released *Lois and Clark* on DVD, I would be in line for it. With bells on.

I took the towel and face cloth and trod over to the shower room, taking a last glance at the lovely Ms. Hatcher on the screen before I flicked on the light switch and shut the door.

♦

I felt considerably more human when I emerged some minutes later, despite the fact that I still had nothing to wear other than the johnny shirt and my underwear. With such limited wardrobe, I did not feel in the least like remaining in a public area. There were robes and slippers available, but they didn't really make the scenario any more appealing. I still would have felt like a sick person sitting around in a hospital lounge area. I was just that, of course, but I didn't feel like immersing myself in the role.

Once I had my own clothes, I'd see about maybe taking a walk outside the unit. They weren't ready to let me outside on my own yet, so I'd just have to wait for some company. Lydia hadn't been to see me since the day before, and she'd been so pissed at me when she'd left that I imagined it would be a while before she returned.

In the meantime, I'd have to find other ways to amuse myself and pass the time. I grabbed a copy of *Woman's World* from the lounge table on my way back to my alcove and decided I'd try and figure out which vegetables went best with my personality.

♦

The Short Stay Unit had five alcoves in total, all of which had been occupied the night before, necessitating my overnight stay in the emergency room. I wondered how often the unit was full. I had a sneaking suspicion that waiting for a bed in the unit was not uncommon. The notion was chilling.

Two of the tenants had left this morning, and with the addition of yours truly, the population was now at four. Over the course of the day, I became aware of two of my neighbors. The first was Albert, whom I had earlier seen in the comfy chair, staring at the television. He rarely looked at anyone, and I hadn't heard him say a word since I'd arrived.

The second tenant, a woman named Edna, who also appeared to be in her sixties, was Albert's complete and utter opposite. She was average height and wiry, with curly grey hair, and she could neither keep still nor stop talking. She paced the unit constantly, and every few minutes she would ask Norma one of a litany of questions: "Should I call my husband?" "Do you think he's all right?" "Do you think he might have killed himself?" And, from her second album, "Do you think the terrorists are coming?"

There, but for the grace of God… and all that. Well, I didn't believe in God, but it was still a good expression. It was also the title of an episode of *Stargate SG-1*, which made it much more palatable.

I was given to understand that I had a third neighbor, but I had seen neither hide nor hair of that individual the entire day. I didn't even know their gender.

As afternoon wore into evening and evening into night, Edna's nattering became worrisome. I wondered how I was going to manage to sleep. I was a light sleeper by nature and often woke up in the middle of the night even under normal circumstances.

The present situation were about as far from normal as I'd ventured.

Fortunately, Norma delivered the solution to me in the form of a cup of water and a tiny blue pill. I could have kissed her.

♦

Lydia came to see me again the next morning. She looked a bit haggard, I thought, but I couldn't be sure exactly why. I knew it was never easy on her being around me, but if she kept coming back for more, it really wasn't my fault, was it? She should know better than to keep beating a dead horse. Well, a horse that tried unsuccessfully to be dead, anyway.

"You doing all right?" she asked.

"Fair to middlin'," I said, sounding much more cheerful than I'd thought I would. "The bed's comfortable, and the food actually doesn't suck."

Her mouth wriggled a bit, as if she couldn't quite decide whether or not to allow a smile. "That's practically praise, coming from the likes of you."

I shrugged with my eyebrows. "Well, I do what I can to keep these people from feeling like complete failures."

She rolled her eyes as far back as they would go. "Oh. Gad. You're impossible."

"I'm impossible not to love."

She wrinkled her nose. "You're awfully chipper this morning."

"I had a good night's sleep. They have these little blue pills here. Wonderful things. I haven't slept this well since I was a preconscious mass of protoplasm."

"Well if that's all it took to improve your disposition, I'd've conked you on the head with a frying pan ages ago."

Seeing me slightly improved seemed to raise her spirits a bit as well. However, I still detected a subtle hint of distress beneath her wrinkly nose and wriggly smile.

"You need anything?" She asked.

"Well, clothes, I think. Toothbrush, comb. Something to read. A million dollars."

She actually laughed at that. "I'll go round your place and fetch some of that for you. You want any food or anything?"

"No, they provide all that here. I'm not all that hungry anyway."

She nodded, a bit solemnly, I thought. My attempts to lighten the mood had not managed to erase the downtrodden look I'd noticed when she'd first come in.

"What's up?" I asked.

"What d'you mean?"

"You look a bit down in the dumps. Everything okay? I mean, other than my constant verbal abuse and casting aspersions on the quality of your character."

"Oh, well, thanks for being specific." She shifted from one foot to the other.

I frowned. "What is it?"

She dropped her shoulders and took another step into the alcove. "Well, actually, there's something I've been meaning to tell you, and I was waiting for the right moment."

"And?"

"Well, there doesn't ever seem to be one, does there? A right moment, I mean."

"Not according to any movie I've ever watched. So just spit it out, will you? You're killing me, here."

She stepped to the bed and sat down on the edge. She grabbed my hands, and gazed into my eyes.

"Oh, Jack. I'm so sorry. I was so stupid."

"Stupid how? What are you talking about?"

"I wasn't thinking straight. I mean, the ambulance was there, and the police—"

"Police?"

"Yes, the police were there."

"You never mentioned the police."

"Well, I had to give them a statement, you know. It was a suicide attempt, after all."

I nodded. "All right. Go on."

"Well, I was in a state. And then Paige called from the store, looking for you, wondering why you hadn't shown up. And I wasn't thinking, Jack. I just wasn't thinking. I'm so sorry."

"Wait a minute," I said. "Are you telling me…?"

She nodded. "I let it slip. I'm sorry."

"You told my boss that I tried to kill myself?"

Lydia nodded.

"Ah, shit." I slumped back onto the bed and put my hand over my eyes. "Shit, shit."

"I thought I'd best tell you before… Well, before it got back to you somehow, that she knew."

I nodded weakly.

"Can you ever forgive me?" she asked.

I sighed. "Well, it's not the most convenient thing that's ever happened, but I'm sure I'll manage to get over it."

Even with my eyes covered, I could hear her swallow.

"Do you mean that?" she asked.

I sat up and looked at her. "I can hardly get angry at you for trying to take care of me, can I?"

Lydia wiped an errant tear from her face. I thought I saw her eyes brighten ever-so-slightly.

She patted my hand. "Let me start to make it up to you. I'll go round your place and fetch some of your things. Okay?"

"That would be fantastic. Thank you."

She stood. "Good. I'll go right now. Back in a jif."

"Just don't bring me any plaid shirts, all right? I'm done with that phase."

"Oooh. I didn't know you had any. Flannel?"

"Yes. Stay away from them."

"Can't I have just a peek?"

"No. Off limits. *Verboten*."

"Right. Well, maybe I'll find something just as ugly for you." She was smiling now. "Serve you right for all you put me through. You ungrateful wretch."

"Guilty as charged, Madam."

"You just take care of yourself. And don't give the staff any grief."

"Too late for that," came a voice from beyond the curtain.

Lydia turned around, laughing, as Norma stuck her head through the slight gap between the curtain and the wall.

"I wasn't eavesdropping," Norma said. "I was just walking by when you said that."

"Don't listen to her," I said. "It's Norma who's been making *my* life miserable. Not the other way around."

Lydia turned back to me, one eyebrow arched. "Yes. And I believe that too. Just like I believe that story you told me about being descended from the Knights Templar."

"Hey, the Knights Templar are in vogue, my love. It's my turn to cash in. Ole Dan Brown really started something there. Everybody's doing it now."

"Will you stop? You're a better writer than that. You don't need to latch onto trends. You just need to be original."

"I just hope I'm a better writer than I am guitar player."

Lydia turned back to Norma. "You see what I have to put up with?

Norma nodded. "At least you can leave."

I sighed. "Great. Now they're ganging up on me."

Lydia stepped over to the bed and gave me a peck on the cheek. "I'm off. Back soon, okay?"

"Okay. Thanks."

The curtain rippled as Lydia left the alcove. Norma stepped in to take her place.

"How are you doing this morning?" she asked.

I looked at her. "Not too bad, actually."

"You do seem to be in a better mood."

"Well, I don't think I'm quite as full of myself today as I was yesterday."

She nodded. "A good night's sleep will do that."

"Those little blue pills… Do you have take out?"

She gave me a slightly scolding laugh. "Nice try."

"You're terrible to me, you know."

"I give what I get."

"*Touché.*"

♦

Just before lunch, Norma popped into my alcove to announce that someone was here to see me. From her tone, it was apparent that she wasn't talking about Lydia. I got up from the chair and stepped towards the curtain. I stuck my head out and looked towards the desk. What I saw nearly caused me to lose my footing.

"Uncle Eric?"

A tall, distinguished, elderly gentleman was making his way towards me. He had a long face, short cropped grey hair, and sufficient height to make his long black coat work. He leaned heavily on his cane as he approached my alcove.

"What in Sam Hill do you think you're doing in this place?" he asked, stepping up to me and stopping at my threshold.

I must not have blinked for some time, because suddenly my eyes felt like they were going to shrivel up and fall out of my head. When I finally did blink, my eyes overcompensated, causing excess fluids to course across my visual field, which made everything, including my erstwhile uncle, look like it was underwater.

"I asked you a question, boy," Uncle Eric said.

"I'm… uh… recovering from an accident."

He glared at me. "Bullshit."

I swallowed and decided to say nothing further.

"Did they stash your manners away with your personal effects when you got here?"

I frowned slightly. "I'm sorry… What?"

"Are you going to invite me in, or do I have to stand here yammering so the whole place can hear?"

I stepped aside and let him through. "Yes. Yes. Of course. I'm just surprised to see you, that's all."

He strode into the alcove and proceeded to settle himself into the chair. "What you mean is, you thought that maybe you'd get away without your senile old uncle hearing about your goddamned stupidity."

"You're not senile, Uncle Eric." I moved to sit on the bed.

"Well, then, don't treat me like I am. I had to hear about this non-sense from that swizzle-stick of an ex-girlfriend of yours."

"Gillian? How the hell did she hear about it?"

"You have friends, you damned fool. They talk to each other. World works like that."

I put my hand to my head and tried to breathe. Uncle Eric's constant and forceful directness was not something I was expecting to have to deal with today.

"Yeah. Okay. I get it. I just didn't expect Gillian…"

"Well, the woman still cares about you. Damned if I can figure out why."

"No, no, Uncle Eric. Don't you go there. I don't need any of that right now."

"I'll go where I damn well please, you ungrateful sonofabitch. I'm eighty-three years old, and I lost a leg in Doubleya Doubleya Two. I think I've earned the right."

I let out a long breath. "Fine. You can say whatever you want. But I don't have to listen."

"That's the problem with you young people. You don't pay any respect to your elders."

"Oh, well, now you do sound like an old man. That's almost stereo-typical old-man talk. You can do better than that."

"So can you."

"What?"

"Never pegged you as a quitter, Jack. Never thought I'd live to see the day."

I just stared at him. Of all the people I knew, Uncle Eric had the biggest knack for cutting through to the heart of things. He also had this uncanny ability to make me feel ashamed of myself for being an idiot.

And I had a knack for being an idiot.

I swallowed hard. "I'm not ready to have this conversation."

He let an accusing puff of air out from between his lips. "Not ready. I'll tell you about not ready. Do you think I was ready to have this leg taken away from me? Do you?"

I shook my head.

"Do you think I was ready to fly to England and serve in the Royal Air Force? Do you think I was ready to be in that Lancaster bomber when our pilot misjudged the runway and crashed her in the fog? Do you?"

I looked at the floor, still shaking my head.

He ran his tongue over his upper teeth and glared at me.

Finally, he looked away. "Don't you tell me about not ready. I don't want to hear it."

I shifted my position on the bed and looked around the room. I didn't honestly know what I could say to him. The man had been through hell, and he was still here to talk about it. My hell didn't seem quite so bad in comparison.

"I'm sorry," I said.

He snorted. "Sorry." He looked back at me, disappointment fairly dripping from his eyes. "That's your answer to everything, isn't it?"

"Well, what am I supposed to say? That I'm weak? That I'm stupid? That I can't do anything right and am a constant disappointment? Because I know all those things are true. But I can't change what I've done, can I?"

He didn't respond to that. He just looked at me for several moments, shaking his head.

I had to look down again.

Finally, he sighed. "If your mother ever got wind of this, by God, I don't know what she'd do."

I raised my head and glared hot molten daggers at him. "My mother," I said, "wouldn't know a teabag from a toaster if you drew her a picture and farted the melody."

He stood then, all six-foot-two of him, and met my molten gaze with an icy one. I immediately regretted my utterance. He stood there, looking down at me, breathing heavily, obviously trying to keep his temper under some kind of control.

"You ever talk about my sister like that again," he said, far too quietly, "and I'll knock you so hard, your grandkids'll come out dizzy."

"Then thank God I'm not planning on procreating."

He picked up his cane and strode to the curtain. "Thank God indeed. I'd hate to see any child that would end up with you for a father."

He paused before exiting, and turned towards me again. "Sometimes I'm glad your mother's where she is. If she was aware enough to know how you've turned out, I think it might kill her."

He turned again and swept out of the alcove.

I flung myself into a lying position and pounded on the mattress with my fist.

"Fuck," I muttered. "Fuck, fuck, fuck." I closed my eyes and clenched my jaw. "You just had to mention her, didn't you, Uncle Eric?"

Chapter Five

After the tumultuous visit from my forthright uncle, I had to move about the alcove picking up my scattered nerves. I loved the old guy, but he had a particular talent for pushing my buttons. And I didn't much like having my buttons pushed. Especially when it came to matters of family. That was a sensitive area for me, and he'd gone there. And he'd done it with his usual grace and aplomb. He'd basically come blustering in like a Nor'wester and had blown out like a backfiring Ford pickup. It had left me dazed and befuddled.

He was right about some things, though, and that didn't help matters much. I knew what I was like. I didn't need him to tell me. I could be a sarcastic bastard at times, and I didn't let people into my little headspace. That was the way I was, and I didn't imagine that was going to change anytime soon. I also knew I had problems. One would have to be a blind idiot not to see that I had problems. That was what had ended me up here in Short Stay.

Add one more item to the list of things at which I sucked: Killing myself.

I lay down on the bed and closed my eyes. I'd cranked up the head of the bed for reclining and reading, and that position suited me perfectly at the moment. I put my hands behind my head, shifted slightly on the horizontal, and prepared for a bit of a tune-out.

But it was not to be.

Just seconds before I would have closed my eyes, I sensed the edge of the shadow of a movement. I figured someone had just walked by briskly and ruffled the curtain with their wake, but for some reason my eyes darted right to the spot.

It was no curtain ruffle.

I took in a sharp breath and sat up straight as my eyes took in my third sighting of the woman in the long retro coat. She was standing in my alcove, staring at me again. The curtain was motionless. The only movement I'd seen had been hers.

"What do you want?" I asked.

She took a step closer to me. Her eyes were boring into me, searching for something. Her frown was deeper than ever, and her expression was one of perplexed bewilderment.

She was quite close to me this time, so I could actually make out her features. Her hair was dark, shoulder-length, and wavy. Her eyes were green. Her mouth was small, but her lips were accentuated by a bright red gloss. She was pale, with a rosy patch on each cheekbone. She wore a hunter green beret, and her long, full coat was a deep burgundy. The coat came nearly to her ankles and revealed what I presumed were the lower part of some very elegant boots. On her hands she wore black leather gloves.

She looked as if she had just stepped out of a Raymond Chandler novel. I almost expected her to light a cigarette and tell me that her husband was cheating on her. *I want you to find out who the rat's two-timin' me with*, she'd say. *The no-good lug's gonna pay for what he's doin' to me.*

But no such words came out of her mouth, which was a good thing, because for some reason, my internal movie studio had made her sound rather uneducated, and that would have completely spoiled the elegant vibe she was giving off as she stood there, silently gazing at me.

I slid my legs off the bed and leaned further forward. "Who are you?"

She took a step backward in response to my forward movement. She looked suddenly frightened, as if I posed some kind of threat. Not to her physical person, but to her worldview. It was as if I represented something she couldn't comprehend.

My internal movie studio was a fairly active one. Staff of fourteen in the front office, seven soundstages, four editing suites.

I stood. She stepped back again. I stepped forward. She stepped back.

"Will you please say something?" I asked.

I went to take another step, but my foot caught the leg of the chair. I reached out to balance myself and glanced down to navigate my foot back out into the open.

When I looked up again, she was gone.

The curtain was still motionless. Not so much as a flutter.

I contemplated the situation for a moment. This same routine had played in three venues now, and it wasn't getting any funnier. Either I had a retro ninja on my hands, or else I was going stark raving bonkers. Neither scenario was particularly appealing, though I had to admit that I rather liked the sound of the term 'retro ninja'.

I stepped to the spot where she'd been standing and looked at the floor. I don't know what I expected to see—imprints from her boots, perhaps—but I saw nothing. No surprise there. Neither ninjas nor spectres leave any traces behind them.

I pulled the curtain back and walked out to the nurse's desk. I looked up and down the unit, but there was no one there except for Norma, who was looking quizzically at me, and Albert, who was now watching some nonsensical game show.

"Something wrong, Mister Richmond?" Norma asked from behind the desk.

I walked up to her. "There was a woman in my room just now," I said. "She came in, stared at me, and then left. She didn't say a word. Do you know who it was?"

Norma looked at me with a neutral expression. I imagined it was fairly well-practiced neutral expression, born of many dealings with people of questionable mental stability.

I found it infuriating.

"I didn't see anyone come in," Norma replied. "I've been at the desk for the last half-hour. Nobody's come in or gone out since your uncle left."

I put my hand on the desk and looked at the floor. "How did I know you were going to say something like that?"

"What do you mean?"

I sighed and looked back up at her. "That's three times I've seen her now. Once when I was still lying in the bed in the emergency room, a second time when I was being taken down the hall to the psychiatric emergency department, and a third time just now, in my little curtained alcove. At no point has anyone else confirmed my sightings by indicating that they, too had seen her. So, either there's a strange woman in 1940s clothing wandering the hospital unseen by anyone other than myself, or I'm losing my mind. And considering where I am right now, the first option is not the one a betting person would go with."

Norma straightened in her seat and looked at me with a soft smile. "Well, I can tell you one thing. People who are 'going crazy', as you put it, are usually quite convinced that they're perfectly fine. If you think you're going crazy, you're very likely not."

I tried to get my breathing under control. "Yeah. I've heard that before. I hope it's true. Because I don't feel at my most stable right now. And I still have no idea who this woman is. That is, if she's not a figment of my imagination."

Norma pursed her lips and unfocused her eyes for a moment. "Well, did she remind you of anyone? Did she look like anyone you know?"

I thought about that for a moment. "Well, you know, now that I think about it, she did look a bit like Susan Hayward."

"Susan Hayward?"

"Yeah. She was an actress back in the forties."

"Yes, I know who Susan Hayward was. I just found it odd that you would come up with her name, that's all."

"Oh, I'm a movie buff. I'm surprised I didn't come up with someone more obscure than that."

"So you're saying that this woman, who looks like Susan Hayward, came into your room and stared at you?"

My shoulders sagged. "It sounds so patently insane when you say it like that."

"Mister Richmond, I'm not making fun of you. I want to help you figure this out. You don't sound like a man who's having hallucinations, but considering that visitors have to be buzzed into the unit, we have to consider the possibility that you slipped into a vivid daydream for a couple of minutes."

"Yeah. Pretty damned vivid."

I ran a hand through my hair and started back for my little curtained alcove.

◆

Lydia returned just after lunch, bearing one of my duffel bags and an armful of magazines.

"The cavalry," I said, getting up from the chair and taking both from her. "You have no idea how glad I am to see this stuff." I held up the magazines. "These especially." I nodded towards the bed, where sat the copy of *Woman's World* I'd been leafing through. "That was slowly draining brain cells from my skull."

I put the deliveries down and gave Lydia a giant hug.

"Well, this is a nice change," she said.

"When people bring me things, I get all gooshy inside," I said.

She rolled her eyes. "Naturally."

I took her face in both my hands and gazed at her for a moment. "Thank you," I said. "I really appreciate everything you've done for me these last couple of days."

I leaned forward and gave her a kiss on the lips. She leaned into it and kissed back.

After a moment, our faces parted slightly.

"You really are in a better mood," Lydia said. Her eyes had acquired a slight luster.

"The thought of feeling like a human again," I said, "is cause for nothing short of celebration."

I practically tore off the johnny shirt and dove into my duffel bag. I pulled out a blue t-shirt, discovering to my delight that it was my favorite *Star Trek* shirt, acquired at a fan convention in Toronto. "Bless you, my love," I said, glancing over at her. I put the t-shirt on the bed and pulled out my favorite pair of jeans, a pair of beige socks, and a fresh pair of boxer shorts.

I peeled off the boxers I was wearing, fully cognizant of the fact that I was now naked in a strange place, and revelled for a moment in the near-naughtiness of it. I turned to Lydia and waggled my dick at her. She rolled her eyes and turned away, but not before I noted the sly smile that made its way to her lips. I hoped that smile held the promise of possibilities when I got out of this place.

I pulled on the fresh shorts and sat down on the bed to don the socks. A moment later I was fastening the jeans and pulling the t-shirt over my head. Digging in the duffel bag once again, I pulled out a pair of sneakers.

The ensemble was complete.

"Let's go for a walk," I said.

Lydia turned around to face me again. "Oh, good, you're decent at last. I thought maybe you wanted to give the staff a little show."

I sneered. "Nah. Too cold in this place. I'd look like a poorly-hung mutant. Or a man with a gummi worm between his legs."

"Will you stop?" Her face was now beet red. "They can hear you out there, you know."

"Yes. Isn't it exciting?"

She shook her head and moved to the curtain. "Come on, then. I thought you said you were stir crazy."

I pulled a sweatshirt out of the duffel bag and followed her.

Norma gave us an odd look as I signed my name in the log book and wrote in the time.

"About half an hour?" I asked.

Norma nodded. "Just push the buzzer when you want to come back in."

We strode down the hall and exited the unit.

"Where to?" Lydia asked.

"Well, there's a Tim Horton's over in the main building. I could sure use a sour-cream-glazed."

"Creature of habit, you are."

"I need my donut, woman."

As we moved through the corridors, I told Lydia about the strange woman I'd seen, or at least thought I'd seen. She was attentive to the story, but I could see concern creep into her expression as I recounted the latest encounter.

"I know it sounds crazy," I said, "but even if I was hallucinating, or daydreaming, or whatever, it felt real. Absolutely real."

"I just hope those drugs you took haven't damaged you in some way," she said.

"It was Gravol and Sleep-Eze-D, for Christ's sake. What kind of damage could they do?"

"Well, they were supposed to kill you, now, weren't they?"

I stopped in my tracks. "Oh. Right."

"Oh, that's lovely. Forget the whole reason you're in here to begin with, why don't you?" She shook her head. "You daft ponce."

"Hey. No fair. I don't understand all those slippery English insults you seem to produce so readily. And they sound so pretty wrapped in that lovely accent of yours, that I hardly feel like I'm being insulted at all. So stop it."

"I have to take what advantage I can, you know. Because your barrage of wordplay hardly ever stops for a breath. I'd've thought you'd've published sixteen novels by this point."

I put my hands to my chest. "Ouch. You strike straight at my heart. Have you no mercy at all?"

"Not if I can help it."

"Strumpet."

"Arsehole."

"Okay, that one I understand."

♦

The next day, my best buddy Brad (so alliterative, I am) came to see me. He shoved the curtain aside and stood at the threshold, looking at me with his head slightly cocked and his mouth in a funny shape. He wore his usual three-days-worth of stubble, and his tousled blondish hair looked unwashed. He was holding a Vachon cake in his hand.

"Dude," he said.

"What's up, Brad?"

"Heard you tried to off yourself."

"Yeah. Word gets around, huh?"

He shook his head. "Fuck, man. That's some heavy shit. Did you see lights or anything?"

"I can't remember a damned thing."

He let out a disappointed breath and shuffled in. He plunked himself into the chair and put his feet up on the bed. He took a bite of his Jos & Louis and stared at the wall for a few seconds.

"That really blows," he said through his mouthful.

"What, that I tried to kill myself, or that I didn't see the Aurora Borealis in the process?"

"Ah, shit, man. Don't do that. I was only talking about the lights for a second. Seriously, I would've been bummed if you'd checked out."

"Well, it's good to know that you care."

"Oh, here comes Mister Sarcasm again. Fuck, man. I hate it when you do that shit."

"I've always been sarcastic. You know that."

"Yeah, but, dude… We're talking about you almost, like, leaving the building. For keeps. You know?"

"Yeah. I know. I was there."

"So, like, why can't you take it seriously?"

"Because you were more interested in whether or not I saw lights."

He took his feet off the bed and leaned towards me. "Don't you put this back on me, man. You're the one sitting here in the loony bin."

"I don't think they like it when you call it that. And, oh, by the way, you're sitting in here, too."

"Stop with the technical grammar literal shit, man. You're always trying to throw me off. And what, they're gonna send the mental health police after me if I call this shithole a loony bin?"

"Well, I don't think they much like it when you call the hospital a shithole, either."

"Yeah? Well, I don't really fucking care."

I shrugged. "At least you're honest."

"Damn straight, I'm honest. I tell it like it is, brother."

"That's what I've always liked about you."

He nodded and continued to munch on his chocolate-coated, disk-shaped sandwich of chocolate cake with vanilla cream in the middle. After a couple of bites, he put his feet back up on the bed again.

"Sorry I didn't come down sooner, man," he said after a swallow. "I was down in the valley, visiting my ex-girlfriend's mother's hairdresser."

"Why didn't you just tell me the dog ate your homework. Fewer syllables and about as credible."

He waved his cake-wielding hand back and forth as he swallowed again. "No, man. I'm not shitting you. I was down in the valley, visiting… "

"Your ex-girlfriend's mother's hairdresser." I paused to take in the full weight of the phrase. "The word that comes to mind is… why?"

"Dude, this chick is, like, seriously, the best hairdresser in the world. I got a haircut from her when Megan and I were still together, and it, like, literally blew my mind."

"Literally, huh?"

"Yeah, man. Litera—" He shot me sharp glance. "I told you to cut that shit out. Don't get all language police on my ass, okay? I'm trying to tell a story here. So stay with."

"I'm all ears."

"Fuck, I hate that expression." He took the last bite of the Jos & Louis and dusted off his hands. "Anyway, man, it was the best haircut I ever had. No word of a lie. And I've been going back to her ever since."

"And I'll bet you're getting more than just a haircut."

He looked at me with a puzzled frown. "What are you talking about?" After a moment, he rolled his eyes. "Jesus, man. I'm not fucking her, if that's what you mean. I mean, she's good looking and all, but she's gotta be… " He paused to think for a minute. "Geez, she's gotta be at least three years older than me."

"Oh, good lord," I said. "She'd be practically robbing the cradle."

"You know I don't date older chicks."

"No, actually, I never knew that."

"Well, that's the way I roll, man. Younger chicks all the way."

"Yeah, well, just don't take that to an extreme."

He gave me another funny look. "What are you talking about, man?"

I raised my eyebrows and shrugged.

He rolled his eyes. "Ah, fuck, man. You've got the dirtiest mind I've ever met."

"And you're the dirtiest slob I've ever met. Thanks for the segue opportunity, and please pick your cake wrapper up from the floor."

He gave me a vacant stare. "Man, I would've thought nearly dying would make you a nicer person."

"I'm crabbier than ever. Don't mess with me."

He leaned over and picked the wrapper up. "Now what do you want me to do with it?"

I rolled my eyes. "Trash can's over there," I said, motioning to the other side of the bed.

Brad got up, reluctantly, it appeared, and stepped over to the can to deposit the cellophane wrapper.

"So how long you in here for?" he asked as he resumed his seat.

"A few days, they tell me. They're going to evaluate my condition."

"What the fuck does that mean?"

"It means I'm going to talk to one of their shrinks, and he or she is going to try and figure out what in holy hell to do with me."

Brad nodded. "Sounds like a plan."

"Well, it beats being sent home with a pat on the ass. Maybe I'll actually get some help this time."

"What do you mean, this time? You try to off yourself before?"

"No. But I've brought myself down to the emergency room a couple of times over the last few years, because I was feeling desperate enough that I thought I might do something."

"Man, that's messed up."

"Yeah, it's messed up. *I'm* messed up."

"Well, at least you know it. That's half the battle, from what I hear."

"Yeah, well. Fat lot of good it's done me so far."

"Man, you are so fucking negative. No wonder you tried to check out. I couldn't stand being around myself either if I was like that."

"Cheap shot, Brad. You can do better than that."

"No, man. You're the Language-Meister. Not me."

"Yes, I keep forgetting what a dim little bulb you are and how your pathetic existence brings no meaning to you or anyone else."

He sighed and shook his head. "Man, you are one piece of work. Why don't you take all that anger and bitterness and… and fucking vocabulary, and finish one of your goddamned novels?"

"Maybe I will, once I'm not crazy in the head anymore."

"Yeah, well, keep talking like that, and you *will* be crazy in the head. Whatever you think is gonna happen is pretty much gonna happen."

"Thank you, Rhonda Byrne."

"Oh, fuck off, man. I'm not talking about that *Secret* shit. That's just a lot of packaging stuck onto something everybody already knows."

"Well, aren't you the wise sage all of a sudden?"

"It's common sense, man. You think about something all the time, it's gonna show up in your life. You don't need to be a rocket scientist or a fucking Austrian filmmaker to know that."

I cocked my head and frowned at him. "Austrian filmmaker?"

"Yeah. You know. That Byrne chick you were just talking about."

"Actually, she's Australian."

"Australian?"

"Yeah."

"I'm pretty sure she's Austrian, man."

"And I'm pretty sure she's not."

Brad frowned and squinted. "Which one has the kangaroos?"

"That would be Australia."

He shook his head. "Fuck. I always get those two mixed up."

He gazed at the floor for a moment, then scratched his chin and shifted in the chair.

"Lydia told me your uncle came to see you."

I frowned. "You talked to Lydia?"

Brad rolled his eyes. "What are you, jealous?"

"No. Jeez. But you and Lydia… You guys don't even click. It just seems odd that you'd see her, that's all."

"She called me."

"She called you?"

"Yeah. She's your friend. I'm your friend. You tried to do yourself in. So she called me. She's considerate like that."

"Considerate. Yeah." I let my eyes unfocus for a few seconds. "She's pretty considerate."

"So how'd your uncle find out you were in here?"

I cleared my throat. "Uh… actually, uh, Gillian told him."

"Gillian?"

I nodded. "Yeah."

"Oh, Jesus, man. That's fucked up."

I put my hands behind my head. "I know."

Brad continued rubbing his chin, then sat forward suddenly. "Wait a minute. How did Gillian find out?"

"I guess either Derek or Winston told her."

"What? That's even more fucked up. Gillian hanging out with your band-mates?"

I closed my eyes and sighed again. "Jesus, Brad. I met Gillian through Derek's girlfriend, remember? And no, I don't think she hangs out with my band. Some subset of these people must have all run into each other somewhere, and naturally, the main topic of conversation would have been yours truly, because, as you well know, there really isn't anything else to talk about—"

"Don't do that, man."

"Don't do what?"

"That whole 'pump yourself up while you're also beating yourself down at the same time' thing. It's not cool."

I looked at him with a slight frown, and chewed on my lip for a moment.

"You know," I said, "for a guy who seems to cruise through life without paying too much attention to the details, that's actually a pretty astute observation. I'm impressed."

Brad crossed his arms. "Fuck you."

"Geez, try to pay a guy a compliment…"

"Yeah, a back-handed compliment."

"Wow, you know that phrase as well. This just keeps getting better."

Brad stared at me for a moment, his face nearly expressionless. "Remind me again why we're friends?"

I shrugged. "I dunno. Because we know each other's secrets?"

He grunted. "Is that all?"

"Well, you also saved my ass from Tommy Frobisher and his goons back in fifth grade…"

"That's a long time ago, man."

I leaned back and closed my eyes. "Well, you know, some things transcend the limits of time and space."

"You're pathetic. You know that?"

I opened my eyes and frowned at him.

"Thanks, Brad. Way to ruin a moment."

"Moment? You don't have moments, dude. You have, like, maybe three seconds a week where you're an actual human being."

"That's harsh, man."

"Well, it's true."

I stared at him for a moment.

"You know you still have chocolate at the corner of your mouth, there."

"No, I don't."

"You do." I pointed at his face. "It's right there."

"Fuck off."

"Suit yourself."

◆

I was in the Short Stay Unit for a total of four days. I had two meetings with the psychiatrist, a Doctor Navarro, who also brought her team in with her: A resident, a social worker, and one of the nurses. It was me and four women, two of whom, the resident and Doctor Navarro herself, were so incredibly gorgeous that it was difficult for me to concentrate on what we were talking about. I behaved myself, for the most part, but once they managed to get my defenses up (which actually happened rather quickly), they stayed up for the remainder of the conversation.

Gorgeousness aside, I liked Doctor Navarro. She was a smart, articulate, perceptive woman, and she had me pegged pretty fast. She asked me a lot of questions and took a lot of notes. The whole pack of them took a lot of notes, actually, and the other three members of the committee also popped in a question here and there. I wouldn't say that I was uncooperative, but I don't think they were entirely satisfied with my level of disclosure. The sarcasm flew fast and furious, as always, and I did occasionally catch a disapproving look on one of their faces.

Evidently, I'm hard to get along with.

The end result of all this was that Doctor Navarro decided to refer me to something called the Mental Health Day Treatment Program, which was a six-week, intensive, group-therapy experience designed to get at core issues and explore feelings. I greeted this news with skepticism and a request that I simply be allowed to go my merry way and try and put some of the scattered pieces of my life back together.

Doctor Navarro did not much like my thinking on the matter. She was, in fact, rather insistent that I take the tremendous opportunity she was offering me to improve the quality of my life.

I said I'd think about it.

♦

After my second meeting with Doctor Navarro and her compatriots, I was told I would be allowed to go home, provided I agreed to participate in the six-week day program.

It was nearly suppertime when the meeting ended, and Norma told me I could partake of the hospital meal if I wanted before heading out. I availed myself of the opportunity, knowing that anything I had at home would either be frozen solid or mouldy.

Lydia arrived just as I was finishing my jell-o. I don't know if it was actually jell-o, the brand name product, but it was a red gelatin dessert that wobbled when I poked it with my spoon. I decided that, if I ever wrote about this experience, I would fly in the face of legal convention and mention the brand name in lowercase letters with no trademark symbol after it. I would do my part to dilute the hold of large corporations on terms which had become common parts of our vocabulary.

At any rate, the stupid red blob tasted like it was made with too much water.

I said my goodbyes to the staff and headed out with Lydia, duffel bag slung over my shoulder and a song in my heart.

Or something like that.

"Glad to be going home?" Lydia asked as I threw my bag into the backseat of her Mini Cooper.

"Well, I have mixed feelings about that," I said. "On the one hand, I'm happy that I can now choose the crap I eat rather than having it chosen for me. On the other, there's now four-day-old vomit waiting for me on my bed. The prospect of going home to that is… unappealing."

She laughed. "Don't be an arse. Did you honestly think I was going to leave that there for you? I cleaned it up after I left you the first night. And I washed your sheets."

I settled myself into the passenger seat and looked at her. She was shaking her head in disbelief and, I thought, a bit of sadness. To believe, as I had, that a friend would just leave the vomit there, was a foreign concept to her. It didn't compute.

Whereas for me, it was just a day at the office. I was pretty uncaring about most people beyond myself, and so I couldn't imagine why someone would do something for me. It was as simple as that.

Lydia smacked me on the shoulder and started the car.

"Let's get you home, you tosser."

The drive home was pleasant. It was early evening, so the traffic was fairly heavy, but the autumn sunlight made up for it, rendering everything in bold colors and sharp edges. It was the kind of weather I loved better than just about anything, and I put my head back and allowed the patches of sun to caress my face as we wended our way through the streets of Halifax towards my abandoned abode.

◆

I walked up the front walk of my small apartment building and pulled out my keys. Stepping into the lobby, I headed for the mailbox and went to open it.

"I've already brought your mail in," Lydia said, stepping in behind me.

I turned to look at her. She was dangling a set of keys between her thumb and forefinger. I noted the smallish one, which resembled the mailbox key I held in my hand at that very moment.

"Oh," I said. "Right. Trusting, aren't I?"

"Who else is going to look after you?"

I caught a hint of melancholy in her expression as she turned towards the stairs. I hefted my duffel bag onto my shoulder again and followed her.

When I unlocked the front door, I caught a whiff of something unfamiliar. I stopped just inside the threshold and sniffed a few times, frowning slightly.

"It's called Mister Clean, you prat," Lydia said, barely hiding the smirk that lay in wait to spring upon me.

"You cleaned my place?"

She stepped past me, whacking me on the arm as she did so. "It's not like I didn't have anything better to do. But the place was in a sorry state, if you don't mind my saying. I thought it might be nice for you to come home to a bit of order, is all."

I moved to the bedroom to deposit my duffel bag. I cautiously entered the room, looking carefully around lest some vengeful fragment of my downtrodden and suicidal self leap upon me and begin the process of strangulation. I placed the bag on the carefully-made bed and let out a long breath. The last time I had been here, I was slowly sinking into a deep unconsciousness that, at the time, I had hoped would be a permanent one.

That hadn't happened.

Fortunately, the room did not look exactly as it had looked then. Lydia had changed the bedclothes, opened the windows, and put an air freshener on my dresser. It was a bit cool in the room, but I didn't mind. The atmosphere had been cleansed. I wondered if she'd burned incense. I sniffed again. All I could smell was the air freshener.

"I tossed out those little glass bowls I found in the dish rack," Lydia called from the kitchen. "I assumed those were the ones you'd put the pills in."

"Uh… yeah." I couldn't believe the care Lydia was taking with all this.

"And that drinking glass, too. The one with the orange swirls on it. There were five of them, and I tossed them all. Cheap things. You need new ones anyway."

I kicked my sneakers off and padded back into the kitchen. "Just make yourself at home, why don't you?"

She put her hands on her hips. "Now don't start with that."

I nodded. "Right. Just don't let me find extra pay-per-view items on my cable bill. I know how you love that girl-on-girl porn."

She stepped up to me and slapped me hard across the face. That made the second time in a week.

"Ow! What the hell was that for?"

"That was for being an obnoxious, sarcastic, uncaring, self-absorbed, pain in the arse. And you've had it coming for three days now. I saved it until you got out of the hospital."

I gave my head a vigorous shake and let out a breath between pursed lips. "I'm glad you didn't save it up any longer. I'd be in the next room with whiplash."

"And deserving every twinge of it."

50

"Well then why the hell did you—"

"Shut up."

She put her hand on the back of my neck and pulled me to her. Her lips were soft and warm, and I immediately felt myself falling into her. I wrapped my arms around her waist, and she wrapped hers around my shoulders. We stayed like that for about thirty seconds or so, and then she pulled away slightly, resting her forehead on mine.

"I liked that a lot better than the slap," I said.

"Me too," she replied. Her whisper was slightly husky.

I took her by the hand and led her into the bedroom.

"What are you doing?" she asked.

"What do you think?" I said, reaching for the buttons of her blouse.

She grabbed my hand and pushed it away. "So that's it, then, is it? A little kiss, and everything's back to the way it was? Is that it?"

"It wasn't so little," I said, smiling my best devilish smile.

"You're a piece of work, Jack Richmond. You know that? A real piece of work. You think you can just waltz back into my life after everything you've done to me, and I'll just lay down, open my legs and let you have a go?"

I swallowed and cleared my throat. "You make it sound so seedy."

She shoved me back and walked out of the room. "That's rich, Jack. That's just bloody rich."

I followed her. "I think you mean Buddy Rich. You know, the drummer?"

She spun on her heel and stomped back to me. "I know damn well who Buddy Rich is, you slimy bastard. And I don't appreciate you slipping in your stupid, deflecting comments when I'm trying to talk to you seriously."

"You weren't talking. You were yelling."

"And bloody well entitled I am. It's always the same thing with you, every time. You don't take anything seriously. You think we can just have a nice little romp now and then, and it doesn't mean anything. You had a girlfriend, Jack. You were with her for nine bloody months. I'm amazed she put up with you for that long. But you still wanted me around, didn't you? You knew I'd always be there for you, just like a damned puppy. Or a fucking doormat. That's what I've been to you, Jack. All this time. A bloody doormat. What does that say about me? What kind of a person does that make me?"

I stood there, letting her barrage of grief and anger pummel me. Every word was like a punch to some vital organ. Every breath out of her mouth was like a burst from a flame-thrower. When she stopped, she stood rigid, her arms at her sides, her fists clenched. Her eyes were red, and they burned into me like hot pokers. A tear ran down the right side of her nose.

"Lydia…" I began.

"Don't," she said. The syllable was sharp and short, like a homemade shank. I wobbled a bit at the forcefulness of it. "I don't want to hear your excuses or your bad puns. I can't take this anymore, Jack. I just can't."

"Then why did you clean my apartment, and why did you kiss me just now?"

She wiped the tear from her face and looked at the refrigerator. "I don't know. I quite honestly don't know." She crossed her arms and took a step towards the sink. "I think I just felt that you needed me. Something like that. You were in trouble, and I was here, and you needed someone to look after things."

She turned back around to face me. The tear she'd wiped had been replaced by a dozen or so of its siblings. "I just wanted to help you, Jack. I wanted to be the one you'd come home to. I was afraid of losing you."

She turned away again. "You selfish bastard. You probably don't even care."

I stepped back and leaned against the stove. A small shudder ran through me as I recalled the image of the pill-filled bowls and the rum-filled glass sitting atop it. I put my hands on the front edge of the appliance and looked at Lydia's back. She was trembling slightly.

"Fine." I said. "You can sleep on the couch, then."

She stiffened. I winced at that, figuring that my tone of voice had gone back into the red "sarcastic" zone. She relaxed again, though, and turned around, wiping more tears from her face.

"What did you say?" she asked quietly.

"I said you can sleep on the couch."

She leaned back on the sink. "That's your idea of a white flag, is it?"

"Well, I'm not sending you home. Not when you're like this."

Her expression softened a bit at that. "Really."

"Yeah. Really."

She crossed her arms and looked at the floor. "Well, that's a *bit* better. I'm still skeptical, of course, because you might just be trying to placate me. But it's a start."

I tried my best to refrain from rolling my eyes, flinging my clenched hands into the air, and proclaiming that it was not I who should have been admitted to the psych ward.

"Go get yourself cleaned up," I said. "I'm exhausted."

I went back into the bedroom, opened the duffel bag, and began putting things away. I had to work hard to focus on each individual task, because parts of my brain wanted to wander all over the place: to the image of the pills and rum on the stove, to the blurry image of the emergency room as I regained consciousness, to the wobbly walks to the toilet, to the strange woman in the long coat whom no one else saw, and back to Lydia, who was causing me as much confusion and frustration as I was sure I'd caused her many times over the years.

I put the last of the clothes into my closet and picked up my electric razor. I began moving towards the bathroom, but stopped short, looking down at my hand. It was clenched around the razor case, and it was shaking. As a matter of fact, my entire body was beginning to shake. It was just like in the hospital, only this time, instead of reacting to an institutional egg-on-croissant sandwich, it was the simple fact of being home and putting my clothes away.

I put the razor down on my dresser and walked to the window. I put my hands on the sill and leaned my weight on them. I closed my eyes, waiting for the trembling to pass.

It didn't.

My jaw clenched, and the hidden emotions began to creep out from their hidey-holes again. Everything began to swirl in front of my closed eyes: anger, grief, hurt, sadness, the whole shooting match. Memories of the last few days, the last few months, the last few years, all tap danced before me. I didn't want to cry out again with Lydia in the apartment, so I bit my lip and made a grunting noise through my nose. My shoulders nearly seized up, and I lifted my hands, bringing them down hard upon the window sill.

It hurt, but I didn't care.

I opened my eyes, breathing heavily. As my body began to settle down, I leaned on the window sill again and looked outside. The familiarity of the view helped to ground me again. Everything was just as it had been before my date with Captain Morgan. The parking lot was still intact, the chain link fence around the edge of the property still stood there. The cobblestone walk was still—

I craned my neck forward and scowled down at the pavement. There was a cobblestone walk running through the middle of the parking lot to the back door of the building. I had never noticed a cobblestone walk there before. As a matter of fact, I was positive that there had never *been* a cobblestone walk at the back of the building. It was certainly quaint, but it was quite impractical. Not to mention incongruous.

I frowned and scanned the parking lot again, just to make sure there weren't any other anomalies awaiting my gaze. Nope. Just the path.

I tried not to let my mind go where it was headed, towards the recollection of the strange ripples in the air at the hospital that knocked the woman into the security guard. I tried, but failed. The comparison was unavoidable.

I looked again at the aberrant path. It was more than just an hallucination this time. It was more than just the fact of my seeing it that bothered me. It was also the fact that, for a moment, I'd been ready to accept it as normal.

It wasn't.

"Lydia," I called. "Come here a sec."

"I'm not coming into your bedroom, Jack."

"Oh, for Christ's sake. I'm not going to—" I steadied my voice and my breathing. "I just want you to look at something out in the parking lot."

"What?" she asked. Her voice was much closer now. I turned around to see her standing in the doorway.

"Down there," I said pointing to the window.

She moved closer. "What?"

I turned to look back down at the parking lot. The asphalt was now a solid surface, unbroken by any lines of any sort. The cobblestone path was nowhere to be seen.

My shoulders dropped. "Never mind," I said.

"Well, you wanted me to see something."

I turned my head towards her. "It's gone now."

She frowned. "What's wrong, Jack?"

I sat down on the bed. "I think I imagined something again."

She sat down beside me. "Did you see that woman again?"

"No. I saw a cobblestone path running through the middle of the parking lot."

Her eyebrows shot up. "A cobblestone path? Well, that's kind of charming, really. If you're going to have hallucinations, you might as well have charming ones."

I closed my eyes. This was not what I wanted to hear right now. I was beginning to doubt my own sanity, and the thought of possible brain damage was never far from the front of my mind since my awakening in the emergency room.

"They shouldn't have released me," I murmured.

"What?"

I looked at her. "I'm obviously going crazy. This is not normal, for me to be seeing things and people that aren't really there, or are there one minute and gone the next. I've damaged myself, and I may never be the same again."

"I think you're being overly dramatic."

I stood. "Oh, you do, do you? Well, you're not the one having the hallucinations, are you? You're sitting there in judgment, telling me to calm down, telling me to behave myself, telling me how to talk, how to think, how to blow my nose. Well, I'm sick of it."

Lydia leaned back onto the bed, propping herself on her elbows. "Now you're getting paranoid."

"Paranoid? I'm scared to death here. I might be losing it. And you're telling me I'm being dramatic and paranoid?"

She let out a long-suffering breath and got up from the bed. "Jack. I'm going home. You obviously need some time to yourself. I don't think I can be any help to you at all right now. So just relax for a while, will you? Watch some TV. Read a book. Have a snack, and go to bed. You need a good night's sleep."

"Well, thank you, Nurse Nancy, for your penetrating diagnosis." I glared at her.

She closed her eyes for a moment, shaking her head slightly. Then she turned and walked out.

A moment later I heard the front door slam shut.

I sat down on the bed again and put my head in my hands.

What the hell was happening to me?

Chapter Six

I didn't sleep particularly well that night. There was simply too much going on in my head. It shouldn't have surprised me. So I got out of bed earlier than I had planned and went to the kitchen to make myself a cup of coffee.

Ah, the java bean. Cure for so many ills.

I made a three-cup pot (just in case) and went into the living room to see what drivel was on the television at this ungodly hour. The couch was comfortable, the coffee was hot, and I had a full battalion of channels to command, so for the moment, life was not unpleasant.

It was almost bearable.

I turned on the Space Channel and immediately recoiled in horror as the stultifyingly horrific comedy of *The Hilarious House of Frightenstein* assailed my senses. I punched the remote with a near-violent enthusiasm as I strove to switch to something else—anything else—to take the vestigial images of bad horror makeup and worse dialogue out of my forebrain.

I finally settled upon an infomercial for one of Tony Robbins' courses on DVD. I figured it was at least good for a laugh.

As I sipped my coffee and watched the toothy behemoth peddle his wares on the airwaves, my eyelids began to droop. I cursed my recalcitrant metabolism, pointlessly asking it why it couldn't have caused my eyelids to droop several hours ago. So I finished my coffee, put the mug on the coffee table, let my head fall back on the couch, and closed my eyes.

Tony Robbins is just as convincing even when you can't see him, I discovered.

I must have dozed a bit (a surprising thing, since I'd just ingested coffee), because the next thing I knew I was not in the presence of Tony Robbins, but of Suzanne Somers, who was selling her latest book. I'd rather been hoping for an ad for "Girls Gone Wild", but this was an okay replacement. Old as she was, our Suzanne still cut a rather fetching figure, and she was wearing tights, after all.

After a few minutes of watching Ms. Somers and occasionally flashing back to memories of watching *Three's Company*, I decided to get my butt up off the couch and head for the shower. If the coffee didn't wake me, the hot water surely would. I left the TV on, put the mug in the sink, and tossed my robe into the bedroom. A moment later I was stepping in to the hot spray. It felt wonderful.

As I dried myself off and got dressed, I tried to figure out what I was going to do with the day. I didn't have to go into work; they weren't expecting me back for a few days. My manager and coworkers knew what had happened, thanks to Lydia, but I didn't blame her for that. She'd been distressed, after all, and it would have been surprising if she *hadn't* blurted out what had happened. My coworkers were all good people, anyway, and when it came right down to it, I really didn't mind that they knew. They cared about me, and I cared for them, too. Well, as much as I was able to care about anyone other than myself.

So I had some time ahead of me, time with no real obligations. I could work on my writing, play my guitar, hit the local coffee shops, watch DVDs, go to the movies, maybe even convince Lydia to come over for some intense make-up sex.

I paused at that last thought. For some reason, I felt a little guilty about the whole Lydia thing. That wasn't like me at all, as my usual *modus operandi* was to basically just do whatever the hell I wanted without much thinking about other people's feelings. Not that I didn't have my limits; I was, after all, a veritable master when it came to customer service at the store. I had a way about me that put customers at ease, and my knowledge of the inventory was exceptional. I was very good at what I did.

I was also fully capable of conducting myself well within social norms when I found myself in social settings. I was well-brought-up, had good manners and hygiene, and could be polite to almost anyone. My inner monologue, however, was rife with judgement and disdain. I didn't have the time of day for most people, but they never saw that side of me. Not, that is, unless they got to know me better. The better I knew someone, the more likely my inner monologue was to become outer monologue.

And that little fact had lost me more than my fair share of friends over the years.

I dressed and went back into the living room. I considered fixing myself some breakfast, but my stomach was not really awake yet, so I decided to wait a while. It was just after six o'clock now, and I rarely broke my fast before eight.

So it was back to the channel flipping again.

I found a kiddies show where frightening puppets were extolling the virtues of the banana. I found a cartoon where a large blue dog was trying to solve a mystery. I found a music video from about 1985. I found an early morning news program where even the reporter looked half-asleep. None of these things interested me.

In desperation, I resorted to the movie channels. They rarely showed anything worth seeing at this early hour, but I figured it was at least worth a try. There might at least be something to make fun of.

The first channel I landed on was showing an old Jean-Claude Van Damme film. I passed on that. The only film of his I liked was *TimeCop* (a guilty pleasure; I loved all things time-travel). The next one was showing a really cheesy adventure film with bad acting and dreadful costumes.

Nearly ready to throw the remote at the screen in frustration, I tried one more time.

This channel, at least, was showing something that caught my attention.

It was a black-and-white film, and the scene playing out was one set at a train station. In the foreground was a woman with her back to the camera. She was watching a train pull out of the station. I didn't recognize the movie, but the woman's coat looked awfully familiar.

I leaned forward and squinted. The woman was wearing a coat identical to the one my strange visitor had been wearing. Of course, I couldn't see what color it was, as the picture was black-and-white, but everything else about it was the same.

The woman was even wearing a beret.

I couldn't place the scene. I had no idea what film I was watching, but I reasoned that I must have seen it before. My confused and over--drugged mind must have latched onto the memory of Susan Hayward in this scene and produced the vision that had appeared to me in the hospital.

I found the realization nearly comforting. At least I knew where the vision had come from. It did seem odd that my mind would focus on this particular image, since I couldn't even remember what film this was, but then, the mind works in mysterious ways.

When she turned to face the camera, I expected to see the large doe eyes and pouty, cupie-doll lips of Susan Hayward. What I saw instead was the face I'd seen in the hospital, similar to Susan Hayward's but different in the arch of the brow, the curve of the jaw, the length of the nose. There was no mistaking it. I'd gotten a good look at her during her last appearance, and it was most definitely the same woman.

I tried to puzzle my way through this: I was watching a movie scene that I didn't remember, with an actress that looked like Susan Hayward but wasn't and who had appeared to me in the emergency room and in the Short Stay Unit.

It made no sense at all.

As I watched the strange scene unfold, I became aware of an additional oddness that only served to compound my confusion: The actress on the screen appeared to be looking straight at me.

The logical part of my mind recoiled at this. Actors in films rarely looked directly at the camera. Why this woman was doing so was beyond me.

I continued to watch, both fascinated and strangely uneasy. The woman on the screen looked worried, almost frantic. She looked as if something bad were about to happen.

"You must protect yourself," she said. "They're coming."

What was she talking about? Was that a message for me? Was I hallucinating again? Was I going crazy? Was I being drawn into Movie World? I had no blessed idea.

For the hell of it, I decided to answer her.

"Who's coming?" I asked. "Protect myself from what?"

Her face fell, almost as if she'd lost hope that I'd ever understand her. "There's no time," she said. "You must be careful. They know about you. They're watching you."

She looked away again, then back at me. She opened her mouth to speak, but the picture suddenly changed. I was suddenly watching an old Steve Martin movie, and it was not in black and white.

"Hey," I said. "Bring her back. She wasn't finished yet."

I looked around the room, feeling suddenly and profoundly foolish. "Great. Now I'm talking to the TV. They shouldn't have let me go home."

But it was the thought of the television talking to *me* that was more troubling.

♦

I did eventually have breakfast, after I'd managed to calm myself down and convince myself that I hadn't really seen what I thought I'd seen. It had been a coincidence, nothing more. There had been a glitch at the movie network, and they'd accidentally fed a scene of an old movie when they'd really meant to show the Steve Martin film. It was obviously a movie I'd seen before, and the actress had been memorable enough to be the source of my imaginings at the hospital. It was probably all just some weird after-effect of taking so much Gravol, Sleep-Eze-D, and rum.

That was all there was to it.

After I'd polished off my scrambled eggs and toast, had another cup of coffee, and washed up the dishes, I decided to go out for a while. I'd probably go crazy if I stayed in the apartment too long, and I knew some fresh air would do me good. So I grabbed my jacket, wallet, and keys, locked the apartment door behind me, and headed downstairs.

I wasn't really sure where I wanted to go at first, but I started walking anyway. I thought I might head downtown, maybe pick up a magazine or something, maybe stop somewhere for a coffee and bagel. I had no set agenda; I'd figure it out as I went along. I was a man at liberty.

It was a beautiful fall day. The leaves were turning the glorious colors of the dance of death, and the air was clear and crisp. The sun was again giving sharp edges to everything it touched, and as I walked along, it seemed that perhaps life wasn't quite so bad after all.

This was a stark contrast to a mere four days earlier, when I had gotten dressed, walked to the mall, purchased some over-the-counter pills and some alcohol, and had systematically attempted to remove myself from the gene pool. I was, yet again, amazed at how something as simple as a different day could produce such a staggering change in one's mental state.

It never ceased to frustrate me.

My feet carried me in the direction I usually walked when I headed for work. I found myself in the center of town, glancing at the shop windows of the Quinpool Road Business District, and wondering what the day would bring. I loved days like these; I could do anything I pleased and go anywhere my feet felt like taking me. The day was like a gift-wrapped box, waiting to be opened.

I found myself feeling suspicious of these optimistic thoughts, and I immediately took their mental mug shots and started a case file on each of them. If they turned out to be bad eggs in the long run, I'd know how to track them down.

At length I found myself nearing the downtown area. It was about a half-hour walk from my apartment building, which suited me just fine. I didn't want to live too close to work, but I didn't want to live too far away from it, either. My location, as Goldilocks might have put it, was just right.

It didn't surprise me that my feet took me towards Barrington Street. It was a familiar route, there was lots to look at along the way, and in the back of my mind I knew I wanted to drop in on my coworkers and show them that I was hale and hearty.

But first, I stopped into Apollo's Coffee, which was right next door to my place of employ.

The aroma hit me like a thrown quilt as soon as I stepped in the door. The familiar setting was a comfort to my troubled soul that no apartment-of-recent-suicide-attempt could ever be. This place had nothing to do with my misery or failure, and I welcomed each sensory fragment as it arrived in my brain.

I stepped up to the counter. Tamara, the owner-slash-manager, was at the cash, ringing in the order of the person ahead of me. As he moved down to the bar, where his beverage would be presented to him, I stepped up and pulled out my wallet.

"Hi, Jack," Tamara said. "Haven't seen you in a few days."

"I've been off," I replied, carefully choosing my words for their double meaning. "As a matter of fact, I'm still off today." I held out my arms, inviting her to take in the non-dress-code splendor of my jacket, shirt, and jeans.

"Must be nice," she said.

I thought about that for a moment. "Nice," I said, "is hardly the word."

She cocked an eyebrow at me. "You feeling okay?"

"Today? Great. Tomorrow? Who knows?"

She stared at me for a moment. "The usual?"

"Yep. No variation from habit there. What muffins have you got today?" I stepped over to the display case to eye the baked goods. "Oh, good. I'll have a lemon-cranberry."

Cranberries always cheered me up.

Tamara called out my drink order—a chai tea latté made with soy milk—and went to fetch my muffin out of the display case.

Tamara was a pretty woman, in her forties, I thought, with shoulder-length dark blonde hair and a face full of tiny freckles. She was always pleasant, and she knew how to run a business. I'd always liked her, and I'd always gotten along well with her. Not that we'd had time for any deep discourses upon the meaning of existence, but we always managed to have a nice chat.

I paid her, took my muffin, and moved down to the bar, where I found another familiar face.

"Hi, Jack," Carol said, glancing up from the container of soy milk she was currently steaming.

I smiled at her. "How are you, Carol?"

She glanced surreptitiously towards the cash, where Tamara was organizing papers of some kind or another. Then she looked back at me, leaned in conspiratorially, and widened her eyes.

"Bored," she said. "It's been dead in here this morning."

Carol had a way of making even grumpy and annoyed facial expressions seem cute and endearing. She was a slight young woman in her twenties, with thick blondish hair that came down to her shoulders and a pretty, pixie-ish face. She was also, to my mind, way too thin.

"Better for me," I replied. "I hate busy coffee shops."

She grunted. "You just hate people."

I nodded thoughtfully. "Well played," I said.

A sudden silence fell upon the establishment as Carol turned off the steamer. I almost felt myself start breathing again. The machines did a wonderful job, but they had an annoying habit of sounding like giant, elderly robots clearing their throats for a really long time.

She poured some of the chai mix into a mug and then added the recently-steamed soy. She stirred the concoction for a moment, topped it with some foam, and handed the delicacy over to me.

"Thank you, my dear," I said. "You steam a mean soy."

"Years of experience," she said.

I smiled at her again and stepped away from the bar.

I took a seat at a table near the front window, so I could watch the passersby on the street whilst I perused a newspaper and drank my latté. I thought I'd relax for a while before going next door to drop in on my coworkers. There was nothing quite like a chai latté to settle my nerves and take my mind off things.

The café was quiet for mid-morning. A couple of students sat at a table in the corner furthest from me, one of them typing assiduously on his Apple iBook G4. (It looked like a fourteen-inch model from where I sat). A couple of businessmen chatted softly about sales figures at a table near the counter. A lone man in a suit took his beverage from the counter and moved towards a table in the middle of the room.

I flipped to the comics page and took a swig of my chai. It tasted wonderful. The soy milk gave it a much smoother taste and texture than regular milk. I was glad I'd switched. I hadn't known how good a chai could be until I'd tried it with soy.

I looked out the window for a few minutes, watching the cars and pedestrians move up and down Barrington Street. It was a perfect fall day, and everyone was going about their appointed business. I was sure none of them had tried to kill themselves in the past week, and I was positive that none of them had seen any strange women dressed in 1940s clothing.

I sighed inwardly. It was so typical of my brain to start rummaging through the bad stuff, even when I was comfortable and enjoying myself. No such thing as just sitting down with a nice hot drink and a paper, just allowing the world to pass by. No, the brain had to go dig up the problems again. I was getting fed up with my brain. It was being uncooperative, and I wondered if I would ever learn how to shut it up.

I glanced into the café again. The lone man in the middle of the café now also had a newspaper, but he appeared to look down at it as I turned my head. It was almost as if he'd been looking up for a moment while I was looking out the window.

Great, I thought. Now I'm getting paranoid.

Just for the hell of it, though, I turned back to the window and started people watching again. I waited a couple of minutes, and then turned my head abruptly to look back into the room.

It happened again. The moment I glanced in his direction, the man averted his eyes and looked down at his paper.

I wasn't sure what I'd accomplished. If he was watching me, it was very likely he now knew that I was on to him. Perhaps if I avoided looking at him from this point on, he'd assume that it had been a fluke, and that I wasn't really aware of his scrutiny.

If that's what it was.

As I looked back at the comics page, I thought that it would be a pretty good idea to start working on my novel again, because it appeared that my imagination was in its top gear and ready to roll. Between the hospital and the hallucinations, I had some great fodder for further plot developments.

I tried to read a few of the comics, but they just weren't funny. I'd been giving them a try every couple of months or so, just to see if there had been any improvement, but I was invariably disappointed. The quality of the humor grew steadily lamer and lamer each time I gave them a glance. It was pretty pathetic, and I imagined I'd soon give up on them altogether. I wondered who their target audience was. Did that many people really find this stuff funny?

I folded the paper and put it on the other chair. Turning to the muffin on my plate, I cut it in half and buttered it. I continued to stare out the window and sip my chai, taking a bite of the muffin every once in a while. I checked to see if there was any reflection from inside the shop visible in the glass, but it was much too bright outside for anything to be discernible. There would be no spying for me today, evidently.

After another fifteen minutes or so, I wiped my mouth with a napkin and got up from the table. I took my plate and mug to the counter like a good citizen and bid my farewells to Tamara and Carol. As I reached the door, I took one more quick glance at the dark-suited man, and once again, I was rewarded with his quickly looking away from me and back at his paper.

I paused outside the café and looked down at my hands. They were trembling again. I took a deep breath and closed my eyes. Maybe if I just waited a moment, the feeling would pass. I tried to calm myself, but the trembling just spread from my hands to my arms.

Nearly panting, I stepped to the right and leaned back against the brick wall. I clenched my fists and looked skyward. This was intolerable. On top of having weird hallucinations, I was now either being watched or becoming completely paranoid. Neither option was particularly appealing. Why couldn't I just have a nice, relaxing day? Why couldn't I just be content and carefree? Even for just one single day? Why?

"Damn it," I shouted, banging my fist against the wall behind me.

The sounds around me suddenly became muffled, as if my head had just been shoved into a large piece of foam rubber. I looked up, expecting to see vehicles and pedestrians stopped, the better to stare at the man who had just cried out in public. Instead, I saw the world in slow motion again, just as I had in the hospital. I glanced at the wall behind me. There were ripples in the bricks, originating at the point where my fist had connected. It was like I had hit the surface of a pond.

I watched, fascinated, as the ripples spread further from their point of origin. They spread up, out, and even down to the sidewalk. They reached the curb to my right and continued onto the pavement beyond, causing the car parked on that spot to wobble slightly.

I squinted, not daring to believe what I was seeing. The car not only wobbled, but flickered a bit, then changed completely. I had been looking at something like a Honda Civic or a Toyota Corolla, but now it was larger, shinier, looking like something out of an old movie. There was a solidness to it that spoke of heavier construction and thicker metal. But it looked odd, like something from a steampunk version of the 1940s.

And then it was over. The ripples were gone, the car was back to normal, and everything around me sped back up and started making unmuffled sounds again.

Suddenly, being watched didn't seem like such a big deal.

Chapter Seven

I looked around. Again, no one had noticed my outburst. Had I even spoken aloud? Had I pounded my fist on the wall at all? Or had I imagined the whole thing?

I took a deep breath and stepped away from the wall, taking a quick look back to ensure that, yes, it was solid brick and not undulating in any way.

I took a deep breath and started moving. Paige's was next door. I suddenly felt a strong need to be in familiar surroundings again.

When I stepped through the door I was immediately comforted by the wood paneling, the subdued light, and the shelves upon shelves of books. I had only been away a few days, but for some reason it felt longer. It wasn't like I was in love with retail or anything like that, but Paige was not just a businesswoman. She was a book lover, a humanist, and a friend. The fact that she was also my boss was just a technicality. She didn't treat us like employees.

The first person I saw as I entered was Nina, one of my coworkers. Nina dashed up to me and hugged me tightly around the waist. Her diminutive stature would not allow her to hold on any higher.

"Jack," she said, her voice muffled by my jacket. "You're okay."

Thus was removed any doubt that my coworkers knew of my recent flirtation with Thanantos.

I returned the embrace and smiled. "Yeah," I said. "I'm okay."

Nina drew back and looked up at me. "You know you could have brain damage," she said, her eyes nearly boring into my skull. "You might not be able to remember where the books are in here."

I smiled and patted her on the shoulder. "The books are right there," I replied, pointing to the walls and shelving units behind her.

She glowered at me. "You know what I mean. You might get all confused about where certain types of books are."

"You mean like the romance novels? I honestly wish I *could* forget where they are."

"You're not taking this seriously, Jack. You have no idea what you might have done to yourself."

"Well, except for a few hallucinations, so far so good," I said. I tried not to let my smile get too large as I waited for her alarmed response to that.

Her eyes grew into shiny circles. "You see? You're having problems already. Why did you do that to yourself?"

"Nina," came a voice behind her. "Could you finish up that shelving in Self-Help?"

Nina scowled again and began to move away. "Keep a close eye on those symptoms," she said. "Let me know if it gets any worse."

"Yes, Doctor," I replied.

Paige stepped towards me, shaking her head. "Some things never change," she said as she threw her arms around me.

"I heard that," Nina called from somewhere in the Self-Help section.

Paige and I both laughed as we disengaged. She put a hand on my shoulder and looked at me intently.

Paige was a woman of average height and slim build, with dark hair cut at the jawline and flipped slightly inwards. She wore dark-rimmed glasses and usually had some kind of sweater on. Today it was a purple one, V-necked, with a frilly white blouse under it. She had a long, narrow face that bore an almost perpetually earnest expression, which made her smile all the more stunning when it revealed itself.

She cared about her employees, and they cared about her right back. At that particular moment, I was gladder than ever to be working for her.

"Are you okay?" she asked.

"Well, you know, that's a tricky word, that 'okay'. It covers a pretty broad territory."

"Jack."

She had her hands on her hips now, a sure sign that she had shifted from concerned-friend-mode back into boss-mode. She knew my penchant for sarcasm and took every opportunity to nip it in the bud. Other than that, I was a stellar employee.

I cleared my throat and nodded. "Yeah. Pretty okay, I guess. Considering the circumstances. A little shaken up, but otherwise unharmed. Except for the hallucinations I told Nina about."

Paige snorted. "Don't encourage her, okay? She goes off at the drop of a hat. You know that."

"I heard that, too," Nina called.

Paige and I started chuckling again.

"I miss her," I said, jerking my head back towards Nina's location. "Actually I miss all you guys."

Paige nodded. "Well, we miss you too. But a short visit is all you're getting today. You shouldn't even be thinking about work."

I shrugged. "I was feeling cooped up, so I decided to get of the apartment for a while. Also, I knew that you—well, some of you, anyway— knew about what happened. So I wanted to check in. Let you all know that I'm still around."

Paige's mouth drew into a straight line. "I'm really glad you're okay."

My eyebrows hiked up a notch. "Yeah. You and me both."

"You take whatever time you need, okay?" Paige said.

"Thanks. I appreciate that. I think a couple more days'll do it."

Paige put her hands on her hips and bit her lower lip. "I don't know, Jack. I think you should take all next week off as well."

My eyebrows shot up. "All next week? What the hell am I going to do with myself for a whole week?"

"You could write," Nina called from somewhere in the shelves.

"Her hearing is remarkable," I said, looking towards the right-hand side of the store. I couldn't see our tiny coworker anywhere.

"Yes. You'd think I'd've learned that by now," Paige replied.

At that moment, another of my coworkers appeared.

"Hey, Jeff," I said.

Jeff bounded up to me and gave me a bear hug. "Jack. It's so good to see you. We were all so worried about you."

"Thanks, Jeff. That means a lot."

"You going to be taking some time off?" he asked.

"Yeah. Next week." I nodded. I turned to Paige. "Which reminds me. I need to talk to you about some further time off in a few weeks."

"Sure. Let's go into the office."

Paige took me by the arm and led me to her personal inner sanctum, the place where the wheels of bookselling were greased and spun.

"Have a seat," she said as she closed the door behind us.

I grabbed a chair and sat down. She took a seat at her desk and turned to face me.

"So, what's going on?"

I took a breath. "Well, these know-it-alls at the hospital have insisted that I enrol in a day treatment program. It's six weeks long, and I'd have to be off work for the duration."

Paige rolled her eyes. "Always the skeptic, aren't you?"

"Well… yeah."

"Think about what you just tried to do. Don't you think something like this could be the best thing in the world for you?"

I twisted my mouth into as many shapes as I could think of. "I don't know. I have my doubts. But they wouldn't let me leave until I agreed to enter the program.

"Good. So when is it?"

"In a few weeks. They're going to call me in a couple of days with the details."

"Good. That's great. You just let me know the dates, and I'll put you on sick leave."

"Just like that?"

Paige nodded. "Yep. Just like that. I want you to take good care of yourself, Jack. And if that means being off for six weeks, then I'm happy to do it."

I sighed. "Thanks, Paige. You always take good care of me."

"Well, somebody has to. Now get out of here. You're not working today."

I stood. "I thought I might pick up a magazine before I head home."

She gave me an evaluating look. "Fine. Just don't bother my staff while you're out there. We have things to do, you know."

"You're a slave driver."

I opened the door and stepped back out into the store proper. Sally, another of my coworkers, was just coming in the front door. Her eyes widened, and she hurtled towards me, her long blonde hair streaming out behind her.

I was beginning to feel that if one more coworker came towards me at vehicular speed, I was going to wind up in the hospital again.

I hugged Sally, and when we stepped apart again, she looked up at me with a frown and a protruding lower lip. "No," she said. "No, no. You don't ever do that again."

I shook my head and put my hand over my heart. "Scout's honor," I said. "True blue."

She nodded, apparently satisfied with my response. "I want to read something you've written," she said, "not something written about you posthumously. You got that?"

"Got it."

She narrowed her eyes at me for a moment. "Because you know," she said, "if you ever do anything like that again, I will have to shank you."

I cocked my head. "Doesn't that go rather against the whole notion of being concerned for my physical well being?"

"You're not accounting for the rage."

"There'd be rage?"

"Oh, yes. Much rage. Red rage. Eyes-glazed-over kind of rage. Directed full on at you and your weakened physical form."

"I think that image will make me think twice if any stupid notions ever enter my head at a future date."

"I should hope so."

As we stood facing one another, sizing each other up like gunslingers in a spaghetti western, Nina floated past.

"Fairy girl was in again yesterday," she said conspiratorially.

I started to laugh, jarred by the sudden shift in milieu, and glanced at Nina's retreating form.

"Which was it this time?" I asked. "The Disney Fairies or the Rainbow Fairies? Or maybe the Pressed Fairies?"

Nina cackled as she headed for the fiction side of the store.

"I don't know," Sally said, thoughtfully rubbing her chin. "She doesn't really seem the violence-against-fairies type. As a matter of fact, last time she spoke to me, she seemed rather concerned that the Catholic Church might be persecuting fairies."

I rolled my eyes.

"Oh, and she's speaking with an English accent now."

I squinted. "When did that happen?"

Sally shrugged. "Last couple of times she's been in."

"Wow. How'd I miss that?"

"Guys."

I turned around to find Paige standing behind me. She'd hiked her eyebrows up a notch, and her mouth was in a funny shape.

"If you're going to talk about the crazy customers, do it in the staff room. Okay?"

Sally and I nodded sheepishly.

"Oops," Sally said abruptly as she glanced down at herself. "Outer-wear still intact. Must go change and clock in before tardiness and chaos ensue."

Sally slunk past Paige towards the staff room.

"And you," Paige said sternly—as sternly as a sweetheart like herself could manage, "get your magazine and get out of here."

"Yes, ma'am," I said.

I gave her a mock salute and headed for the magazine section.

All that remained was for me to decide what kind of mood I was in, *Popular Psychology* or *Rolling Stone*. Considering my recent foray into the world of mental institutions, the former seemed less and less likely as I approached the racks.

♦

I bopped around downtown for another hour and a half or so before heading home. My feet were starting to get a bit tired, so I grabbed a bus back to Halifax Shopping Centre, which was near enough to my abode to lessen the footwork considerably.

As I approached the front of my building, I slowed my pace. Someone was sitting on the front step reading a book. I frowned and squinted. The concrete step was not a comfortable place to sit, and the entryway was not in the direct path of the sun at the moment, so I couldn't imagine why anyone would choose that particular spot for an early afternoon read.

As I drew closer, I noticed that the seated person's lips appeared to be moving. I smiled, recalling the few times I'd seen someone moving their mouth whilst reading and how amusing it had looked. Moving a few steps closer, however, I realized that this was not a case of subvocalization at all; the person was talking to someone on their cell phone as they looked at the book.

I could now faintly hear the seated person's voice, which meant that I was close enough for them to hear my footsteps. The reader/speaker looked up, saw me, and—somewhat hastily, I thought—put the cell phone away. Now that he was looking right at me, I recognized his face, and I began to relax. The round face and dark-rimmed glasses belonged to Winston Chung, friend and keyboard player. I was no longer wary, but I still had no idea what he was doing there.

"Hey, Winston," I said.

He blinked a couple of times and put down his book.

"You didn't have to cut your conversation short on my account."

As I reached his position, he stood to greet me. "Hey, Jack," he said. "I was just talking to Derek. He came here with me, but since you weren't home, he went off to do some errands, and I said I'd wait for you to get back."

He stepped over to me, a bit tentatively, I thought, and gave me a timid hug. Winston was not a demonstrative man under normal circumstances, so this display was akin to gushing.

I returned the hug, so as not to discourage his foray into the world of human contact, and smiled slightly as we stepped apart again. I was oddly touched by the gesture.

"It's good to see you," he said, pushing up his glasses. "How are you doing? I mean, are you—?"

I smiled. "I'm doing pretty well, all things considered."

Winston nodded. "That's good to hear."

There was something odd about Winston's demeanour. He seemed a bit nervous, and his story about Derek dropping him off had sounded rehearsed. I felt my wariness returning. Given my recent bout of paranoia, however, I decided to refrain from saying anything. Also, Winston had a tendency to be a bit on the geeky side, so I might have been completely misreading him.

"Come on in," I said, giving him a gentle slap on the back of the shoulder as I headed for the door.

Winston picked up his book from the step—I noted it was the paperback edition of Harry Turtledove's *The Victorious Opposition*—and followed me inside.

"Still on the alternative history, are you?" I asked.

"Yeah," he replied, a hint of defensiveness in his tone, as if I'd been calling his choice of literature into question. "It's a good series."

"I read *The Guns of the South*," I said. "Really enjoyed it. But for some reason I've never picked up any of his others."

"That's too bad," Winston said as we ascended the stairs to my floor. "The other books are really good."

"Yeah," I said, heading down the hall to my apartment, "but no time-travel. You know me. Always about the time-travel."

"Is that why you like *Doctor Who* so much?"

I pulled out my keys and unlocked the apartment door. "*Doctor Who*,"

I said, ushering my companion inside, "is just plain fun. *That's* why I like it so much."

Winston shook his head. "Way too cheesy for me. And that movie they did back in ninety-six—"

"The movie they did in ninety-six shall not be spoken of again on these premises," I proclaimed. "It was ill-conceived and ill-executed. Thankfully, we shall soon have new *Doctor Who* to help erase the memory of Doctor Number Eight." I gestured towards the living room. "Have a seat."

Winston padded into the living room and took a seat on the couch. "You mean they're dragging it out again?"

"Yep. The BBC is producing new episodes. Christopher Eccleston as Doctor Number Nine. You want a cold drink?"

"Sure, thanks."

I stepped into the kitchen and opened the fridge. "Coke okay?" I called out to my guest.

"Yeah. Great."

I put ice cubes in a couple of glasses and poured some trademarked, brand-name, brown, fizzy, sugary liquid into each.

Stepping back into the living room, I placed the glasses on coasters on the coffee table and sat down in the chair next to the couch.

I had just settled myself into my seat and was reaching for my beverage when the door buzzer sounded. I sighed, took a quick swig, and raised myself out of my chair again. I stepped over to the door and pressed the speaker button on the intercom panel.

"Hello?"

"Hey, Jack. It's Derek."

"Hey, Derek. Come on up."

I pressed the door button on the panel and held it for a few seconds.

"Your partner in crime has completed his mysterious errands," I said, turning back towards Winston.

It was a fairly innocuous comment, but I saw Winston's expression flicker ever-so-slightly. I knew something was up.

"Well, I get no information from that face. You're inscrutable as always."

Winston frowned. "Dude. That's racist."

I frowned right back at him. "Excuse me?"

"That word. 'Inscrutable.' You're only using it because I'm Asian."

"Since when did the word 'inscrutable' become racist? I missed that meeting."

"Come on, man. It's been a stereotype ever since Hollywood started making movies."

I opened my mouth to say something else, but a knock at the door preempted me.

"Saved by the bell," I said. "Or the knock, in this case."

I opened the door. On the other side was our illustrious drummer, Derek Simmons. "Come on in," I said. "We were just discussing the racism of the word 'inscrutable'."

Derek smiled. "Why do I always miss the good stuff?"

He stepped into the room and gave me a hearty pat on the shoulder. "It's good to see you, man. We were all really worried about you."

"Geez. If I'd known I'd get this much care and attention, I would have tried to do myself in years ago."

Derek started laughing as he sat down next to Winston. "You kill me, man." Winston looked at him askance.

"Well that didn't work out at all," I said. "It was actually me I was trying to kill."

Derek laughed even harder, actually slapping his knee as he did so.

"You want a Coke?" I asked him.

"Yeah, man. That'd be awesome."

I suppressed a smile as I walked back into the kitchen. Derek said "man" at the end of nearly every sentence. That, combined with his round glasses, his shaggy brown hair, and his moustache and goatee, made him look and sound like a beat poet from the fifties or sixties.

I poured Derek's drink and returned to the living room.

"So," I said, placing Derek's glass on the table and reseating myself, "what've you been up to?"

Derek took a sip of his Coke and eyed me suspiciously. "What do you mean, man?"

I sat back in my chair and smiled. "Your reaction serves to confirm my suspicions. You guys are up to something. Winston, despite his usual inscrutability—"

"Stop doing that," Winston muttered.

"—has appeared just ever-so-slightly uncomfortable since he got here. And now you, with your suspicious glance and 'who, me?' attitude. You look like the man who just ate my last sardine."

Derek put his glass down and stared at me. "What?"

"Never mind. I just made that expression up this minute, and it didn't work out at all. Regardless, you guys are both looking pretty shifty."

As if on cue, the two conspirators shifted in their seats. They looked at each other, then looked back at me and shrugged. I was having a helluva time not breaking into laughter.

"Hmph," I said. "Then I guess I must just be paranoid. Not surprising, really. You know. Mental health issues and all."

This statement was met with silence. I was uncertain whether the discomfort hanging in the air was due to their conspiratorial behavior—at which they were proving to be anything but adept—or to their uncertainty about my mental health. At this point, I didn't care. I decided to let it hang for a moment, just for pure devilment.

Finally, Winston cleared his throat.

"So, um… how's your mom?" he asked.

This was among the most ill-advised of courses he could have pursued. I narrowed my eyes at him and began to bare my teeth.

Derek whacked him on the arm. "Jesus, Winston."

Winston looked at him, mouth half open. "What?"

"Don't ask him about his mom. What the hell are you thinking?"

"I was just trying to make conversation."

"Man, you have a memory like a sieve."

Thankfully, before this line of discourse could develop into the train wreck it was destined to become, another knock sounded at the door. Derek and Winston immediately sat up a little straighter and turned their gazes towards the source of the sound.

"Isn't a knock at the door usually preceded by a buzz at the buzzer?" I asked no one in particular.

Neither of my guests said a word. I squinted at them, and they shifted in their seats.

"Well, I'm not getting up again." I looked at the door and raised my voice. "It's open."

The knob turned, the door opened, and a head poked into the room. It was a female head, topped with long blonde hair and adorned with freckles. It was a rather cute head, and it belonged to Tina, Derek's girlfriend.

"Hey, Tina," I said. "Nice to see you. Come on in."

She stepped into the apartment, but kept her hand on the doorknob.

"Sorry," she said, glancing back out into the hall. "My cell rang when Derek and I were coming in, so I took the call down in the lobby."

This scenario was becoming more entertaining by the minute. None of these people had any kind of poker face at all. They were telegraphing nervousness and discomfort across the miles.

"And so," I said, "here's the third member of our merry band of conspirators."

"What?" Tina looked startled at my comment. "Wha-what do you mean?" She glanced out into the hall again.

"What's going on out in the hall, Tina?" I asked.

"Hmm? What?"

"You keep looking out into the hall."

I glanced again at Derek and Winston. They were both examining the carpet.

"Yeah," Tina said. "Well, there's someone here who wants to see you."

"Wow. A fourth person. Why didn't you guys tell me we were having a party here? I would have picked up mixed nuts and a shrimp ring."

Derek laughed in spite of himself.

Tina stepped further into the room, and the door opened slightly wider. As I watched my fourth visitor come into view, I felt a cold knot begin to tighten inside my stomach.

"Hello, Jack," Gillian said. "Sorry for the cloak and dagger."

I stared at her for a moment. She wore a black leather jacket and a dark red skirt. Her jet-black hair was coiffed and shaped and perfect, and her exquisite brown eyes were slightly moist as they regarded me.

I had to clear my throat before I could speak again. "This is not even remotely funny," I said, a slight rasp in my voice.

"It's not meant to be," Gillian replied. "I just wanted to see you."

"You mean you wanted to see what's left of my smouldering carcass."

"That's not fair, Jack," she said.

"Oh, 'fair'," I said. "You want to talk about 'fair'? I can talk about 'fair' until the cows come home. Because I know exactly what it means and how it does not in any manner whatsoever apply to my life."

"Jack, give her a break, will you?" Derek said.

"You," I said, whipping my gaze at him. "You have no part in this. Except for bringing her here against my will. You will remain silent. Do you understand?"

Derek resumed his examination of the carpet.

Tina stepped forward with a growl. "Will you stop being so fucking dramatic? Gillian was worried about you, and she wanted to see you. Is that so hard to understand?"

"No," I said. "No, not really. But what *is* hard to understand is why you, someone I hardly know and who knows absolutely nothing about me or my lot in life—"

I stood now, the muscles in my neck and shoulders tightening, my jaw beginning to clench, my voice gradually becoming louder.

"—is standing there in righteous indignation—"

I half shouted and half spat the last few words at her.

"—and judging *me*!"

She took a step back, her eyes widening slightly. Gillian placed a steadying hand on her shoulder, then stepped forward and glared at me. "Nice, Jack," she said. "Real nice. Take it out on someone who's just trying to help."

I gaped at her. "Help? Is that what you call this? 'Cause it looks like some kind of twisted intervention to me."

"Is he a drug addict?" Winston murmured to Derek. "I didn't know he was a drug addict."

"Shut up, Winston," Derek whispered.

I narrowed my eyes, took a deep breath, and turned towards Derek and Winston. "Good advice," I said, more quietly and evenly than I'd thought I could manage. "Shutting up is an activity I highly endorse at this juncture."

"Jack." Gillian, said, a hint of exasperation creeping into her tone.

I turned back to her and pointed an accusing finger. "No," I said. "Not another word. This shutting up activity, it applies to all of you. And it is to be immediately followed by another activity I like to call getting the fuck out of my apartment."

I could hear Tina's breathing now. When I looked at her, I understood why. Her nostrils were flared, her fists were clenched, and she was glaring at me with such heat in her eyes that I thought for a second or two she might laser me in half. We stared at each other for a moment, like two gunslingers from a Sergio Leone movie, and then she snorted, turned on her heel, and stormed out the door, slamming it behind her.

I gaped at the door for a moment, and then allowed a slight chuckle to emerge from my throat. "And that's how it's done," I said. "It's quite easy, though I doubt any of you could quite match Tina's style."

Gillian was suddenly inches from me. Her proximity had scarcely registered when I noted her arm being raised and her hand moving rapidly towards my face.

The slap connected impressively, and the force and sting of it were enough to turn my head to the side and send me staggering backwards and into my chair. My legs could go no further backwards, but the rest of my body wanted to, so my knees bent, and my ass descended onto the arm of the chair. The landing was unbalanced, and so my next act was to topple unceremoniously onto the carpet.

Winston was no longer looking downwards in discomfort. As I hit the floor, I noted his wide-eyed stare, which was moving back and forth between Gillian and myself.

Derek stood up and grabbed Winston's arm. "Come on," he said. As he dragged Winston to the door, he paused to look at Gillian. "We'll be in the car, okay?"

Gillian nodded perfunctorily, and my two musician friends exited.

I sat up, rubbing my cheek. "I already have someone who does that for me," I said, "but that was really quite impressive, so if the position ever opens up, I'll let you know."

Gillian bit her lower lip and shook her head ever-so-slightly. "God," she said. "I'm amazed I stayed with you as long as I did."

"And I'm amazed," I said, struggling back to my feet, "that I never discovered what a temper you have. Not to mention your killer right arm."

"Talking wasn't cutting it," she said.

Her jaw was set, and her eyes were boring into me. They weren't lasers, though, like Tina's had been. They were more like those huge drill bits that oil companies use to dig into the ground for some bubblin' crude. I found myself swallowing hard.

"Sit down, Jack," Gillian said quietly. Too quietly, I thought.

"I really don't think this is such a—"

"Sit. Down."

For a small and slight person, Gillian wielded a hefty presence. I'd always likened her to a little fireball. She was ably living up to that assessment.

I held her gaze as I stepped slowly to the left and lowered myself back into the chair.

"I really don't know what you expect—"

She held up her index finger to cut me off. She kept it raised as she stepped over to the sofa. She looked down briefly as she sat and arranged herself, and then she looked back up at me again.

"All I want," she said, "is for you to drop the bullshit and tell me what happened. That's all. I still care about you, Jack, and I was worried. So I want to hear the story from you. Okay?"

"Gillian—"

The finger went up again. "Stop protesting," she said. "And no bullshit."

My shoulders sagged, and I sank further into the chair. I didn't want to deal with her right now, but she wasn't giving me much choice.

Why the hell did she still care? And if she cared so much, why had she left me to begin with?

I knew very well the answer to that second question, and it didn't do much to console me in my present circumstances. I could feel rage starting to boil up in me. Rage at her, for leaving me, for continuing to care, and for being in my face with her index finger stuck up in the air.

I loathed her and loved her at the same time. I despised her, and I adored her. She was a strong woman, stronger than I had ever imagined, and her coming here to confront me was an act that filled me with both terror and an odd sort of admiration. She was impressive. Most impressive.

Her hands were now quietly folded in her lap. Her expression had not softened, but her eyes were not drilling quite so furiously now. She was simply waiting.

She knew she had won.

And I hated her for that.

"All right," I said. "Fine."

♦

I sat in my chair for a long time after Gillian had gone. I tried not to think, or to feel, or to do anything other than simply sit and stare at the opposite wall. I let the world wash over me, like I was a stone on the beach. I thought maybe if I sat there long enough, the waves would eventually reduce me to nothing, and I would no longer be subjected to the onslaught of sensory input that seemed to twist me into uncomfortable shapes every time I so much as opened my eyes.

Under normal circumstances, I was absolutely no good at meditation, but I understood the concept and purpose of it sufficiently to know that if there was ever at time that I needed to be free of thoughts, this was it. I basically froze. Nothing moved. Not my arms, not my legs, not my brain, not anything. I just sat, breathed, and turned off the hurt. Self-protection was paramount.

I don't know exactly how long I sat there, but it seemed like an eternity. For a moment or two, it even felt like I was really turning off the world. I almost dared hope that I might maintain this blessed state for an indefinite period.

It was not to be, however. At some point in my self-imposed stillness, my willpower proved weaker than my intentions, and stray thoughts and feelings began to re-enter the council chamber and make their opinions known. My reverie subsided, and the world returned to its normal place in my consciousness. It felt not unlike coming back from a wonderful vacation and realizing you have to return to a job you don't much like.

I was also returning to a house that was awash in clutter. Fragments of ideas, scraps of memories, bits of emotions, were all strewn about the inside of my skull like discarded toys in a child's bedroom. It was chaos, and I wished that I could turn it all off again. I knew, however, that I'd already shot my bolt, and that the thought-free state I'd just experienced was now far from my grasp.

Thoughts were everywhere now… on the ceiling, in the bedroom, in the closet, under the coffee table, in the refrigerator… everywhere. Thoughts of Gillian, of Lydia, of the hospital, of the mysterious man in the coffee shop. Thoughts of death. Thoughts of despair.

Thoughts of my mother.

Twice within four days someone had mentioned her. First Uncle Eric, during his explosive visit to the Short Stay unit, and now Winston, in a clumsy and ill-fated attempt to make conversation.

I had been successfully avoiding thinking about her, at least up until the day I'd decided to call it quits and check out of Hotel Earth. On that day, all the things that I had ever done wrong and all the things that had ever happened to me had all piled on top of one another in an attempt to crush my brain. My mother's situation and my inadequacy as a son had been but two of the many satchels in the heap, but their presence had been keenly felt.

And now they were staring me in the face.

My mother was locked away in a mental institution, and I, ungrateful wretch that I was, was dealing with the situation by simply not dealing with it. I stayed as far away from her, both physically and mentally, as I possibly could.

♦

My mother, Priscilla Richmond, *née* Stevens, had been a journalist, and a damn good one. She'd written for both the *Herald* and the *Daily News* at various points in her career, and she'd later switched to television, where she'd continued to excel.

Where she didn't excel was being a single parent.

My father, William Richmond, had disappeared when I was a teenager. We never found out what had happened to him. He could have died, or lost his memory, or been abducted by aliens, or he could simply have run away. We just didn't know.

Needless to say, this took its toll on my mother. She coped by throwing herself more and more into her work and less and less into her parenting. I would later develop a theory that she had become so terrified of losing anyone else that she simply shut down her family instincts so future losses wouldn't matter as much.

Any dime-store psychologist will tell you that's a sure road to disaster.

Meanwhile, the teenage me was left flapping in the breeze, believing that the whole shemozzle was my fault.

You don't do that to a kid.

Mom was a great provider, but a lousy nurturer. So for me, material possessions became symbols of love and affection. And I had no shortage of those. She bought me all the comic books and novels I wanted, and when I wanted to learn to play guitar, she spared no expense. It was great, for what it was worth, but it wasn't parenting.

So I adopted the family strategy. I pushed the warm-fuzzies as far away as I could reach, and I built my little fortress out of words and notes and pop culture.

But that's not the interesting part.

It so happened that one day—a day like many others before it—while Mom was in one of the editing suites at the TV station, putting the finishing touches on a piece that was to air that night, she had what I have come to refer to as a "psychological event". One minute she was pressing buttons and trimming video clips, and the next minute she was out of her chair, out the door of the suite, and wandering down the hall, a strangely vacant look in her eyes. (I wasn't there, of course, but that's how one of her colleagues described it in the police report.)

The next few minutes were, to put it mildy, chaos. The report contains conflicting details here and there, but the overall gist of the story is consistent throughout.

According to witnesses, my mother stopped at an emergency cabinet, broke the glass, and removed the fire extinguisher. She then continued down the corridor to the main reception area, where she proceeded to crack open the skull of one of the secretaries with said fire extinguisher.

Apparently, this act did not generate enough blood for my mother's current tastes, so she took advantage of the fact that everyone around her was utterly stunned, and she went back to the emergency cabinet, dropped the fire extinguisher on the floor, and grabbed the axe.

She managed to get good solid hits on two more skulls, a couple of arms, and a thigh, before being brought down by police. When it was all over, two people were dead, one was in a coma, and three more were in serious to critical condition. My mother's kneecap had been shot out, and her mental state was anybody's guess.

I was in my twenties when all this happened, so I was self-sufficient. I didn't have to suffer the vagaries of foster home placement or rearing by some unknown relative. I simply went on with my life, minus the physical presence of the already emotionally absent mother.

I went to the mental hospital after I received the phone call, and I saw her there, locked up in a padded room, in her straight jacket, drool foaming at the corners of her mouth. I observed a little metal door in my brain slam shut, and I walked out of the hospital, never to return.

From what I understand, she's never spoken a word since.

♦

And now, thanks to some serious button-pushing by my uncle, my bandmates, and my ex-girlfriend, I was revisiting this horrible story, watching it unfold again in the bubbles of my memory. My limited capacity for meditation had been reached, and my thoughts had returned.

All of them.

With a vengeance.

And now I had to make them stop.

I groped around in my cluttered mental room in search of something, anything, that would divert my thought processes away from family history. Something intellectual would work, perhaps a puzzle, or a mystery, something I wanted to figure out. Yes, that would do the trick.

And in a moment, I had it.

I got up, exited the apartment, and walked down the stairs and out the front door. I walked down the driveway, into the parking lot, and headed straight for the chain link fence at the back of the property. I positioned myself about halfway along its length and turned to face the back of the building. I stood there for a moment, just surveying the area.

This was where the imaginary cobblestone path had appeared when I'd looked out my bedroom window the day before, and I was pretty sure that the simple fact of that imagining meant that I was headed down a road from which there was likely no return.

No, no. This is a puzzle. I want it to be a puzzle. A mystery. Not an hallucination.

I'd latched onto the wrong thing. Why did all roads seem to lead to mental health? Or lack thereof?

There's a padded room waiting for you, a little voice said.

But part of me railed against that. I'd heard it time and time again: People who think they're crazy rarely are. People who are mentally unstable are often convinced they are absolutely fine.

So, if I thought I was going crazy, what did that mean?

And if I wasn't going crazy, then why was I seeing things that weren't really there?

The imaginary path I'd seen had started right at the spot where I was standing and had run directly to the back door of the building. I stood there, looking up and down the length of the parking lot, seeing in my mind's eye that strip of cobblestones, willing it to be there.

I'm going to find out how this works. Because it's a puzzle. Right?

I closed my eyes and concentrated, visualizing the cobblestone path. I imagined it starting right at my feet and running all the way across the lot to the back door.

I opened my eyes.

There was no path. Not even a single stone.

Of course not. Nothing ever really worked that way. Nothing mental, at any rate. Whatever you want your mind to do, it's almost guaranteed to do something else.

I could feel frustration welling up inside me. If something weird was happening, I wanted to be able to control it. But no, this was not going to be the case. The hallucinations were going to control me instead, and my mental state would deteriorate until I was no longer able to function in society at all.

There was now a hard knot in my stomach. If I didn't keep a close watch on myself, I'd start to panic. I didn't want that to happen.

But fears of mental instability were not sufficient. Oh, no. Not for my overactive brain. Not even images of mothers in straight jackets were sufficient. Now thoughts of Gillian were starting to creep from the back of my mind towards the giant IMAX screen at the front. One more brick. The wheelbarrow had already been full. It was straining under the weight of the load now. I didn't know how much more I could take.

I turned around and kicked the fence. "Fuck," I shouted, and kicked the fence a second time for good measure. I closed my eyes, put my hands on the fence, and tried to get my breathing back to normal. After a moment, I turned back towards the building. I started to move towards the driveway, but stopped short.

The cobblestone path was once again before me. It led directly across the lot, just as it had before, bisecting the huge rectangle of pavement and ending right at the back stoop of the building.

"This is nuts," I muttered to myself.

I stared at it for a long time. It didn't waver, or flicker, or fade in and out. It just sat there, a perfectly normal-looking cobblestone path, waiting for someone to walk along it.

So I did.

It was not solely a visual phenomenon. I could feel the stones under my sneakers. I could hear the crunch of my soles against them. I took step after step, slowly making my way towards the other end. I kept my eyes on the ground, thinking the stones might vanish if I so much as glanced away from them.

I was about halfway along the path when I realized that my passage was suddenly blocked. As much as I hated to take my eyes off the stones, I looked up to see what was in my way.

It wasn't a what. It was a who.

My hospital visitor had returned. She stood there in front of me, big as life, her hunter green beret and burgundy coat just as I remembered them, her black leather gloves, her fancy boots, her bright red lipstick.

Her deep green eyes.

I took a ragged breath and considered the possibility that I had just entered the realm of the rubber room. Somehow, however, it didn't feel like that. Everything was entirely too real, and I no longer felt agitated.

I was a bit concerned, but I wasn't distraught.

I gazed at her for a moment, just taking in the realness of her unreality. I didn't know what else to do.

She, for her part, seemed content to do the same thing.

Finally, the silence and the suspense became too much for me. The dominant part of my personality reasserted itself, and I was compelled to speak.

I doubted much good would come of it.

"I'm going to go out on limb, here," I said, "and hazard a guess that you're not actually present, and that I've really managed to do a number on myself with that pills-and-booze stunt I pulled a few days ago."

She smiled. It was a lovely smile, but it really didn't help me much.

"You don't look like you're out of the silent movie era," I said. "So why don't you speak?"

"I prefer to listen," she said.

It was my turn to smile. Her voice was lovely, but it held undertones of brashness, even brassiness, that reminded me exactly of the way many actresses delivered their lines in old 1940s movies. She not only looked out of place; she sounded out of place.

"Listening is a good skill," I said, "but I was hoping you might be able to tell me a few things."

She cocked her head slightly. "Like what?"

I shrugged. "Oh, I don't know… Like, for instance, who you are… and why you keep appearing… and why no one else can see you… and why you dress like Ingrid Bergman. Just to name a few factoids I seem to be lacking."

She laughed this time. "What a wonderful way with words you have."

"Um… Thanks. And if I may say… you have quite the way with alliteration."

She smiled again. "You may. And thank you."

I let out a long breath through my nostrils. "This isn't actually getting us anywhere. I still don't know anything, here, except that you have a nice smile and speak in fairly short sentences."

She cocked her head again and looked at me, her eyes sparkling like emeralds in a glass bowl. She seemed genuinely entranced by the encounter, and as flattering as that was, it was beginning to unnerve me.

"Look, uh, Miss…?"

"Yes, of course," she said, shaking her head slightly as she pulled in her gaze a bit. "How rude of me. It's Irene. Irene DiFalco."

"Well, Irene, it's nice to meet you, if in fact this is real at all and not just taking place inside my head. My name's Jack."

"Yes. Jack Richmond. I know."

"Really." I looked at her hard. "Have we met before?"

She shook her head. "No. We haven't met. But, as I said, I listen."

"So you were listening in the hospital."

She nodded. "I needed to know about you."

I put a hand to my head. "You needed to know about me?"

She nodded again.

"Why?"

Her smile faded, and her gaze drifted down. "I don't really think I'd best get into that right now."

I crossed my arms. "Right. Because you're really an hallucination, and you can't give me any information that I don't already have in my sub-conscious. Right?"

She looked back up at me, her eyes slightly wider now. "No. No, that's not it at all. You have to understand how real this all is. I just—" She looked away again. "I just can't tell you everything right now. You wouldn't understand."

I closed my eyes and shook my head. "Right. I get it. I'm just sup-posed to go along with whatever game you're playing and just—" I glared at her and took a step forward. "And just forget about how fucking weird this all is?"

She recoiled, nearly stumbling backwards. "You mustn't speak like that."

"Oh, right. I forgot. No swearing in 1940s movies. You can smoke cigarettes, but you can't swear."

Her eyes narrowed. "What's a… movie? And what are… cigarettes?"

"You don't know what a movie is? Or cigarettes? Well, you're in a movie, aren't you? Isn't that what this is? My movie-buff imagination playing tricks on me and presenting me with a lovely damsel from the Humphrey Bogart era? Isn't that it?"

"I don't understand what you're saying. I've never heard that word movie before. And is that a name? Humphrey… Bogart, is it? I don't know that name."

I took a step back and looked her up and down. None of this was making any sense. If this was all an hallucination—or better yet, a dream—why would my subconscious conjure up the image of a woman who was the very epitome of the forties heroine and have her ignorant of movies and cigarettes? It didn't add up.

But then, this was my subconscious I was talking about here.

I turned back to her. "Look. When I saw you on my TV this morning, you said they were watching me. You said there wasn't much time. What did you mean?"

She shook her head again. "I was… where? On your… what?"

I was getting nowhere with this. "You spoke to me this morning. Don't you remember? You were standing at a train station. You were watching a train leave."

She squinted and looked down, rubbing her chin. Finally, she looked up again. "Oh! I think I understand now. I must have projected myself without realizing it."

"Projected yourself?"

"Yes, yes. Sometimes, when we're feeling especially strong emotions, we can project our essences across great distances and give someone a message."

My head was beginning to throb at this point. "Now I'm the one who doesn't understand. You're saying you projected yourself into my television to give me that message?"

"Well, I don't know what a television is, but I suppose you must have gotten my message." She frowned. "Even though I really didn't know I was sending one." She looked up at me again. "What did I say?"

"You said there wasn't much time, and that they were watching me."

"Yes. That's right. I had only just learned of it myself. And it distressed me terribly. I must have projected that to your… What is a television, anyway?"

Considering that she didn't know what movies or cigarettes were, or who Humphrey Bogart was, it should not have surprised me that she was also unfamiliar with the concept of television. This, however, was turning out to be a surprising day, and I found my mouth hanging open at nearly every turn.

"It's… um… well, it's a device that… um… lets us see images from far away. They're usually recorded, but sometimes they're happening at the same time as we see them."

Her smile was returning. Her eyes were getting their lustre back.

"That sounds fascinating," she said. "How does it work?"

"How does it work?" I repeated. I couldn't believe I was having this conversation. "Well, I don't claim to know the ins and outs of it, but it's basically a device that translates an electrical signal into images and sound. It used to be just done with something like radio waves, but now it's more often done over a cable system."

"We have nothing like that in my world," she said.

"Your world?" I asked. "What do you mean, your world?"

"Well… I mean… I come from…" She frowned slightly. "It's difficult to explain."

I closed my eyes and let my shoulders droop. "Great. Back to that again. How are we supposed to have any kind of conversation if you won't tell me anything?"

She looked suddenly sad. "I'm terribly sorry. I didn't mean to confuse you." She took a tentative step towards me. "Can you forgive me?"

The look on her face was so earnest, so entreating, that if I didn't forgive her immediately, I would have felt like I was kicking a puppy.

"Um, yeah. Sure. But, uh, listen, can we get back to this whole 'being watched' thing?"

"Oh, of course. I came here to tell you about it, but it appears you already know."

My frustration level was rising rapidly. She seemed a decent sort, but none too swift. I was beginning to see that the information would come to me at her speed, not mine.

"Well, the funny thing is, Irene," I said, trying to keep the sarcastic edge in my voice as blunt as possible, "I actually don't know that much at all. Just that you're worried about time, and that somebody's watching me. Why would someone be watching me?"

"Well, because they know, of course."

I kept my hands at my sides and breathed deeply. Lashing out was not going to get me anywhere.

"They know what?"

"Well, about your ability to see." Her tone was one of surprise.

I breathed again. "That's not so very unusual. Most people have the ability to see."

Her eyes widened again. "Good heavens. Of course they don't. Why, that would mean—utter chaos."

I was beginning to suspect that we were talking about completely different things.

"What kind of, um, seeing are we talking about here?" I asked.

"Well… Oh. You thought I was talking about…" she waved a hand in the air. "No. I'm not talking about seeing." She pointed to her eyes. "I'm talking about seeing." She opened her eyes wide as she said this and made a sweeping gesture with both arms.

"Okay. I'll bite. Seeing what?"

"Why, seeing between worlds, of course. What else would I be talking about?"

But of course, I thought. What else could she possibly be talking about? Why was I being so dense? Wasn't it obvious? I was seeing between worlds. It made perfect sense.

"Between worlds?"

She nodded. "Yes. Between your world and mine."

"Well, I'm glad to know there's a reason for this communications gap we seem to be experiencing here. Different worlds, huh? Sounds like a few sitcoms I've seen in my day. We could have some wacky misunderstandings, you and I. And a maid, of course, one from the other side of the tracks. Probably get great ratings."

She just stared at me.

"Right, right, I know. Sitcoms, ratings… more words you've never heard. I'm guessing there's not a lot of technology in your world."

Her eyes flew open wide, and she looked nervously around, as if she feared someone was watching or listening.

"What's wrong?" I asked.

She pulled her focus back to me. She looked as if she were trying to calm herself down. "That word. We don't use it."

I thought for a moment about what I'd just said. "Which word? Technology?"

She winced. "Yes."

"That doesn't make sense. You don't use it, but you still know it?"

She sighed. "Yes, we know the word. But it's taboo."

"Taboo?"

"It's forbidden."

"Yes, I know what taboo means. 'Technology' just seems an odd choice of word to put on the list, that's all."

She winced again at my repetition of the word. "It's not just the word that's forbidden. It's the entire concept."

I was ready to wake up now. The scenario had gone from novel to bizarre, from bizarre to incredible, and now it was moving from incredible to ludicrous.

"Look. Irene. This is all fascinating, and you're really quite a lovely hallucination. I've enjoyed chatting with you, really I have. But it's time for me to pack some things and check myself back into the psych ward again. Okay?"

She stepped towards me. "You're not safe here," she said.

I nodded. "I agree. If this keeps up, I might try to hurt myself again. So, yes, the psych ward it is."

She grabbed my arm. She felt surprisingly solid, for an hallucination. "You can't stay here," she said.

"What? What are you talking about?" I pulled my arm from her grasp. "This is ridiculous."

She kept her hand in the air for a moment, then let it drop. "You don't believe me," she said, looking at the ground again. "I've failed. There's no more time."

"Time for what?" I asked, exasperated.

My brain couldn't take much more of this, I knew. I rubbed my temples for a moment, then my eyes.

When I refocused my gaze, she was gone. So was the cobblestone path

"Women," I muttered, as I turned towards the driveway.

Chapter Eight

(Thursday, 3:40 A.M.)

I awoke in the middle of the night, feeling that something was amiss. I couldn't recall hearing anything, and it didn't feel like I'd been in the midst of a bad dream, so I was curious as to why I'd awakened and why I felt as I did.

I was fully awake, so I decided to get up and go to the bathroom. I usually had to do so at least once each night anyway, so I figured I might as well do it now. The room was almost completely dark, but a faint light coming in through the window was sufficient for me to see my way to the hall.

As I passed the window, however, something caught my eye. I thought I'd caught a glimpse of a moving light down on the ground below, so I stopped and looked down at the parking lot. It was extremely dim outside, but I could see a small colored light moving back and forth down there. I could also just make out the general shape of a person holding this light.

As I squinted and craned my neck, I could see that it was not a light I was seeing, but some sort of display. It looked like a tiny screen with several colored LEDs beside it. My first thought was that some drunken neighbor of mine was staggering through the parking lot, waving his MP3 player around. Or perhaps his GPS unit.

But the movement wasn't random. It was a back and forth motion, like someone taking a reading of some kind, or looking for something.

It wasn't lost on me that the place he was standing was the exact location where I'd had my conversation with Irene DiFalco.

Without turning a light on, I grabbed my clothes off the dresser and pulled them on. I stepped to my apartment door, opened it quietly, and moved out into the hallway. I figured my best chance of not being heard was to go down the back stairs to the rear door of the building. Then I'd pop out and surprise him, and find out what he was doing.

When I reached the bottom of the back stairs, I stepped up to the door and put my ear to it. I heard nothing. If he was moving around out there at all, he wasn't making any noise.

I knew I had to act quickly. If I waited much longer, he'd probably finish up what he was doing and leave. So I took a deep breath, counted to three, and slammed myself against the door's crashbar.

"What are you doing?" I called out as I dashed towards him.

I had thought to catch a glimpse of his device before he tucked it away, but as I reached his position, I suddenly found that he was holding something quite different in his hands.

A gun.

A Glock 17 semi-automatic pistol, to be precise.

I screeched to a halt and put my hands in the air.

"Whoa," I said. "What's this all about?"

He was motionless as a gargoyle. He held me in his steely gaze, not blinking, not swallowing, not even visibly breathing. His handgun was at the level of my throat, and the hand holding it didn't waver a millimeter.

Even in the dim parking lot light, I recognized him.

"You were in the café," I whispered. "You were watching me."

He said nothing. He simply took a step towards me and raised the gun to my face.

I jumped back nearly a foot. "All right," I said. "Shutting up now."

He waved the gun towards the driveway, the international sign for "Start moving".

I swallowed. He waved the gun again.

I started moving.

"I think you'd find me a lot more cooperative if you'd just tell me what's going on," I said. "Giving me the silent treatment isn't really going to much endear you to me, you know."

Apparently, shutting up was not one of my great strengths.

My companion must not have liked my witty banter, because a moment later I felt something cold on the back of my neck and heard a faint hiss.

I thought of *Star Trek* again as my knees betrayed me and the edges of my vision began to blacken.

♦

When my senses returned to me, the first thing I noticed was a massive headache. I reached up to put a hand on the back of my neck. Whatever device my assailant had used had left no trace that I could feel.

So maybe I'd imagined the whole thing. Maybe I was still in my bed.

I opened my eyes and discovered just how wrong I was. I was seated in a metal chair at a metal table. The room was small and drab, lit only by a bare bulb hanging from the low ceiling. There was one door, no windows. Across the table from me was a second chair, in which sat the silent man from the coffee shop and, more recently, my back parking lot.

"So where'd you get the hypospray?" I asked. "You pay a little visit to the twenty-third century or something?"

"You talk too much, Mister Richmond."

My companion's lips had not moved. The voice had come from another part of the room. I looked around, an act which brought me great physical discomfort, and finally discerned a shadowy shape in the corner to my left.

He stepped forward. I still couldn't make out his face, but I could see he wore a dark suit, just like his compatriot.

"My ex-girlfriend used to tell me that a lot," I said. "I think it's some kind of defense mechanism. You know, to keep people at arm's length."

The man took another step forward. I could see now he was older than his colleague, perhaps in his sixties. His face was gaunt, wrinkled, tired. His hair was mostly grey.

"I'm surprised you're not smoking a cigarette," I said. "You know… go for the full effect."

He looked down at the seated man. "Well entrenched in popular culture, this one," He said.

The other man nodded slightly.

"What surprises me, Mister Richmond," the older man said, "is that you don't seem to be afraid of us."

I tentatively stretched my neck and quickly decided to stop.

"Look, pal," I said. "First off, I'm only halfway conscious right now, so things aren't really reaching all the way in here." I pointed at my head. "Secondly, I tried to kill myself a few days ago, and frankly, I don't know if I'm ever going to be successful at anything. So, if you want to save me the trouble, go right ahead. Just give me a heavier dose this time."

The man's mouth straightened into a line. "A man who has nothing to lose is a dangerous man indeed."

I closed my eyes and sighed. "Okay, now you really do sound like the dude from *The X-Files*. Could you cut the melodrama and tell me what the fuck I'm doing here?"

"I'm not sure if I really want to do that yet."

I squinted at him. "Well, I know your silent friend here was measuring something out in my back parking lot, and I'm pretty sure it has something to do with that woman I was talking to out there, so why don't you just fill in the blanks for me so I'm not guessing at everything else."

A look passed between the two men when I mentioned "that woman". Either I'd just confirmed something they suspected, or I'd just told them something they didn't know.

"Look, guys. I was just minding my own business. Really. I didn't go seeking her out. She just appeared. Five times now. Three times in the hospital, once on my TV screen, and then once in the parking lot behind my building. I don't know why she's coming to me, but it's getting annoying. I just want to get back to my life. Or what's left of it, anyway."

I wasn't exactly sure why I was telling them all this. I was probably giving them exactly what they wanted. I didn't know if they were good guys or bad guys or in-between guys. I guess I figured if I just kept talking, I might avoid further physical injury. Dying wasn't a big fear for me; I just didn't want to be in a lot pain when it happened.

"So, it's true, then," the older man said.

"What I just told you? Yeah, it's true. I wouldn't make shit like that up. Well, I mean, I would. I'm a writer. This sort of thing would make a really great story, you know? So in that context, sure, I'd make something like that up. But it really happened to me, so no, I'm not making it up. I would never claim something like that happened if it hadn't. I mean… I may be crazy, but I'm not insane. Well, you know what I mean…"

"Yes, Mister Richmond. I get your meaning. But now, you see…" He raised his eyebrows and shrugged slightly, turning the palms of his hands towards me. "Well, I have a problem."

I looked up at him. He didn't look angry. He didn't look upset. He didn't even look irritated. He just looked tired and maybe a bit perplexed.

"Great." I slumped in my seat. "So I've added a new wrinkle to whatever scheme you're hatching here. Is that it?"

The seated man looked up at his older colleague. The older man nodded thoughtfully for a moment.

"You're an observant man, Mister Richmond," he said after a moment. "I imagine that comes from being a writer. Always paying attention to details. Always using your imagination to figure out plot problems. Plus, your evident affinity for movies and television seems to be standing you in good stead."

"Well, it doesn't take a genius to figure out that you guys work for some kind of secret organization, and that you're involved in some kind of research into... I don't know... into whatever this woman represents. Unless, of course, she's really just a figment of my imagination, in which case maybe it's my brain you're interested in. And if that's the case, you're welcome to it, 'cause it's caused me nothing but grief."

This elicited a slight smile from the older man.

"You're very perceptive, Mister Richmond," he said. "Perhaps a bit too perceptive."

I frowned. "Perceptive? I was thinking maybe nut-house crazy."

"Oh, don't sell yourself short, Mister Richmond. You're hardly crazy. You have your issues, of course. We all do. Yours appear to be holding you back somewhat. But crazy? I think not."

"Well, then, what? Am I actually on to something? The whole 'woman from a different world' thing? Or is it my fucked up brain chemistry?"

"Well, I doubt that it would be prudent for me to go into much detail, but one thing I'll tell you: Something's different about you now. I'm not sure precisely what that is, but I think it would be useful to find out."

"So, what, you're going to dissect me? Is that it? Because if that's the case, I'll just take door number one, if it's all the same to you. The one with 'quick and painless death' behind it."

"Calm down, Mister Richmond. We don't want to dissect you. We just want to run some tests. That's all."

I narrowed my eyes at him. "Oh, that's much more reassuring. Run some tests. I don't even know who you people are."

"And you're not going to know. We have no intention of telling you any more than we already have. We'll run some tests, we'll send you home, and you won't remember a damned thing."

"Oh, great. Now we're into the whole *Men in Black* deal. Why are you even telling me that? Why are you even talking to me?"

He smirked at me. He actually had the gall to smirk.

"Because," he said. "I know how much you enjoy melodrama."

I stood up. "You son of a bitch," I said through gritted teeth. "You wanted me to entertain you? By playing Fox Mulder to your Cigarette-Smoking Man? What kind of fucked up mind would do something like that?"

"My job is not as interesting as you might think," he said. "I add a bit of spice whenever and however I can."

He moved to the door. His colleague got up to join him.

"Sit down, Mister Richmond. Someone will be along in a moment to take you to a more comfortable room."

I sat down, fuming. If he'd wanted to get my goat, he'd succeeded. I'd been genuinely curious about what was going on. My fear instincts hadn't fully kicked in, but my general inquisitiveness had. He hadn't appeared threatening or evil, so I'd given him the benefit of the doubt. But to stand there so smug and superior and tell me how much he'd enjoyed watching me think, well that was another thing entirely. I would not be fodder for someone else's weak imagination. That was taking things too far.

A few minutes later, the door opened again. A man in a grey uniform stepped in. He was tall and muscular and had a shaved head and goatee. He looked like a wrestler stuffed into a corporate setting.

He stood aside and crossed his arms.

"I take it I'm supposed to go with you…?" I said.

He glared at me. I sighed and stood up.

"Doesn't anybody talk around here?" I asked as I stepped past him into the corridor.

He poked me in the back with some kind of baton several times as we moved through the corridors. He'd whack me on the right shoulder when he wanted me to turn right, and on the left shoulder when we were heading left. I refrained from turning around and telling him off, as someone of his build could and probably would inflict injurious pain upon me if I didn't do exactly what he wanted.

I was not a big fan of injurious pain.

Finally, after what felt like ten minutes of wandering through dimly lit corridors and riding in dimly lit elevators, we arrived at a grey door, set into a grey corridor wall with a dozen other evenly spaced grey doors. My burly friend pulled out his keys, opened the door, and ushered me inside.

I turned to say something to my taciturn escort, but by the time I turned to face the door, it was already nine-tenths closed. I opened my mouth, but I managed nothing more than a slight "ah" sound before the gap closed, the door thundered shut, and the room shook.

I turned away, strode into the room, and kicked the first thing I could find, which was the uninviting cot that sat by the far wall.

"Fuck," I yelled at the wall. "Fuck and shit. What in Jesus fuck damn hell is going on here?"

I dropped my butt onto the cot and put my head in my hands. I tried not to think too much. I just focused on my breathing, which was none too meditative at this point. I stared through the gaps between my fingers at the concrete floor and tried to stop my brain from latching onto any particular concept. I figured maybe if I zoned out for a while, I might calm down.

After a few minutes, my breathing slowed a bit, and the pounding of the blood through my head diminished somewhat. I took my hands away from my face and took in my surroundings.

The room was like a prison cell. Besides the cot upon which I sat, there was only a chair, a sink, and a toilet. My heart sank further into my bowels as I realized my stay was likely to be an extended one. If I was being provided with a bed and a toilet, it was unlikely I was just here for dinner.

I got up and began to pace the small room. I had a lot of pent up energy, and it wasn't going to dissipate just sitting on the cot. I had to move.

Part of me was numb, but another part of me was terrified. I'd never been in a situation like this, one where I had absolutely no control whatsoever and knew absolutely nothing about what was going to happen. A little ball of panic began to form at the bottom of my esophagus.

I didn't much relish the thought of pain or death being inflicted upon me by the hand of another. If I was going to die, then I wanted it to be on my own terms. This—this mystery, uncertainty, and waiting—it was unconscionable.

I tried to figure out what I had done to bring such a dramatic set of circumstances upon myself. Was I really that bad a person? Was my attitude so fully and royally fucked up that this was what I deserved? Had I wronged someone that egregiously? Pissed off just the wrong people? What was it?

Well, I *had* tried to kill myself. But that was self harm. I wasn't trying to hurt anyone else by removing myself from the mortal coil. I was trying to improve it, by taking away a malfunctioning unit. Plucking the bent eyelash. Chucking the bruised apple. I thought what I had tried to do was a logical thing.

It wasn't, of course, but that's the spin my troubled mind put on it.

I stopped at the sink and placed my hands on the edge. I leaned my weight on my arms and hung my head. I once again tried to breathe evenly, but it was still proving difficult. My thoughts were racing, and my conscious mind was beginning to see flashes of things that my subconscious mind had been screaming at it for a while now.

I closed my eyes and gripped the edge of the sink. It was beginning to occur to me that the events of the last few days had not been merely a bunch of random things that just happened to occur in the same small space of time.

There was something more to it than that.

My suicide attempt was not just a thing I'd done earlier in the week. I knew that now. It was not just a bad decision made in a bad frame of mind. It had been the beginning of all the madness that had ensued. It was only after I'd regained consciousness in the hospital that my odd experiences had begun.

So what did that mean?

I returned to the cot and sat down. For some reason, I hadn't connected the dots until now. But it was all starting to make sense. Something about what I had done had triggered these events. I'd brought this insanity on myself, simply by trying to leave the world.

But what was it about what I'd done? Was it the drugs themselves? The rum? The combination? Did I get closer to death than I'd originally thought? Did my brain chemistry change?

And which would be worse? Finding out that this was all an elaborate hallucination brought on by my very active imagination, or finding out that it was real?

I swallowed hard. That was a tough call; as much as I disliked the circumstances in which I now found myself, the thought of losing my sanity was a bitter notion indeed.

I stood up and returned to the sink, this time to splash some cold water on my face. It felt good, and for a moment my head felt clearer.

For a moment.

I had nothing to work with here. I'd had a conversation with a woman who couldn't possibly exist, and I was now in the clutches of an organization that, in all likelihood, didn't officially exist. I knew nothing. And armed with that kind of knowledge, I was absolutely powerless. I didn't know where I was. I had no way of communicating with anyone, I didn't know the names of the people who'd put me here, and I didn't even really know if I was actually in full possession of my mental faculties.

Which meant I was helpless. I'd have to endure whatever tests these people wanted to perform on me, and after that, who knew? I might be taken home, or I might disappear forever, and no one I knew would ever find out what had happened to me.

The suicide thing was starting to look like a walk in the park.

I wiped my hand across my still-damp face, and then turned to the toilet. My bladder was calling to me—it had been calling to me for some time, actually, as I'd missed my middle-of-the-night wizz—so I unzipped and watered the water. I rinsed off my hands, flushed, and went back to the cot. All I could do now was lie down and wait.

As I sat on the edge of the cot and made ready to recline, I glanced at the wall to my left. I'd thought that it was plain and unadorned when I'd first entered, but I now saw that there was a shape drawn on it. It looked like someone, probably a previous occupant, had tried to imagine his way out of here by drawing an archway.

I smiled. A nice thought, that. Just like *Simon in the Land of Chalk Drawings*. Whatever you draw comes to life. If I'd had a pencil or a piece of chalk on me at that moment, I would have added some detail to the lines there and made it a bit more realistic.

Not that I was any artist, mind you, but I would have given it the old college try.

But as I continued to look at the simple rendering, I began to see that there was more detail in it than I'd originally noticed. What I'd first seen as lines forming a simple shape was in actuality a more complex drawing, with depth and shadows. I was sure that if I looked at it from the right angle, it would appear to actually recede into the wall.

And was that color I saw there, down in the corner? Had the prior occupant found something green with which to add a little grass at the bottom?

But there was red there, too, I now noticed. Red bricks, just above the grass. How could I not have noticed that when I first looked? Was I that caught up in my own thought processes?

I stood and approached the wall. This was insane. It wasn't me. I hadn't failed to observe the details. The details simply hadn't been there when I'd first looked. They were appearing, one by one, as I looked at it.

The red bricks now reached halfway up the wall. The edge of the archway was now rendering itself in large stone blocks, sandy in color. The mortar between the bricks was pale grey, dry and cracking. There were stones now amongst the blades of grass. Within the archway itself, I could now see the beginnings of a street-scape. A sidewalk. The side of a building. A newspaper vendor. An old truck. Passers-by.

And then, she was there. Walking towards me. Walking towards the archway. She smiled as she approached, her green eyes glistening. She stopped inside the arch and extended her hand. Her glove entered the room.

"Come," Irene said. "There isn't much time."

Chapter Nine

I looked at her, basically a vision in wool gabardine, and very nearly burst out laughing. If this was an hallucination, it was a damned fine one, and I'd be crazy not to go along with it.

After all, I was in a small grey room with a cot and a toilet. The scenery looked much better on the other side of the imaginary archway.

She waggled her hand at me. "Come on," she said, urgency creeping into her voice. "We can't keep this open for long. We're taking a big risk even opening this into your location. They'll know within minutes that we've done this."

"They?"

She flared her nostrils and glared at me. "I'll explain later. For now, just come through."

What did I have to lose? It was either stay in the dingy grey room and await unknown tests followed by an unknown fate, all courtesy of an unknown organization, or go through a magic archway with a beautiful woman into what looked like a scene from a 1940s movie.

The math wasn't hard.

I took her hand, and she pulled me through. There was an odd sensation for a moment, kind of tingly, and a bit like I was walking into a stretchy membrane that finally split and reformed behind me. My ears popped as I reached the opposite side of the archway. When I looked behind me, there was nothing but a brick wall.

"It's a bit disorienting the first time," she said. Her smile had returned.

I looked around. I was standing beside an old brick building at the end of an alleyway. It wasn't a dingy alleyway like many of those I'd seen in films, where it was the only place the hero could run to escape his pursuers. It wasn't dark or creepy or damp or anything like that. It was just a narrow street-like entity running between two buildings. It was an odd alley, though, in that it was a *cul-de-sac* rather than a through-way. The wall through which I had come was at the end of the alley, effectively blocking passage. No film characters, pursued or otherwise, could use this alley to get anywhere. Except for people like Irene, of course, who seemed to be able to extend the alley into other places. Like my little grey holding cell.

Nothing I was seeing was unfamiliar to me. There were brick buildings, stone buildings, cement buildings. Out the end of the alley I could see asphalt, sidewalks, curbs, more buildings, and a few automobiles. They were really old automobiles, mind you, but they were recognizable to me. I'd seen their kindred in many scenes of many films.

"Are you all right?" Irene asked.

I looked at her. "Yeah. I'm fine. Just getting my bearings." I glanced around again. "Uh... where are we, exactly?"

She laughed. "Oh, this is Halifax."

I looked askance at her. "Excuse me?"

Her green eyes were fairly dancing with merriment. "I thought that would get your attention."

"Well, you were right. Now what are you talking about?"

"This isn't your Halifax. It's my Halifax."

I didn't reply. I just stared at her for a moment. She had this infuriating habit of making short, simple statements that made absolutely no sense at all.

She could evidently sense my discomfiture, as she immediately took me by the arm and began leading me out of the alley.

"You'll find a lot of similarities between the two, I'm sure," she said. "Based on what I've seen of yours, the geography is quite similar, but of course your world has a lot of... um... advancements, shall we say, that my world doesn't."

"It looks like you're in a completely different time period here," I said.

"I know that's what it looks like," she said, "but that's not the reason. I actually have no idea what the time difference is between our worlds. The main reason for the differences you're seeing is that there are certain things we don't do here. And there are other things that we do here, that you don't do in your world."

We were now out of the alley and on the main street. We stopped, and she turned to me, an earnest expression on her face.

"You have to promise me something," she said. "While you're here, you must respect certain things."

"Like what?"

"You remember when we were speaking outside your home? You said a certain word, and I told you it was taboo?"

I recalled the conversation. "Oh. You mean—"

She put her hand on my lips. "No. You mustn't say it. Not here."

"But it's just a word."

She shook her head. "No. It's not just a word. Not here."

I frowned. "You know, I really wish this all made some kind of sense."

"This isn't your world. Remember that."

I nodded vaguely. "Okay. All right."

She nodded sharply, evidently satisfied with my response. "And to be on the safe side, you'd better not mention any of the things in your world that have come about because of…" She paused, almost chuckling. "…because of what we just talked about. People here won't understand you, and I don't think it would be a good idea to draw that kind of attention to yourself."

"But how am I supposed to know what things I can mention and what things I can't?"

"It'll become evident to you very quickly. You'll notice a certain absence of certain types of things. If you don't see it, don't talk about it." She leaned towards me and put a hand on my arm. "Okay?"

I let out the breath I'd been holding and gave my head a mild shake. "All right…"

I looked again at my surroundings. It must have been approximately the same time of day here as it was back in my version of Halifax, because the shops near us looked like they were just opening. Some of the shop-keepers were putting their wares into bins outside their storefronts. People were bustling up and down the sidewalks, and vehicles of varying types and sizes were rumbling up and down the street.

"Well, you have vehicles similar to the ones I know, so I guess that's a valid topic of conversation."

"That's right." Her smile was almost like that of a teacher praising a prize student.

I continued scanning. "And you have fire hydrants, so that leads me to believe you also have indoor plumbing."

"Very good."

I frowned. It all looked so normal. Antiquated, but normal. What was missing?

I continued my scan. There were houses. There were shops. There were vehicles. I knew that Irene was unfamiliar with movies and television, so I was probably right in assuming that those things had never been developed here. I looked at the houses, trying to imagine what forms of entertainment were inside them. Certainly no pay-per-view and video-on-demand. I saw no cables attached to any of the buildings.

Then it struck me. There were no cables attached to any of the buildings. Not just TV cables. No cables at all. No telephone cables. No power lines. Nothing.

I looked at the street again. There were streetlights, but they weren't electric. They looked more like gas lights.

These people had no electricity.

I looked at Irene. "You have no—"

She put her hand on my lips again. "No. We don't. And that's another word you'd better keep to yourself."

So she knew what electricity was, but she didn't know what movies or television were.

I narrowed my eyes at her. "Again with the knowing about something but not having it. This place is making my head spin, and I just got here."

"We'll speak no more of it for now. It's far too easy to misspeak and incur the wrath of some passerby. We don't want that."

I frowned. "Because…?"

She patted me on the arm. "We just don't want that. Trust me."

She was still smiling, but there was something unnerving about what she was saying and the way she said it. I was beginning to get the impression that the social conventions here were very different from those in my world. Maybe even the laws.

My world, her world… I was beginning to think in those terms, and that bothered me. I still didn't know if I was experiencing something real, or if my mind had simply decided that it had had enough and had transported me to a place of whimsy and intrigue, just to keep me interested.

Then a more solemn thought occurred to me: What if I had actually died? What if everything I'd experienced since taking those pills was a product of my now-deceased mind? What if I had never awakened in the emergency room? What if I had never been admitted to the Short Stay Unit and released to go home.

What if I had actually succeeded in my suicide attempt?

I looked at Irene. Her expression was neutral, but something in her eyes told me she had a pretty good idea what I was thinking.

"This is all very strange to you," she said quietly.

"What was your first clue?"

"You feel you've lost your mind," she continued, "or are in the process of losing it."

"Something like that. Yeah."

"You wonder if you even survived your attempt to end your life."

"What, you're a mind reader, too?"

She laughed. "No. Good Heavens, no. That would be wrong."

It would be wrong. Not impossible, just wrong. They might not have electricity here, but they sure as hell had something else.

"Well, you seem to know what I'm thinking."

"We're very intuitive here. We learn how to read each other, to judge others' moods. The very attuned among us can almost tell what a person is thinking."

"And you're very attuned."

She smiled, but she averted her gaze. Her faced reddened slightly. "I do have a gift, yes."

"Does this gift also enable you to travel to other worlds?"

She looked up again, her gaze falling sharply upon me. "No. That's not something I can do alone."

I took her reaction as an indication that I should not pursue this line of inquiry. I put my hands up.

She took a step towards me. "I'm sorry," she said. "I didn't mean to react so harshly. I know you don't understand our world yet. So please, when you meet other people here, be careful what you say. Not everyone will be as understanding as I am."

I nodded slowly. "Thanks for the warning."

She took my arm in one hand patted it with the other.

"Come along," she said. "We have a bit of a walk ahead of us, and there's someone I really think you should meet."

◆

We walked along the street past a few houses and a couple of shops. I knew I wasn't in my home city, but the surroundings felt eerily familiar. At one point, I stopped and turned in a circle to get a sense of the place.

"The harbour's that way," I said, pointing to our right.

She nodded. "See? Not so different from your Halifax."

"I haven't seen any street signs," I said.

She cocked her head. "Street signs?"

I looked sharply at her. "You know… signs… posted at intersections… telling people what the names of the streets are."

"You name your streets?"

"Well… yeah. We kind of need street names in order to get around."

She had a strange frown on her face now. "I see. Your navigation of cities is quite different from ours."

"Well, if you don't have street signs, then yes, I guess it is."

"I'm not sure you'd understand our way."

I was pretty positive she was right.

She took my arm again and we continued.

"Where are we going?" I asked.

"I told you. We're going to see someone."

"Who?"

"You'll see in due course."

I didn't like the sound of that at all.

We continued on, the eerie familiarity of the street growing stronger with each step. I knew that I knew the street. I knew I'd been on it before. But the maddening thing was, I really hadn't. I'd been on a different version of this street, on another world, far distant but easily accessible by those who knew how.

Probably the thing I found most unnerving about it all was the fact that everything looked so normal. Sure, there were no power lines, but that was a small absence. The buildings looked like any I'd see at home. They looked historical, but they looked "normal" historical. The streets were paved with what looked like asphalt, the trees bore green leaves and looked like maples, oaks, elms. The grass was green. The cars were old-fashioned, but they were made of metal and had rubber tires. I couldn't identify any of the makes or models, but they looked like normal antique cars.

But underneath it all, beyond these surface similarities, I now knew there were fundamental differences. Our worlds might have been developing along a parallel course, but somewhere along the way, they took a very drastic departure from one another. I was curious to know what the crucial moment might have been, and what had happened—or failed to happen—as a result.

My attention kept returning to the vehicles parked on the streets and in the driveways. While much of what I was seeing around me was similar to what I knew back home, the cars were different enough to keep me reminded that I was in a completely foreign place. It wasn't just the fact that they were old-fashioned-looking; that was more quaint than anything. There was something more fundamentally unfamiliar about them, and it had been bugging me since I'd arrived.

Finally it hit me. I stopped, staring at a sleek but sturdy roadster parked along the curb.

"What is it?" Irene asked.

I strode towards the vehicle. "If you people don't have…" I let the sentence trail off, knowing that finishing it might get me in trouble.

"What are you doing?" Irene started moving towards me.

"Just taking a closer look," I replied.

I stepped up beside the car and squinted into the driver's side window. There were dials and gauges on the dashboard, but they were large and clunky. They didn't look like they were driven by electricity. And how could they be? This place had no electricity.

Irene was now beside me. "Please don't touch other people's property," she said, concern creeping into her voice.

I turned to her. "I wasn't planning on it. I just needed to know what these things had on their dashboards."

I stepped around to the front of the car and crouched. There were headlights, all right, but I could see right away that they weren't electric bulbs.

I stood up, shaking my head. Irene was looking at me oddly, her head cocked slightly to one side.

"It's all gas and steam, isn't it?" I asked.

Irene frowned slightly. "Yes, of course. What else would it be?"

I rolled my eyes. She could sound a bit patronizing from time to time. The teacherly demeanour will only get you so far in my books.

I found myself shaking my head again as I stepped back onto the sidewalk. Apparently I'd walked into some kind of steampunk novel. The notion both amused and disturbed me. I really wasn't in Kansas anymore.

We'd barely walked two more blocks when I found myself stopping again. We were now in an area that contained more shops and fewer houses. My neck was becoming sore from all the turning back and forth my head was doing. I was nearly getting dizzy.

"Wait a minute…" I said.

"What is it?" Irene asked.

I stopped dead in my tracks. Just ahead, on the right, was a large brick building with what looked like smokestacks jutting from its roof. What the stacks emitted, however, looked more like steam than smoke. The distinctive smell of brewing hops was nearly overpowering.

"That's a brewery," I said, indicating the building.

She nodded.

"That's wild. This is Agricola Street." I indicated the street we were on. "And that's Young Street." I pointed towards the intersection just ahead of us.

She smiled that disarming, ingenuous smile again. "This is a quaint concept, these street names of yours. It's rather pleasant, really, in a curious sort of way."

I was still turning, looking, inspecting. "This is so weird. I mean, I know this intersection, but it's also completely foreign to me."

I shook my head and started moving again.

Irene's smile broadened. "I know what you mean," she said. "I had similar feelings when I first visited your world."

Irene led me three more blocks, at which point we turned right down one of the side streets. About a block and a half down she stopped.

"We're here," she said. "Please be careful what you say when we go inside."

"Or else I'll be a ritual sacrifice?"

She rolled her eyes. "Don't be silly."

I stopped her as she turned towards the front door. "Umm… What about my clothes? Are they going to offend anyone, do you think?"

She looked me up and down. "No. I don't think so. They're a bit odd, but nothing offensive. I don't think you need to worry."

She turned and proceeded up the front walk.

"What, me worry?" I muttered to myself.

Irene knocked on the door of the house. A moment later, the door opened. A woman in a maid's outfit appeared. She smiled, greeted Irene, and stepped back to allow us entrance.

"This is Jack Richmond. I think the councillor is going to want to speak to him."

The maid nodded as she closed the door behind us. "I'll get him, ma'am. May I take your coat?"

Irene removed her outer garment and handed it to the maid.

"Councillor?" I asked.

"Yes. You're about to meet the councillor for this district."

"Interesting. We have city councillors in my version of Halifax, too."

Irene smiled again, and we stepped into main room of the house.

Again, things looked fairly normal. There was a fireplace, a mantelpiece, curtains on the windows, a sofa with a low table in front of it, a few upholstered chairs, a rug in the middle of the floor. There were gaslights above the mantle and numerous candles at various strategic positions around the room.

Except for the slightly more modern furniture, the place looked almost Victorian.

"Please, have a seat," the maid said. "The councillor will be down in a few minutes."

"Isn't it a bit early in the day to be calling on someone?" I asked Irene.

She shook her head. "No. He'll have been up for some time already. He has an office upstairs. I assume he's working."

"I don't want to interrupt him…"

"No. It's fine. He'll want to see you."

I tried to imagine what a councillor in this world would possibly want from the likes of me. I was probably a novelty, being a visitor from elsewhere and all, but I couldn't tell him much about my world if talking about technology was such a taboo here.

I hadn't realized that sitting down would feel so good. I was more exhausted than I'd thought, and I was having trouble focusing. My brain seemed to be distancing me a bit from my situation, and that was probably a good thing. A little numbness went a long way towards staving off the hysterics, which would no doubt kick in later.

I consoled myself by reiterating that my current circumstances were a marked improvement over sitting in that grey holding cell, waiting for God-knew-what.

"By the way," I said. "I never did thank you for rescuing me from that little room I was locked in."

She drew her mouth into a straight line. "I'm glad you're safe. I just hope that the people who were holding you didn't…" She trailed off.

"Didn't what?"

Footsteps coming down the stairs prevented me from getting my answer. Irene stood and looked expectantly at the room's entrance. She flashed me a quick glare, and I followed suit. This was evidently an important man.

A moment later, the councillor entered. He was not a big man, not nearly so impressive-looking as I'd imagined. He was actually rather short and a little bit stooped. He was thin, not excessively so, but enough that his expensive-looking suit seemed overly roomy. He wore little round wire-framed glasses and had tufts of white hair sticking out like a fringe all around the back and sides of his otherwise bald head.

Irene bowed her head and curtsied. "Councillor Greaves," she said.

I followed her lead and bowed towards him.

"Irene," the man said in a surprisingly strong voice. "Good to see you, my dear."

Irene stepped forward. "Councillor, this is Jack Richmond. He comes to us from another place."

The councillor pursed his lips and nodded, looking me up and down.

"Welcome, Mister Richmond," he said after a moment. "I hadn't thought to meet someone from your world so soon."

I raised my eyebrows slightly.

"Councillor Greaves knows of your world," Irene said.

"Oh, yes," Greaves said, nodding thoughtfully. "A number of us do. Irene here has given us quite detailed reports on what she's seen. It was a most exciting discovery." He coughed and stepped further into the room. "But let's not stand around talking. Come and sit down. I'll have Charlotte get us some tea. Would you like some tea, Mister Richmond?"

I nodded. "That would be nice, yes."

"Good." He gestured to the center of the room. "Please. Sit down." He turned towards the front hall. "Charlotte, fix us some tea, will you?"

The maid appeared in the doorway. "Yes, Councillor. Right away." She disappeared again.

He toddled over to the sofa and sat down. "Now, I imagine you have a lot of questions, Mister Richmond. As it happens, I have some of my own, but we'll start with you, since you suddenly find yourself in a strange place with little frame of reference."

This seemed all a tad too civilized. I had lost my bearings a long way back, and I didn't see much hope of regaining them anytime soon. I'd been cruising along, allowing events to unfold and really trying not to think too much about them. There was precious little that had happened to me over the last few days that made any real sense, and suddenly being presented with an opportunity to have some questions answered was almost too much to take in.

"I don't mean to be rude," I said. "But I'm having a hell of time convincing myself that any of this is real."

Irene winced and drew in a sharp breath. I looked at her. Her brow was creased, and her lips were tight.

"What?" I asked.

She shook her head slightly. "We're… um… we're not accustomed to such strong language."

I frowned, trying to figure out what I'd said. "Strong language?"

Irene leaned towards me and spoke in an almost inaudible whisper. "You said…" She paused to steel herself, then spoke even more quietly. "You said 'hell'."

I could feel my shoulders sag. If 'hell' was a taboo word in this society, then I was going to have a most challenging time here.

"I use a lot worse than that one back home. It's just part of the way I talk."

Greaves was nodding. "Yes, Mister Richmond. I understand. Unfortunately, we have a fairly conservative society here, and it's probably a good idea not to draw too much attention to yourself."

I suddenly felt like I was in the episode of *Star Trek* where everyone acted like Mormons until the noonday bell chimed and everyone ran into the street and started whaling on each other.

"Right," I replied with a sigh. "I'll shelve that in the same compartment as the list of topics Irene's told me not to discuss."

Greaves nodded. "Yes. We mustn't discuss anything too advanced."

I narrowed my eyes. "Yeah. About that. There's something I don't understand. How can you know about something and not use it?"

Greaves exchanged an amused look with Irene.

"Mister Richmond," he said after a moment, "I think your question opens up a rather weightier topic than would be wise for us to discuss at this early stage in your visit. I would invite you to get to know our world a little better first, and then, when you have a more comfortable understanding of our ways, we can discuss these concerns of yours."

That was, without a doubt, the most polite, respectful, and elegant blow-off I had ever received in my life. There was no doubt in my mind that this man was a skilled politician.

"You're not going to try and correct my wild preconceptions?"

Greaves laughed. "No, not at all. You'll come to adjust your view of us over the time you spend here. I think you'll find, as you get to know us, that we're a fairly peaceful and agreeable people. We have our rules, of course, but within that structure, we're pretty easy to get along with."

"I hope you're not claiming to have a Utopia here."

Greaves laughed. "Good Heavens, no. We're not perfect. We have our problems. But I think you'll find perhaps there's somewhat less to worry about here than in your own world."

I sat forward in my chair. "Okay, that brings up another question. How do you know so much about my world?"

Greaves nodded his head. "We don't know a lot about your world, truth be told. In fact, we only just discovered it a few months ago. We've been quietly observing what we can, but it hasn't been easy."

For some reason, I found myself becoming agitated. "You're not making any sense," I said. "I don't understand any of this. This whole 'alternate worlds' thing… It's impossible. It's the stuff of science fiction. We can't detect other worlds or universes back home, so how can you possibly do it here? We're way more advanced than you people are."

Greaves shook his head. "That's a relative term, Mister Richmond. You may be more advanced than we are in some ways, but I can guarantee you that we are more advanced than you in other ways."

I put my head in my hands. "I've only met two of you so far, so I'm really hoping that not everyone here speaks in such cryptic statements."

Greaves laughed. "I'm simply trying not to overload you with information. You've been through quite a lot, I understand. So I want you to take in new facts at a pace that's reasonable and comfortable for you."

"Thanks a lot," I said. "But you don't have to coddle me. I'm a big boy. I can handle it."

Greaves nodded again and looked at Irene. "What do you think, Irene? Is he ready for this?"

Irene scrutinized me for a moment. When I sat up again and looked at her, I saw that luminous smile again. I had forgotten for a moment how incredibly lovely she was.

"I think he's quite strong, Councillor," Irene said. "He has a stubbornness about him that I've rarely encountered before."

Greaves raised his eyebrows. "So you believe his stubbornness is a strength, do you?"

Irene nodded slightly. "In this case, Councillor, yes. I do. I don't believe he'll rest until he knows what he needs to know."

Greaves smiled. "And what do you think he needs to know?" He appeared to be enjoying this interchange.

Irene looked at me again for a moment before returning her attention to the councillor. "He needs to know that this is real. That he's not imagining it. He needs to know that he's sane."

I managed to refrain from mentioning that in my world, it was rude to talk about someone while they were sitting right there in front of you.

"Ahhhh…" Greaves put his head back and looked at the ceiling for a moment. "Well, Mister Richmond, I'm not sure that I can give you the evidence you need to prove that you are not dreaming. However, I can give you my assurances that, as far as I am aware, this place in which you find yourself is quite real. It's certainly real to me. And I believe Irene would tell you the same thing."

Irene nodded.

"Yes, that's very nice. But I'm sure that the inhabitants of a dream or hallucination would tell me the same thing." I shifted in my chair and looked him in the eye. "The thing is, I don't know if I can trust my mind anymore. I recently attempted to kill myself with a large amount of medication, and I think I might have caused myself some brain damage. I'm not discounting the possibility that I'm actually dead, and that this is all some elaborate creation of my own recently-departed consciousness."

At that moment, Charlotte re-entered the room with a tea tray. She stepped into the middle of the room, placed the tray on the coffee table, and took a step back.

"Will there be anything else, Councillor?" she asked.

"Not for the moment, Charlotte," he replied. "Thank you."

She curtsied and stepped out of the room.

Greaves leaned forward and began distributing teacups to the edges of the table. "Do you take milk?" he asked.

I nodded. "Yes. Thanks."

A moment later I had a steaming cup of tea in my hands. The china pattern was unusual but attractive. The cup and saucer bore tiny pastoral scenes, all done in a rust color on a bone background.

I took a sip. "This is nice," I said. "It tastes a bit like Earl Grey."

Greaves pursed his lips and raised his eyebrows. "Not familiar with that one," he said. "This is Grimsby tea. It's imported from England."

"From England?" I asked, startled. "I thought you'd only just—"

Greaves grinned at me as I caught myself. I'd forgotten for a moment that we were sitting in a house in an alternate version of Halifax. Of course there would be an alternate England.

"Oh," I said. "Right. I guess there'd be a lot of places with the same names."

"Indeed, there probably are," Greaves replied. "Care to try a few?"

His good cheer was infectious. He seemed to be honestly enjoying my visit. I glanced at Irene, whose own serene smile continued to have a strangely calming effect on me. These were happy people, I thought. My muscles relaxed a bit just thinking about it.

"Okay," I said. "Canada, obviously, if we're in Halifax."

Greaves nodded. "Oh, yes."

"France?"

"Yes."

"Germany?"

"Uh-huh."

"East and West Germany, or unified?"

"Oh, fascinating," Greaves said. "Did they reunify in your world?"

"Yes," I said. "The Berlin Wall came down in 1989, and Germany reunified shortly after that."

"Mmmmm…" Greaves nodded thoughtfully. "Continue."

I thought for a moment. If they still had a divided Germany, they probably also had…

"Czechoslovakia?"

Greaves nodded. "Yes."

"Yugoslavia?"

"Yes again."

"No such thing as Slovakia, Slovenia, Croatia…?"

"Yes, but they're provinces of those countries."

"What about Russia?"

"Well, as I understand it, Russia is just one small province—"

"Of the U.S.S.R.?"

He gave me a puzzled look. "Of the what?"

114

"The U.S.S.R. The Union of Soviet Socialist Republics."

Greaves shook his head. "No. I don't know that phrase. Here, Russia is a province of the Eternal Grand Empire. Or whatever that is in Russian."

"The Eternal Grand Empire?"

"Yes. I don't claim to know how it's all organized, but it's the largest country in the world—if you can even call it a country. It dominates everything."

"And what about the United States?"

"Yes, they're there. Right to the south of us. A bit tarnished, since the southern states seceded, but still alive and kicking."

I took a sip of my tea, feeling suddenly like I'd stepped out of the steampunk milieu and into a Harry Turtledove novel. The U.S. split in two. The Eternal Grand Empire. This was going to take some getting used to.

I felt a sudden pang as my mind quickly flashed me an image of Winston holding his copy of *The Victorious Opposition*. Part of the pang was due to the realization that I was very far from home, about as far from home as a person can get. The other part of the pang owed itself to the recollection that my last words to Winston, and to Derek, had been less than kind.

"Mister Richmond?" Greaves asked.

I shook my head slightly and returned to the current situation. "Yes. Sorry."

"Are you quite all right?"

I nodded. "Just a bit overwhelmed. I'll be fine."

I sat back in my chair and took another sip of tea. My brain was tired, my body exhausted, and I couldn't understand why I was so calm. It was interesting to observe myself. I often did this. I had a sufficient level of self-awareness that I could sometimes detach a bit of myself and step back to watch the rest. And right now, the rest of me was sitting quietly, asking and answering questions and taking in all the information. The detached, observing part was quite impressed with this and wondered how long it would last.

I imagined that at some point I would have a meltdown and become suddenly unable to accept anything that was happening to me. But for the moment, it hadn't come to that. I knew that I'd best enjoy the calm before the storm and take in as much information as I could.

"I have another question," I said.

"Of course," Greaves replied. "Please…"

"I saw Irene five times in my world. The first three of those were in the hospital. That's a busy place. Lots of people around. So why is it that no one else saw her? Why am I the only one? I mean, she was right there, in my room."

Greaves and Irene exchanged a look.

"Well," Greaves said after a moment, "I figured you'd get to that eventually. It's actually a tad complicated." He looked over at his companion. "Irene, would you like to take this one?"

Irene gave me a nervous smile. "Well," she said. "I suppose on the most basic level, you could say that I wasn't really there at all."

I slumped in my chair. "Right. So I was hallucinating after all."

Irene leaned forward. "No. That's the strange part. You saw me when I didn't wish to be seen."

I put a hand to my forehead. "This just keeps getting weirder and harder to understand. What do you mean, you didn't wish to be seen?"

Irene extended a hand towards me, as if to calm me down, even though she couldn't reach me. "Let me backtrack a bit," she said.

"That would be good," I said. "I can deal with backtracking."

"You might recall that you didn't actually hear me when I was in your hospital room. You only saw me."

I nodded. "The first three times, actually. Twice in the emergency department and then in my room in the Short Stay Unit."

"I don't know those terms, but I remember the occasions."

I frowned. "I thought it was weird that you never said anything. I didn't hear you speak until I saw you on my—"

Irene put a hand up. "Please. No mention of such things."

I let my head hang forward. "This is going to be difficult," I said. "Those things are all part of my everyday life."

"I understand. But please try." She sat back in her chair. "At any rate, I didn't expect to be observed by anyone. I wasn't… how shall I put it? I wasn't fully present in your world those first three times."

I gaped at her. "Not fully present?"

She shook her head. "I was travelling…" She sighed. "This is quite difficult to explain."

Councillor Greaves sat forward. "Irene is what we call an adept. She has the ability to cross planes of existence with her mind."

"Cross… planes of existence… with her mind?"

The two of them nodded simultaneously.

"Yes," Greaves said. "It is a rare talent, and one we use sparingly."

I leaned forward and put my arms on my knees. "So this is like… what? Astral projection?"

Irene pursed her lips. "I'm not familiar with that term."

"Yeah, yeah. Same tune, different lyrics. You're not familiar with half the things I say. How are we supposed to communicate without a common frame of reference?"

Greaves sighed. "We have more in common than you think, Mister Richmond. After all, are we not speaking the same language? Do we not live in the same city, use many of the same implements and machines? I'm sure you would have much more trouble if you travelled to a foreign country in your world."

I raised my head and looked at him. "You're talking about surface things," I said. "I'm talking about deeper stuff than that. I'm beginning to realize that we have very different ways of living, and some very fundamental differences in mindset and philosophy. I'm finding that difficult to cope with right now."

"Yes, yes. Of course." Greaves batted the air with his hand. "You're quite right. I do apologize for putting so much on you so quickly. But you did say you could handle it. You remember?"

"Yeah. I remember. I think I might've been overly optimistic."

Irene leaned forward. "Do you wish to take a break from this conversation?"

I looked over at her. Her green eyes were practically brimming with concern. She'd been nothing but kind to me since I'd arrived in her world, and I was beholden to her for that. I don't know what I would have done if I'd suddenly found myself here without any guide.

Her gaze gave me an extra shot of strength.

"No, it's okay," I said. "I think just another cup of tea is all I need."

"Done," Greaves said as he leaned forward to take my cup and saucer from me and refill it.

"There's something else I don't understand," I said. "Well, there's a bunch of things I don't understand, but one stands out at the moment."

"Please," Greaves said. "Let's hear it."

I shifted in my seat and crossed my legs. "Why are you being so hospitable? I'm a stranger from another world. Why aren't you suspicious of me? Why are you serving me tea and explaining all these things?"

Greaves smiled. "I do this because of Irene," he said.

I turned my head to look at Irene again. She was smiling, as usual.

"The councillor trusts my instincts," she said, "a fact for which I'm truly grateful. He could see as soon as he looked at us that I felt safe with you. And I do. I don't feel that you're a danger to us. I feel, rather, that you might be able to help us."

I sat upright at that. "Help you? How on earth could I possibly help you?"

Irene leaned towards me. "There's something about you. You could see me when no one else around you could. There may be others on your world who can see as you do, but I didn't encounter them."

"But how did you end up in my room? Of all the places on the whole planet you could have visited, how did you end up with me? The chances against that are astronomical."

"Oh, I don't think so," Irene said. "You see, I believe there's something about you that drew me to you. I didn't realize it at first, but when you looked at me and spoke to me, I knew there was a reason I'd arrived in that room. I still don't know what that reason is, but I'm sure we'll find out in time. That's part of the reason I wanted to bring you here."

"Part of the reason?" I asked.

"Well, yes. You know the other part. You were in danger. I wanted to see you to safety."

I looked at the floor for a moment and nodded. There was too much happening here. Too much new and unfamiliar. And that was just in this world. I still had no clue about what was happening back in my own. I didn't know who the men in the suits were or why they wanted to talk to me and run tests on me. There was so much still unknown.

I bent forward again and started to laugh. Irene glanced at Greaves, who returned the look.

"Is this a good sign or a bad sign?" Greaves asked her.

"I don't know," she replied. "It's very odd."

I sat up again and looked back and forth between them. "You know what the irony of all this is?" I asked. "A few days ago I attempted to kill myself. I really wanted to bring an end to my troubles and to the way I felt. And now, here I am, beset by a whole new world of problems and weirdnesses. Doesn't matter if they're real or not. I'm experiencing them.

And I'm pretty sure that if I hadn't attempted to check out, none of this would be happening."

I sat back in the chair and picked up my tea again. I took a sip. It was so much like Earl Grey that, if I closed my eyes, I almost felt like I was back in my living room with my *Battlestar Galactica* mug, watching something delightfully distracting on the Space Channel.

I wished like hell it were so.

"Mister Richmond," Greaves said. "I feel very bad indeed for what you've been through."

"Listen," I said. "If we're going to be spending all this time together, then you're going to have to start calling me Jack." I looked at Irene. "That goes for you too."

They both nodded.

"Fine," Greaves said. "Jack. I can see from looking at you, and I can hear from listening to you, that you're a troubled man. And I would not wish to add more troubles to those you already bear. But I hope that you'll understand why we need to learn more about your world."

"Well, I was kind of hoping you'd explain that to me. That was another of the bazillion questions I still had rattling around in my head. Never mind why you were visiting. How did you even know my world existed to begin with?"

"That is perhaps the crux of the matter." He looked to Irene again. "My dear, would you continue?"

Irene nodded. "As the councillor mentioned, I'm what is known as an adept. I discovered this when I was a teenager. And as my skill with this kind of travelling grew, I began to realize that I could travel to places beyond my world. It was confusing at first, because I was seeing all sorts of things that were unfamiliar to me, and I couldn't understand how they could exist. As I began to share what I saw with my family, it became clear that I was tapping into something that few people ever do. That's how I came to be here in Halifax."

Greaves nodded emphatically. "Halifax has one of the finest adept training facilities in the world," he said. "It was established here many decades ago. You see, our planet has an energy field, and that energy ebbs and flows much like the tides themselves. But there are currents as well, and Nova Scotia sits on a spot where two of these currents meet. It is a very powerful place, and those with the ability to travel have always come here seeking to tap into the energy of that confluence."

119

Irene picked up the narrative again. "My time here has been an incredible adventure. My senses have developed, and I've travelled places and seen things that few will ever know."

I was waiting for more. "So, I get that you're extremely sensitive."

"Yes. So sensitive, in fact, that I was eventually able to pick up on disturbances in the Earth's energy field."

I closed my eyes and tried to keep a straight face. "A disturbance in The Force," I murmured.

Irene looked at Greaves, her eyes glistening. "I've never heard it described in such terms," she said.

"Very poetic, Mister Rich—I mean Jack," Greaves said with a smile.

I put my teacup down on the coffee table. "So you sensed something that had to do with my world?" I asked.

Irene nodded. "Yes. I sensed something was wrong. The energy around me would occasionally vibrate in ways I'd never felt before. So I tried to figure out where it was coming from."

"And…?"

Irene leaned towards me. "Jack, there are people in your world who are trying to breach the barrier and cross to this one."

I squinted, confused. "Okay. I guess I can believe that. But so what? I mean, you people do it."

"No, you don't understand." Irene's jaw was tight now as she spoke. "They are using unnatural means."

"Unnatural means…?"

Greaves cleared his throat. "Jack. These people are building… implements. They are not using their minds. They are using tools."

I was beginning to understand. They couldn't say exactly what they meant because of their cultural taboos. But it sounded to me like whoever they were talking about on my world was using some kind of advanced technology to travel between worlds.

"So, they're doing things and building things that you can't talk about here," I said.

Greaves let out a breath and sat back. "Yes," he replied. "Precisely."

"And this kind of… travel… It's not a good idea?"

Irene hissed. "It's an abomination."

I half-closed my eyes and dipped my head forward slightly. "So, am I to understand that this sort of travel—this non-mental sort of travel—is harmful in some way? Dangerous, maybe?"

"Most assuredly," Greaves said solemnly. "It disrupts the energy field."

Great, I thought. How typical of the humans on my world to tear the hell out of something in an attempt to make use of it. God knew what they'd do if they ever managed to actually cross the barrier.

I shuddered.

"My people," I said to them, "are well known for abusing resources. I had no idea that anything like this was happening."

"I doubt many on your world are aware of this," Greaves said.

"So these people who had me locked up over there. They're part of the organization that's doing this research?"

"I can only assume so," Irene said. "They must have detected my entry into your world. When I spoke with you the first time, behind your residence."

I nodded. "Yes. There was a man there that night, measuring something. He was standing in the same spot where you and I were talking. I tried to find out what he was doing, but he had a weapon."

I described to them the events of my kidnapping, interrogation, and subsequent incarceration, up to the point where Irene traversed the barrier for the sixth time with her imaginative cosmic doodle.

"I don't know exactly what would have happened to me," I concluded, "if Irene hadn't opened that arch just then, but I do know they were planning on running some kind of tests on me."

Greaves seemed to sink into his armchair a bit.

"So," he said after a moment, "they suspect, as we do, that you are an important part of what is happening."

It was my turn to sink into my seat. This was not what I wanted to hear.

"I'm just a regular human being," I said. "There's nothing cosmic, magical, supernatural, or inter-dimensional about me. I just get depressed a lot and make snarky comments about everything. That's the exent of my powers."

Greaves snorted. "I sincerely doubt that that's the case," he said.

I rolled my eyes slightly. "Okay, fine. I can write fairly well, and I play guitar a bit. But that's it. Seriously, I'm no great shakes. No cosmic significance here."

"That remains to be seen."

"What, you're going to tell me that I'm descended from the great planes-travellers of yore, and I'm destined to overcome my humble upbringing, learn of my great powers, and dispatch evil from the universe?"

Greaves glanced at Irene, whose smile was now threatening to take over the room.

"It may well be something like that," he said.

I was instantly struck by the notion that reading the works of Joseph Campbell might have been a serious mistake.

Chapter Ten

(Thursday, 11:35 A.M.)

After a couple of hours of fairly intense conversation, both Councillor Greaves and Irene could see that my energy level was rapidly sinking. Greaves suggested that we have some lunch, after which I could retire to one of his guest rooms for some much-needed rest. Charlotte prepared a sumptuous midday meal for the three of us, and when we'd all had our fill, Irene took her leave, and I headed upstairs to take a nap.

I lay in the bed, which was unexpectedly comfortable, and stared at the ceiling. I knew I wouldn't sleep well, especially in the middle of the day, so I just lay there, allowing my brain to do whatever the hell it wanted. The thoughts rolled around and tumbled over and under each other, leaving the inside of my skull littered with dents, footprints, and scuff marks. I didn't bother trying to reign it in. There was simply too much going on in there.

But sleep I did. When I awoke to darkness, I couldn't have been more surprised. I was not a sound sleeper at the best of times, and to sleep uninterrupted from noon until darkness was the rarest of occurrences. I must have been more exhausted than I'd imagined.

The darkness was welcome, even if the returning cacophony in my head was not. I doubted I'd sort anything out in the dead of night, so I didn't try. I knew, in fact, that the middle of the night was the worst time to think about anything. If there were problems, they became magnified. If there were fears, they grew out of proportion. If there were worries, they spun faster than in the daylight. "The Hour of the Wolf" was a phrase I'd once heard applied to that dismal time between three and four in the morning. It was also the title of an episode of *Babylon 5*.

My mind I could ignore to some extent, but my bladder was another matter. I sat up, yawned, and stretched my arms above my head. I had no idea what time it was, but my eliminatory system didn't care one whit.

I had already investigated the bathroom situation, and thank God no electricity was needed for good indoor plumbing. There was hot and cold running water and a flush toilet. I assumed there was some kind of coal or oil furnace heating the water, because electric water heaters would be unheard of here.

I fussed with details like that to distract myself from the larger issues at hand. Issues such as: Was any of this real? Why had I been able to see Irene when she had mentally travelled to my world? Why did those men in the suits want to interrogate and run tests on me? How does one travel between worlds?

And the big one: Why did they think I was so special?

For the answers to these, and other questions, I would have to do more than tune in to tomorrow's (now today's) episode. I would have to start taking a more active role in what was happening to me.

That was really the crux of the matter, I now realized. I wasn't making things happen; things were happening *to* me. The one thing I had tried to make happen, my own death, had not come to pass and had instead, I now thought, played a pivotal role in all the unfortunate things that had followed.

I rubbed my eyes and wobbled to the bathroom. Councillor Greaves had been good enough to provide me with one of his nightshirts, which spared the household a semi-conscious nude excursion to the toilet by the otherworldly guest. I didn't know if Charlotte was a live-in maid, but it gave me great pleasure to envision her standing in the hall as I staggered, half-asleep, naked, and with a blooming, dream-induced erection, to the porcelain pot.

I had to take comfort where I could find it. At this point, including a maid in my naughty imaginings would have to do. Chances were that everyone else in the house was sound asleep at this hour anyway, so I probably could have safely walked around naked if I'd really wanted to.

As I splashed a bit of cold water on my face, I returned to my analysis —such as it was—of my long road to Bizarro World. If it had all begun with the suicide attempt, then something must have happened to me while I was unconscious. I couldn't imagine that something as simple as Gravol, Sleep-Eze-D, and Captain Morgan would cause changes to my brain significant enough to alter how I perceived things. I was pretty sure that I was not the first person to try that particular combination.

I'd never heard of anyone having their perceptions augmented from ingesting such a cocktail, but then again, I didn't make a point of keeping abreast of the latest suicide trends. Besides, if someone did gain new abilities from those or any other circumstances, they would surely be whisked away to a government facility somewhere, and no one would ever hear from them again.

I froze in the midst of drying my face. Slowly, I let go of the towel and stood upright. I had just hit the nail on the head. I *had* been whisked away. If it hadn't been for Irene, I might still be in that godawful grey room. I'd most likely have already undergone God-knows-what kinds of tests.

I sat down on the edge of the bathtub. This was a revelation. It was the piece I'd been missing. I was different now, and some agency—some government agency, I now felt certain—*knew* that I was different. I would probably have been kidnapped even if I hadn't leapt out the back door of my apartment building to confront the man with the measuring device.

I stood up again, shaky now for reasons other than sleepiness, and returned to the bedroom. I crawled back under the covers and nestled myself into the most comfortable position I could find. I didn't expect to fall back to sleep, but I figured I'd at least be polite and not start moving around too much until the household started its day.

The "household" appeared to consist of just Councillor Greaves; I hadn't met anyone else. He might have had a wife and children, for all I knew, but there had been no sign of them. Just the councillor and his maid. Perhaps they had more than an employer-employee relationship; I just didn't know. If so, it wasn't a May-December romance. It was more like an Ides of March-New Year's Eve romance.

Deciding I didn't particularly want to continue that line of thought, I turned over again and closed my eyes.

The next thing I knew, there was light outside the window.

No shit, I thought. *I dozed off again.*

I sat up, rubbed my eyes, and stretched. I could scarcely believe my luck. Hours upon hours of sleep with only a brief visit to the waking world. And most miraculous of all: There was no assistance from the friendly little blue pills.

To be honest, though, given a choice between that and the massive roundhouse to the worldview I'd lately experienced, I'd still opt for the little blue pills.

Within minutes I started hearing sounds elsewhere in the house.

Footsteps, doors, pots, and pans. *Charlotte must be starting to prepare breakfast*, I thought.

I sighed and swung my feet out of the bed. She was downstairs, but she was making the Devil's own noise. Perhaps it was her way of letting the councillor know that it was time to get up. Or perhaps she was just a really clumsy cook. Whatever the reason, I decided to go downstairs and investigate.

I put on my clothes of the previous day—vowing to take a nice hot bath before the morning was out—and headed downstairs. I could hear the intermittent running of water in the kitchen sink, the opening and closing of cupboard doors, and more clanging.

I stuck my head into the kitchen. Charlotte was chopping things and mixing things and putting pots and pans on hot elements. Gas stove, I figured.

"Morning, Charlotte," I said sleepily.

She shrieked, and a wooden spoon and a bowl of eggs went flying into the air. I stepped forward to try and catch them, but to no avail. The bowl and spoon clattered onto the floor, and the eggs splattered up onto the nearest cupboard.

Charlotte had her back against the counter and her hand on her chest. "Mister Richmond," she said through sharp, rapid breaths. "You frightened me out of my wits."

I put a hand to my forehead. "I'm sorry. I didn't mean to startle you. I didn't realize you were so focused on what you were doing."

Her breathing began to slow a bit. "I'm completely immersed when I'm cooking," she said. "It's almost like I go to another place."

I smirked. "Another world?"

Her face reddened, and her eyebrows tilted towards each other. "Good Heavens, no," she said. "I don't have such abilities. That's why I'm a servant."

I put my hands up. "I'm sorry. I didn't mean to offend you. I didn't realize—"

She nodded, then looked down and straightened her apron. "Of course," she said. "Of course you wouldn't know. I shouldn't have scolded you. You're our guest, after all."

"Well, don't make any special concessions for me. Please keep letting me know when I say something wrong. I'll never learn about this place otherwise."

"Don't worry," she said as she reached for a cloth. "There are plenty of people who'll be only too happy to set you straight if you don't follow our customs."

She crouched to pick up the bowl and spoon, then knelt on the floor to wipe up the egg.

Maybe it was just my tired brain, but I thought her utterance held sinister undertones. I suddenly felt as if I were in an episode of *Stargate SG-1*, and I had just stepped through the gate to a world where ritual sacrifice was commonplace for those who broke convention.

I shook my head to clear the cobwebs. For all this world seemed a friendly place, it was also giving me a strange undercurrent of dread. All this talk of taboos and customs was starting to make me queasy. Not to mention that Charlotte had just hinted at some sort of class-based system, where some types of people were more worthy than others.

I was beginning to wonder just what in hell I had stepped into here.

Charlotte shooed me out of the kitchen after that, and I went back into the living room to sit down until breakfast was ready. Councillor Greaves came downstairs about ten minutes later.

"Good morning, Jack," he said, his voice full of bluster and enthusiasm. He reminded me of an old English admiral, come to give his sailors a morning pep talk.

"Good morning, Councillor," I said, standing to greet him.

"Sleep all right?" he asked.

"Surprisingly, yes. Soundly and solidly, and for an extremely long time. Interrupted by only one siphoning of the serpent."

Greaves looked at me oddly for a second, then let out a solid chortle. "Yes, yes," he said. "Quite a way with words you have, there. Never heard it put quite like that before."

"Well, if nothing else, I can provide you with hours of entertainment."

The councillor smiled again as he moved towards a chair opposite me.

He was in the midst of settling himself into the chair when Charlotte called from the kitchen that breakfast was ready. Greaves sighed, hoisted himself back up again, and gestured me towards the dining room.

Charlotte brought out a tray with two covered platters upon it. She set it down and removed the covers. Steam rose in two great shafts from the just-cooked food. Once the steam had cleared a bit, I could see on one platter a gigantic mass of scrambled eggs. On the other was a heap of sausages, stacked like a cord of firewood.

Charlotte took the platter lids away and returned with another tray. Again two columns of steam rose as she revealed the contents of two more platters. This time it was a pile of French toast and a heap of regular toast.

The jam and syrup were already on the table.

I looked up from the morning feast and gave Councillor Greaves my best nonplussed look. "You're kidding me, right?"

Greaves chuckled. "Not at all. Dig in."

"I mean… There's enough food here to feed a dozen people."

He smiled. "Irene will be here shortly. And Charlotte will have her share once we're finished."

"Even so…" I said, letting my eyes rove across the feast one more time.

He lifted his plate and scooped some scrambled eggs onto it. "Please help yourself," he said as he took four sausages and plunked them next to the eggs.

I shook my head in bewilderment and lifted my own plate towards the center of the table.

Conversation was limited during the meal, as both of our mouths were full most of the time. Charlotte's cooking was tremendous, and I couldn't remember enjoying breakfast so much in a very long time. The good folks at the hospital did their best, but their works were but a pale shadow of the marvellous comestibles I was currently consuming.

After a couple helpings of eggs, three sausages, two slices of French toast and a bit of toast and jam, I sat back, overstuffed and content.

"That was amazing," I said.

"Thank you, sir," Charlotte said as she entered the room again to clear the dishes. "I do try my best."

Greaves waved her away. "Stop being so impertinent," he muttered at her.

Charlotte made a face at him and left the room again.

Greaves pulled out a pocket watch and opened it. "Irene will be arriving shortly. Why don't you get yourself cleaned up? I'll have Charlotte put out some clothes for you. I doubt you want to be travelling in yesterday's attire."

"Travelling?" I asked. "Where are we going?"

He got up from the chair, wiped his mouth with his napkin, and set it down on the table. "You'll see soon enough," he said, patting me on the shoulder as he exited the room.

I finished my tea and started for the stairs. Before heading up, I poked my head in the kitchen to ask Charlotte if it would be okay to take a bath.

"Oh, that's perfectly fine, sir," she said. "That bathroom is yours. His Nibs has his own."

"I heard that," came Greaves' voice from the living room.

Charlotte winked at me and turned back to her cleaning activities.

Eagerly anticipating the feel of hot soapy water against my skin, I went upstairs and practically dove into the bathroom. The water from the taps was hot and plentiful, and the room had been amply supplied with both towels and soap. I even came across a bottle of bubble bath in the medicine cabinet.

Mere minutes later, I was stepping into a veritable oasis of suds. I lowered myself into the tub—a big old-fashioned affair with clawed feet and a back support at just the right angle—and sighed audibly.

I found myself musing about the peculiar nature of this world in which I found myself. I didn't know the ins and outs of it, but its anachronisms were at once charming and confusing. Despite the presence of cars, trucks, and the like, and despite the gangster-era appearance of the buildings, clothes, and furniture, it seemed rather like I'd been taken back to Victorian days. The gas lights and pocket watches completely confused my sense of era.

I had the strange feeling that these people were really living in the same year that my world was, but the lack of certain technologies had held them back. I couldn't be sure of that, of course, but the jangling in the back of my noggin told me it was so.

I soaked and scrubbed for about twenty minutes and then, reluctantly, hauled myself to my feet and pulled the stopper from the drain. As the water seeped out of the tub, I reached for a towel and began to dry myself off. Once I was no longer dripping, I wrapped the towel around my waist and grabbed my clothes.

I stepped down the hall towards my room just as Charlotte was coming out of it.

"Oh," she said, averting her eyes. "I beg your pardon, sir. I've just put out some fresh clothes for you."

I grabbed the edge of the towel to ensure it stayed where it was. "Thanks," I said. "Thanks very much."

The irony of the situation was not lost on me. I had mere hours earlier imagined her catching me naked on the way to the bathroom. Now, here she was, catching me pretty damned close and heading the in other direction. She slipped past me, but not before I managed to catch a glimpse of the slight smile she was trying to hide.

The towel seemed tighter all of a sudden.

Once I'd managed to calm down all my various brain cells and body parts, I began to examine the clothes that had been laid out for me. I raised my eyebrows in appreciation as I picked up the shirt, pants, and suit jacket. All were exceedingly well made, and all were of a style that I thought would suit me pretty well.

They were vintage, of course, as were so many other things here, and I was once again beset with an image from *Star Trek*, as I recalled Kirk and Spock in their 1930s gangster attire in the episode "A Piece of the Action".

As with jell-o, there was always room for *Star Trek*.

I raised my eyebrows again as I tried on the garments and found that they fit almost perfectly. Why Councillor Greaves would have clothing of my size in his home was beyond me. He was much shorter and thinner than I was. I couldn't imagine what these clothes were doing here. Unless he'd had Charlotte run to the haberdasher's late in the night. But that seemed equally unlikely.

I stepped to the mirror and checked myself out. I was pleasantly surprised. The suit fit like a glove, and I had to admit to myself that it helped me to cut a rather dashing figure. "Clothes make the man," I'd heard it said. I'd always thought it was just an old saying. Evidently, there was more to it than that.

I went back downstairs a few minutes later. Greaves was sitting at the dining table with Irene, who had evidently arrived whilst I was bathing and was now enjoying some of Charlotte's delicious breakfast goods. She wore a tailored, cream-colored blouse and a beige skirt. They were well cut, but I thought the colors a bit drab for her, especially considering how dramatic she'd looked in her long burgundy coat.

She looked up as I entered the room, and her green eyes lit up.

"Good morning, Jack," she said, standing and stepping towards me.

"Good morning," I replied.

She took my hands in hers and looked me up and down. "You look ever-so-handsome," she said, a wide smile spreading across her face.

A slight flush rose into my face. "Thanks," I said.

Greaves stood and moved towards us. "Yes, indeed, Jack," he said. "That outfit suits you to a tee." He moved towards the door, but stopped and turned back. "Perhaps that's why they call it a 'suit'." He smiled to himself as he turned towards the door and headed into the entry hall.

Irene took my arm. "Shall we?" she asked.

I shrugged. "Whatever you say. I'm just a passenger here."

She patted me on the arm and led me towards the entry hall. Charlotte was waiting by the front door, coats in hand. She gave Irene hers first, another long dramatic coat, but dark green this time. She handed Greaves a long black woolen coat and a dark hat, and then she handed me a dark trench coat and a fedora.

I inspected both items before putting them on. They were the perfect completion to my ensemble, and the giddy child in me stepped out to play for a moment. I nearly scanned the area in search of a Tommy gun.

I looked up at Charlotte, shaking my head in amazement. "Awesome," I said.

She winked at me again. "Thank you," she said.

Irene gave me a dark look as we stepped outside the house. "I'd be careful if I were you," she said.

"Jealous?" I asked.

She snorted and stepped ahead of me.

A car was waiting for us at the curb. To me it looked like an old Rolls-Royce from about 1935, but in reality it bore no brand insignias that I recognized. The driver, who'd been standing patiently beside the rear end of the car, opened the back door. Greaves gestured for Irene to get in and then stood aside to allow me to climb in and sit beside her. He followed and took the seat facing us.

It was an extremely roomy vehicle.

The driver closed the door behind us and moved around to the front of the car. In a moment, we were off and running. To what destination, I knew not.

We travelled along what felt like the equivalent of my Gottingen Street, and before long, the immensity of Citadel Hill loomed before us.

"This is supremely weird," I said.

"What, specifically?" Greaves asked, genuine curiosity in his tone.

"Well, I've known that hill all my life," I said. "It's been part of my day to day landscape. But now I'm seeing it in a completely different context, and it's messing up my head."

He laughed. "That's a strange turn of phrase, but I think I know what you mean."

Irene had been silent since we'd left the house. I glanced at her, but she was paying no attention to my conversation with the councillor. She was looking out the window, lost in her own thoughts. I decided it would be best if I left her that way.

We turned left at the base of the Citadel and began to travel down towards the harbour. I had a good view of the water now, and the sight was remarkably like that of my own Halifax. The buildings were different, but the harbour was the same. I shook my head in wonderment.

"You're still not going to tell me where we're going?" I asked.

"In time," Greaves said.

We crossed what should have been Barrington Street and turned right a couple of blocks later. I looked around, getting a feel for the area. I was pretty sure we were now driving along what would have been Hollis Street in my own world.

A few minutes later, we turned into the parking lot of a large hotel, but that, apparently was not our destination. The car continued past it, towards a smaller building that appeared to be attached.

"Here we are," Greaves said as the vehicle pulled up beside the front door.

The driver got out and stepped around to our side. He opened the door, and we all piled out, stretching our various limbs and surveying the landscape.

"Bring the bags, will you, Wilson?" Greaves said to the driver.

Wilson nodded and opened the trunk of the car.

Greaves led the way towards the entrance, and Irene and I followed. The building and the hotel it adjoined both had an art-deco appearance about them. I looked up at the ornamentation as we approached the door, admiring the workmanship and the design. I was suddenly a bit ashamed of the modern world I'd left the day before, with all its prefabricated homes and metal studs and quick-as-you-please construction. It just wasn't the same.

Inside was a polished marble floor, wooden benches, and a long row of counters. I suddenly clued in. This building served the same function as its counterpart in my world.

"This is the train station," I said.

Greaves turned back to me and nodded. "Yes. Yes it is. Wait here a moment, and I'll fetch our tickets."

As he stepped over to the first available counter, I turned to Irene.

"This is a beautiful building," I said.

Irene nodded absently. "Yes," she said.

I stepped closer to her. "Are you okay?" I asked.

She looked at me, but immediately turned away again. "I'm fine," she said.

I rolled my eyes. That was the standard answer on all worlds, evidently.

"I guess I was rude," I said. "I'm sorry."

She turned her head halfway back to me. "Yes," she said. "You were rude."

I let my shoulders sag. I tried to think of something to say in response to that, but I was at a loss. I didn't know how to treat her anymore. Her reaction to me as I'd descended the stairs in my new attire had seriously confused me. The look on her face as she'd taken my hands in hers had been one of near-adoration.

I couldn't imagine I'd made that much of an impression on her. I figured it had to have been the suit.

As I opened my mouth to utter some platitude, a couple of puzzle pieces in my brain clicked together. Without even realizing it, I'd been thinking about the suit the whole time.

"Oh, my God," I murmured.

Irene turned towards me again, her face displaying both displeasure at my choice of language and mild alarm at my tone of voice.

"What is it?" she asked.

I glanced down at my trench coat and suit before fixing my gaze squarely upon her.

"He was expecting me, wasn't he?"

Irene's eyes widened slightly, and she took a halting step towards me.

"Jack," she said. But the sound of Greaves' footsteps returning to our location prevented her from saying anything further.

As the councillor stepped up to us with our train tickets, Wilson came in the main entrance with three suitcases on a trolley.

"Follow me," Greaves said, immediately turning around again and heading for the opposite end of the cavernous room.

Irene and I followed him in silence, our footsteps interspersed with the squeak of the trolley's wheels behind us.

"Get that fixed, will you, Wilson?" Greaves said.

We stepped through the doors at the far end of the room and onto the platform. A train awaited us.

Again I was transported into a 1940s movie, as we were greeted by a veritable fog bank of steam. As we moved along the chain of old Pullman-style cars, I looked ahead, towards the front of the line, where I caught the occasional glimpse of a majestic black steam engine, poised to leap into action.

I laughed aloud, unable to contain myself. "Where are we headed?" I asked. "Hogwarts?"

Irene gave me a sharp look, while Greaves just chuckled and shook his head. "I will never get accustomed to your odd words and phrases," he said.

I turned up one corner of my mouth. "Yeah, another lost reference," I said, suddenly disappointed that there was no one around from my world who could share my mirth. "It's from a well known story on my world. About a place where there's actually magic."

Irene and Greaves exchanged a telling look.

♦

We found ourselves in a comfortably appointed compartment. A sliding wooden door separated us from the corridor, and two upholstered benches faced each other inside the cozy space. Through the window, I could see the landscape passing us by.

I knew it was Nova Scotian landscape, but I was hard pressed to recognize anything I saw. There were no familiar landmarks, no signs, no nothing. Just lots and lots of land and the occasional building. It was, for all intents and purposes, a foreign country. Sure, if I had a good topographical map and some orienteering equipment, I'd probably be able to find my way around, but beyond that, I might as well have been in Siberia. Or whatever the Eternal Grand Empire called that region of its domain.

I put my head back and sighed. Too much. Too much.

"Are you cold?" Greaves asked.

I raised my head again. "Hmmm?"

He gestured towards my torso. I looked down, realizing he was talking about my coat. I hadn't taken it off yet.

"It is a bit chilly in here," I said. "But mostly I just like the outfit."

Greaves smiled and nodded, returning his attention to his newspaper.

I was suddenly restless. We hadn't been travelling long, but not knowing our final destination was making me antsy. I suddenly realized that I was holding my fedora in my lap and fidgeting with it.

I glanced at Irene. She was staring out the window, a wistful expression on her face. The sunlight was touching her cheekbone in a way that nearly made my heart break.

She was beyond lovely.

I let out a quiet sigh. As much as I enjoyed meeting beautiful women, my reaction to Irene was not making things any easier. My life was messed up enough without musing about romantic entanglements.

And that was exactly the word. Romantic. Whereas my thoughts about Charlotte were lusty and naughty, my thoughts about Irene were almost... pure. That in and of itself was enough to convince me that something was wrong with my brain.

I simply didn't think like that.

After a few more minutes of sitting in silence, Councillor Greaves rustled his paper, put it down beside him, and stood up.

He stretched his arms in the air, let out an almighty yawn, and toddled towards the compartment door.

"I shall return anon," he muttered as he exited to the corridor.

I watched the door close, then turned to Irene.

"Where's he going?" I asked.

She glanced at me for a moment, but quickly returned her gaze to the passing scenery.

"That's just his little phrase," she said.

I shook my head slightly. "Little phrase?"

She nodded. "His little expression."

"For what?"

She turned her head to look at me. "For answering the call," she said. Her tone suggested I was an idiot.

I leaned my head forward and widened my eyes expectantly.

"The call?" I asked. "The call of what? The call of the wild?"

She frowned. "No." She leaned forward, blushing slightly, and whispered, "The call of nature."

I leaned back. "Ooooooh."

She turned her attention to the outside world again. I watched her for a moment, then leaned my head back against the seat.

After a minute or two of further silence, I could take it no longer.

"Look, Irene," I said, sitting up straight again. "I'm really sorry if I offended you back at the house. You've been nothing but decent to me, and I feel bad about my offhand comment."

I didn't know why I was doing this. Or at least part of me didn't.

She looked at me. Her expression had softened somewhat, but there lingered a hint of wariness in her eyes.

"Thank you," she said. "I appreciate the apology."

"Well... I mean it."

She nodded. "I know you do."

This was like pushing sand uphill.

"The thing is," I said, "I've never met anyone like you before."

She laughed lightly at this. "Of course, not. You're not from this world."

I waved my hands erratically in front of me. "No, I'm not talking about the whole 'adept' thing. I'm talking about someone who... I don't know... someone who makes me... aware of myself. In ways that I wasn't... aware..."

I let my shoulders droop and looked at the floor.

"It's hard to put into words," I muttered.

When I looked up again, she was looking at me in a most peculiar way. Almost like she was studying me. I gazed back at her. Her loveliness had expanded tenfold since I'd watched her looking out the window. Her eyes glistened more brightly than ever.

It took me a moment to realize that it was because her eyes were wet.

She blinked rapidly a few times and turned towards the window again. She didn't stare out at the passing world this time, however; instead she looked down at her handbag, which was tucked between her leg and the windowed wall. She rummaged inside it for a moment and then took something out.

"I want you to have this," she said, reaching her closed hand across the gap between the seats.

I extended my own hand and opened it, slightly cupped, under hers. She lowered her hand towards mine and opened her fingers, dropping a small object into the center of my palm.

I pulled my hand back and examined what she had given me. It was a small green crystal, as smooth as any stone, but as clear as tinted glass. I could see the lines on my skin through it, slightly magnified.

I briefly wondered if I could make it into a ring and join the Green Lantern Corps.

I looked up a Irene.

"It's beautiful," I said.

She smiled. "I want you to have something to remember me by."

I frowned, puzzled. "Remember you by? That sounds a bit—"

"Jack." She was looking intently at me now. "If you were to remain here in my world, I have no doubt that you could, with training, become easily as talented an adept as I am."

"What?"

"Shhhhh." She reached an index finger towards my mouth. "But I know your path lies elsewhere. You'll eventually have to return to your own world."

I nodded.

"But I want you to know," she said, leaning forward, "that I cherish this time with you."

I noticed an unfamiliar lump in my throat. I opened my mouth to speak, but before I could utter a word, shuffling footsteps sounded outside the compartment.

"Put it away," Irene said, nodding sharply at the crystal.

I tucked the gem into my jacket pocket.

The compartment door slid open, and Councillor Greaves re-entered. He closed the door behind him and returned to his seat.

"Much better," he said, picking up his paper again.

I looked at Irene again, and we shared a brief smile.

The councillor's return reminded me that my own bodily functions were still operating mostly normally.

"I think I'll take a turn at that," I said.

I stood, placed the fedora on my head at a rakish angle, tugged slightly on the brim, and winked at Irene.

"I shall return anon," I said in my best Humphrey Bogart.

Greaves looked up from his paper. "You need a hat for that in your world, do you?" he asked with a twinkle.

"Indulge me," I replied.

Greaves smiled and returned his attention to the paper.

I stepped out of the compartment and slid the door closed behind me. The corridor was deserted. I put my hand against the wall to steady my steps as the car rocked rhythmically back and forth.

As I neared the end of the car, one of the other compartment doors opened, and man in a black cloak stepped out. I figured he was a clergyman or monk of some sort or another, as he wore a hood and moved with his head down. He stepped along the remainder of the corridor, his steps much more sure than mine, and finally paused at the door to what appeared to be the washroom.

He turned suddenly and bowed to me. "I did not realize you were there," he said.

I still couldn't see his face. His hood was deep enough to keep his face in shadows.

"That's okay," I said. "Please go ahead."

"No, no," he said, stepping to the side. "My urgency is not so great. I insist you go first."

Not wanting to cause any possible offense to any possible spiritual or religious sensibilities this fellow might possess, I nodded and stepped towards the door.

"Thank you," I said.

If he replied, I didn't hear it, because what I stepped into was not a washroom at all, but open air. I fell a good five feet to the ground, twisting my right ankle and bruising my right arm in the process. Beneath me were railroad ties, but the train on which I'd been travelling was nowhere to be seen.

I sat up and looked around. There was no sound, nothing to indicate a train had passed mere seconds ago. It was as if it had never existed.

I tried standing. My ankle was tender, but I didn't think I'd sprained or broken it. It would probably work itself out after a while.

I took a few steps along the track, craning my neck to get a better look at my surroundings. I could see houses in the distance, but I couldn't make out much in the way of detail. I had no idea where I was.

A few feet ahead of me, a small dark shape was visible between two of the railway ties. I hobbled over to it and bent down.

I picked the object up. It was a flattened Tim Horton's coffee cup.

"Oh, boy," I said, thinking of Scott Bakula as I did so.

It appeared I was back in Kansas again.

Chapter Eleven

I dropped the deceased coffee cup to the ground and stared at the land around me. It looked like mostly farmland to me, and the few buildings I could see looked like barns and farmhouses.

I stood still for a moment and listened. A very faint intermittent whooshing sound reached my ears. It sounded like cars going by on a road. I turned my head slowly around to orient myself to the soft noise. After a few moments I was fairly certain which direction it was coming from.

I dusted myself off, stepped back a few paces to pick up my fallen fedora, and began moving towards what I assumed was the highway.

I stepped off the tracks and over the gravel bed to the grass beyond. Stopping every minute or so to reorient myself to the whooshing sound, I finally began to sense it getting louder. As I moved closer, I could tell that the vehicles I heard were moving at quite a clip. I didn't think that the roadsters I'd seen in Irene's world could travel that fast. Just one more clue that I was no longer in that domain.

I swallowed hard. I just hoped that I was back in my own.

I climbed a fairly steep embankment and found myself standing beside a guard rail. A bright yellow guard rail. Within seconds an even brighter yellow Nissan Sentra sped by.

The Tim Horton's cup should have been all the information I needed.

I climbed over the guard rail and sat on its sloping top edge. I presumed I was back in my world, but I had no idea where I was geographically. If the two worlds were similar in the way they were laid out, then I would have to presume that the rail line in Irene's world was heading towards the equivalent of Truro, which was north of Halifax. That being the case, I was probably stranded somewhere between Halifax and Truro now that I was back home.

I hoped that my logic would hold up.

I watched a few more vehicles whizz past. The speed at which they were going, combined with the width of the road, gave me to believe that I was perched on the edge of Highway 102. That was a comforting thought; if I collapsed from lack of food and water, at least I knew that someone would eventually see me.

I considered my options. I could hitchhike, but that would be a last resort; the notion didn't appeal to me at all. I could walk to the nearest town, but I didn't know exactly where I was, so I didn't know how long a walk that would be. Then it hit me; I could just pull out my cell phone and call someone.

As I put my hand to my jacket pocket, a memory seeped back into my consciousness, a memory of leaving my cell phone, wallet, and keys in my own clothes. Those clothes were now separated from me by the fabric of the universe. They were an entire world away, back in the land of Irene, Greaves, Charlotte, and no electricity.

I let my hand drop back to my side, suddenly deciding that it would be a good time for another self-whack-on-the-head. I felt as ridiculous as I was sure I looked.

My options were severely limited. I had no cell phone, no money, no credit card, no identification, and an anachronistic outfit. Even if I did decide to hitchhike, it was unlikely that anyone would pick me up, dressed as I was.

The phrase "I'm fucked" drifted into my mind.

I could hear it now: "I'm sorry, officer. I don't have any ID on me. You see, I left it in my other clothes, which are over in this other universe I was visiting. Somebody pushed me through an interdimensional portal, and now I'm back here again. It's the damnedest thing…"

It would be a quick ticket to further psychiatric evaluation.

It was a warm day, fortunately, so I decided to at least remove the trench coat and hide the fedora within its folds. I might look a little less ridiculous wearing just an outdated suit. Not much, but a little.

I decided to start walking. I didn't know how long I'd last in unfamiliar wing-tips, but I thought I'd at least give it a try.

As I secreted the hat and draped the coat over my arm, I heard a car horn honking. I turned to look, and a small red Dodge Omni was pulling over to the side of the road.

"Hey, man," someone called. "Are you heading for the convention?"

"Convention?" I asked.

The man who had spoken was skinny, with dark tousled hair and a two-day growth of stubble. He wore a t-shirt that bore the number 42 on the front. The driver of the car was a heavy man with a full beard and long, dirty-blond hair. He also wore a t-shirt, but I couldn't see what was printed on it.

Something in the back of my mind began to jangle with familiarity. The look of these two individuals, combined with the word 'convention', brought images to my mind that I wasn't all that happy to see again.

"Yeah," I said. "Yeah. The convention."

"Man, that's a killer costume. You look just like Kirk out of 'Piece of the Action'. You hitchhikin'?"

Yep, they were headed for a science fiction convention. It never ceased to amaze me how these people continued to perpetuate the stereotype by being the stereotype.

"Yeah. Hitchhiking. Never done it before. Maybe not such a great idea."

"Well, we're here now, dude. Hop in."

There was a tiny slice of space in the backseat. The skinny guy got out, tipped his seat forward, and shoved some duffel bags over towards the driver's side. This left just enough room for someone of my general width to squeeze in. If I'd had even a few extra pounds on me, the deal would have been off.

The car smelled of sweat and Doritos, but not strongly enough to make me gag. I simply resolved to breathe through my mouth for a while, until my senses became accustomed to my new environment.

"My name's Dan," the skinny guy said. "And this is Rick. We live in Truro."

"I'm Jack," I said. "Nice to meet you. And thanks for the lift."

"No worries, Kimosabe. We gotta stick together, right?"

I nodded. "Right." Inwardly, I rolled my eyes. As a fan of many science fiction and fantasy shows and movies, I had met my share of other individuals who shared those interests. Unfortunately, I had met more than a few who did not share my interest in social skills, hygiene, and decent clothes.

"We're going to run a panel this year," Dan said. "It's on the social customs of alien planets. We're going to draw examples from *Star Trek*, *Stargate*, *Doctor Who*, and *Farscape*. Well, those are the shows that Rick and I are most interested in."

"Speak for yourself," Rick said.

"Hey, there, big guy," Dan said. "What are you so pissed off about?"

"We need to include *Sliders*," Rick said.

"Ah, geez, Rick. They didn't travel to alien planets. They travelled to different versions of Earth. How many times do I have to tell you?"

"Hey, man. There's nothing more alien than a different version of Earth. I'm telling you, we need to talk about it."

"I think we've got enough material with the other shows, okay?"

It was at this point that I began to tune out. I'd heard my share of discussions like this, especially during my ill-fated and short-lived tenure as the president of a *Star Trek* club, and I'd resolved to avoid further such situations if I could at all manage it.

This time, it was a necessary evil. I needed to get back to Halifax.

As Dan and Rick droned on about interdimensional travel versus interstellar travel, I put my head back on the seat and closed my eyes. If it hadn't been for the fact that I'd just experienced interdimensional travel myself, I would have tuned out a lot earlier.

The vibration of the car and sound of the tires on the road were oddly soothing. I found myself occasionally nodding off, hauled back to awareness by the sound of "That's lame, dude," or "What are you on?"

As I drifted in and out of consciousness, images from the past few days drifted past my mind's eye. Mostly, though, I found I was seeing images of Irene and Charlotte. The elegant beauty and the saucy, sexy maid. I almost wished I was back there talking to them instead of here with the two buffoons in the front seat of the car.

It was Irene's sincere gaze and moist eyes as she spoke to me on the train that dominated my thoughts, however. I couldn't recall anyone ever looking at me like that before.

I reached into my jacket pocket. The smooth green crystal was still there. Irene didn't need to worry. There was no possibility of my ever forgetting her.

Both Irene and Charlotte had captivated me, in different ways, in a very short time. Perhaps it was their interest in me that sparked my own interest in them. I was a stranger, a visitor from an exotic place. Certainly there was intrigue in that, but I was a human just like they were. What made me so special?

And I supposed the reverse was true for me. Both Irene and Charlotte were representatives of an exotic world that I knew next to nothing about. They were almost polar opposites in type, but they each had an undeniable allure about them. And, if I really thought about it, I was doing what I normally did. If I found myself in an unfamiliar or unplanned situation, I would usually focus on the women.

I must have actually fallen asleep at some point, because I was pulled to consciousness by the slowing of the car. Rick was pulling us into the parking garage below the Holiday Inn on the corner of Quinpool Road and Robie Street. The entrance to the hotel was actually on Pepperell Street, which was a side street off Robie, but the intersection of Quinpool and Robie was a major one that had come to be known as the Willow Tree, despite the absence of anything even remotely resembling such flora. So I always thought of the hotel as being at Quinpool and Robie.

Dan and Rick got out of the car and stretched their backs. I climbed out and did the same.

"Hey, man," Dan said. "I just realized you don't have any bags."

"Yeah," I said. "I'm staying with friends in town. They have everything I need. And I'm going to buy some stuff. I was due for a new toothbrush anyway."

Dan nodded thoughtfully and reached into the back to pull out some of the bags. I didn't know exactly what they had planned for their panel discussion, but from the way he strained to pull some of his stuff out of the car, I imagined that they had some serious audio/visual equipment with them.

"Need a hand?" I asked.

"Yeah, thanks," Dan said. "If you could grab that last one out of there…"

I reached in and pulled out the indicated satchel. Rick had already grabbed two handfuls and was heading for the elevator. Dan locked up the car and picked up his share. I tagged behind them with my lone bag.

When we reached the lobby, they dumped their bags beside a sofa and headed for the check-in counter. I put the bag I was carrying with the rest and sat down for a minute. I was still tired, despite my snooze in the car, and I needed to get home. That would be a difficult proposition, I surmised, without my keys. I wondered if the superintendent would let me in.

The issue of my ID was a slightly thornier one. With no way to retrieve it, I would have to go through the laborious process of finding my birth certificate, filling out a form to get a new Social Insurance Card, then doing the same for my Health Card and Driver's License. Plus, I'd have to cancel my credit card and get the company to issue me a new one.

There was also this small issue of the shadowy organization that wanted to test and interrogate me.

I put my head back again and willed my brain to shut off.

It didn't work.

♦

I finally decided that I needed to call someone. I'd get nowhere just sitting there on my own with no possessions other than a retro three-piece suit. I thought about calling Lydia, but I didn't want to deal with her at the moment. She'd probably tear off into a rant of some kind, and I didn't need that just now.

I decided to call Brad.

With great effort, I raised myself up out of the lobby sofa—which was more comfortable than I had anticipated—and made my way over to the front desk.

"Yes, sir," the pretty brunette behind the counter asked. "How can I help you?"

I put on the most pathetic face I could muster. "My wallet was stolen," I said, "and I was wondering if I could use your phone to call a friend of mine. It would just be a local call."

Her face nearly crumbled. "Oh, I'm so sorry, sir. That's horrible. Just follow me to the end of the counter, and I'll give you the courtesy phone."

She moved to my left and stepped to the far end of the counter, where she lifted a phone from her lower countertop up to my higher one.

"Thank you very much," I said, still trying to sound like someone who'd lost his wallet. Which wasn't difficult, because I had, in fact, lost my wallet. I knew where it was. I just couldn't get at it. Nor did I have any expectation of being able to get at it any time in the near future. *Ergo*, I had lost my wallet.

I picked up the phone and poised my finger over the buttons. It wasn't until that very moment that I realized I couldn't remember Brad's number.

The day was going exceedingly well, I thought.

"Excuse me," I said to the gal behind the counter. "Would you happen to have a phone book?"

She smiled and returned to my location. "Certainly, sir." She reached under the counter and produced a phone directory.

"I seem to have lost my memory as well as my wallet."

She smiled at my brave attempt to be humorous through my obvious misery. "I'm sure the same thing would happen to me in that situation," she said. "It's very stressful, I can imagine."

She couldn't imagine, really. No one could. I'd been through things in the last couple of days that no one would believe, let alone imagine. I didn't say anything of the sort to her, though. I just smiled and thanked her again.

I flipped to the back of the phone book, to the "W" section, and scanned for "Williams". There was a metric ton of them, but fortunately only a few "B"s and only a couple of "Bradley"s. I smiled quietly to myself at Brad's unfortunate full first name, and began dialing the phone.

I chuckled slightly as I recalled Mister Spock, in his awkward gangster imitation, saying "I would advise youse to keep dialin'" as he held a Tommy gun on one of the bad guys.

The phone rang about five times before Brad picked up.

"'Lo?" he said, his voice croaking with what I assumed to be sleepiness.

"Brad? It's Jack."

"Dude. Where've you been? People are looking for you."

A bolt of panic surged up from my stomach through my chest as I imagined the shadowy and mysterious organization that had taken me to their lair.

"What kind of people?"

Brad cleared his throat. "Jesus, man. Paranoid much? Lydia and your other band guys. And a couple of people from your store."

I hadn't realized I was so popular.

"Christ, I haven't been gone *that* long. What the hell's their problem?"

"Are you even, like, on this planet, man? People are fucking worried about you. You tried to off yourself, for Christ's sake. You think people aren't going to worry?"

I closed my eyes and rubbed the bridge of my nose. "Yeah, okay. I understand that. I just wasn't able to call anyone until now, that's all."

"Well, that's pretty fucking inconsiderate of you, dude. You didn't even tell anyone where you were going."

"I know. It couldn't be helped." I tried to control my breathing, but my rising agitation was making it difficult. "Listen, Brad. I need your help, okay? I'm at the Holiday Inn on Robie and Quinpool, and I don't have my wallet or keys or anything. Any chance you could come and get me? I'm in kind of a tight spot."

I could hear faint breathing on the other end of the line for a moment.

"Jesus fuck, man. Did you hook up with some chick and she stole your wallet? Cause you're an idiot like that, you know."

"Brad, the last thing I need right now is to be told that I'm an idiot. Whether or not it's true, I don't want to hear it. Okay? And no, I did not hook up with some chick, as you so tactfully put it. I'll explain the situation to you when I see you, if that isn't too much trouble."

Another pause.

"You're one demanding sonofabitch, you know that? You expect everyone to drop whatever the fuck they're doing because you need something. I don't even know why these people are worried about you. You're just about the most selfish prick I've ever met. I don't get you sometimes. Hell, most of the time."

My breathing continued to struggle against me.

"This is one helluva time for a lecture. Can you not tell from the tone of my voice that I'm in real trouble here? Can you, even for a minute, forget about all that and just come out and help me?"

"Jesus." He muttered something unintelligible, which was just as well as far as I was concerned. "Where'd you say you are?"

"Holiday Inn. Robie and—"

"Yeah, yeah. I know where it is. Gimme fifteen minutes."

"Thanks, Brad. You're a prince among men."

"You owe me, dude."

"I owe you big time."

"You'd better remember that."

He hung up before I could say anything else. I put the phone down, hung my head, and let out a long, drawn-out breath.

"Are you okay, sir?" the girl behind the desk asked.

I nodded without looking up. "My friend's giving me a hard time, but he's coming to get me."

"Aren't you staying for the convention?"

I raised my head and gave her a puzzled look. "Why on earth would I stay for—?" I began, but realized before I finished the question that I looked very much like a costumed convention attendee.

"Oh," I said. "Right. The convention. I'm going to come back after I take care of a few things."

She smiled. "That's good. I'm glad you're not going to miss out."

I returned the smile and handed the phone book back to her. "No, I don't think I'll be missing anything," I said.

I turned to face the lobby. I gave my head a slight shake and took a deep breath. The adventure would continue. I had a ride away from here, but I was now faced with the prospect of explaining to Brad what I was doing in this getup.

I decided to return to the comfortable sofa and await Brad's arrival.

"Nice costume," someone said as I passed by a small knot of people waiting to check in.

I turned to look and saw that the words had come from a young woman dressed up as Princess Leia. "Thanks," I said, trying to ignore the bagel-shaped hair constructs on each side of her head. "Yours too." I simply didn't have the energy to get into my usual fan-bashing schtick. Besides, I was outnumbered here.

I turned my head away and focused on the sofa. It was my only goal at this moment. I recalled its firm but yielding seat and its high, neck--supporting back. It called to me. And I was answering the call.

As I sank my tired butt into the cushion, Dan and Rick arrived at my location to retrieve their many and sundry bags.

"You checking in?" Dan asked.

"No, my friend's coming to get me. I'm going to go to his place for a bit and then come back."

"Don't be too long," Dan said. "You don't want to miss the opening ceremonies."

I decided against telling him that, yes, in fact, I did very much want to miss the opening ceremonies.

"I don't think I'll miss too much," I said, opting for the same cleverly disguised sardonic cynicism that I'd used on the desk clerk.

"Well, come and look for us when you get back," Dan said. "If you miss us down in the convention rooms, we're staying in Room 2110."

I nodded weakly.

"Okay, then," Dan said. "See you later."

He and Rick hoisted some of the bags onto their shoulders and carried the rest in their hands. As they walked away, I plunked the folded trench coat on my lap and pulled the fedora out from within its folds. I leaned my head back and perched the fedora on my forehead so that it covered my eyes. I was spent. I would take whatever rest I could find.

As my eyes closed, I had a sudden image of Dan and Rick as the geek versions of Jay and Silent Bob. Instead of profanity, Dan would come out with a constant stream of science fiction and fantasy references, whilst Rick would say precious little at all.

I then had another uncalled for image, this one of the actual Jay and Silent Bob playing *Dungeons and Dragons*. I started to laugh, glad for the slight diversion from my miserable existence.

My pop culture references were pretty much all I had at that moment.

♦

It was more like twenty-five minutes before Brad arrived. I had actually dozed off on the couch and was snoring slightly when he came into the lobby.

I had a sense of someone standing over me, so I lifted the fedora and opened my eyes.

"Jesus fuck," was all he said.

"Nice to see you too," I mumbled.

He gestured towards me. "What the fuck is all this?" he asked.

"I've switched tailors. Nice of you to notice."

He dropped his arm to his side and skewered me with a glare. "Will you cut the crap? If you're not going to tell me what the fuck this is all about, then I'm just going to turn around and drive home without you."

I sighed and sat up. "Can my tale of woe at least wait until we're out of this godforsaken geek fest?"

Brad looked around. "They're having fun, dude. You know? Fun? Ever hear of it?"

I rolled my eyes and got up from the sofa. "They're making bloody fools of themselves, is what they're doing."

"Said the man in the gangster suit."

I stood up and batted his comment away with my fedora. "Yeah, well, it's easy for you to talk. You don't know how I got this way."

"Well, I'm waiting to hear, aren't I?"

"And I'm going to tell you. Just not in this throng of misfits, okay?"

"Jesus. What is it with you?" Brad turned and headed for the door. "Come on."

I put the fedora back on my head and followed him.

"Hey, nice costume," said a man in a Jedi cloak as I followed behind Brad.

"I would advise youse to keep walkin'," I said.

This, to my chagrin, only served to elicit a loud hoot of a laugh from the Jedi in question.

"You love those movies and shows," Brad said as we stepped into the sunlight. "Why are you so down on these people just because they go to conventions. It's, like, their hobby or something."

"A great many of those people," I said. "Lack a little something known as social skills. And some of them smell bad."

"You're a prick, man. I've said it before, and I'll say it again."

"And you're a slob. Can we move on?"

Brad led me down Robie Street to one of the side streets, where we turned right.

"Jesus," I said. "Where the hell did you have to park?"

"Oh, yeah. Complain about my parking choice now that I've come all the way down here to rescue your sorry ass. You know what the parking's like down here. The hospital's right there, in case you forgot."

I had not forgotten. Not in the slightest. The spectre of the hospital loomed long and dark to our left as we proceeded along Robie. It was not a happy place. Not to me, anyway. I tried not to look at it. It reminded me of things I didn't want to think about at this particular moment.

♦

When we reached Brad's place, he parked on the street about two houses down. Brad lived in the upper flat of a three unit building in a reasonably quiet neighborhood. It was a small place, but he lived alone and didn't seem to mind the sloping ceilings in the bedroom and living room too much.

We went upstairs to his flat, and Brad unlocked the door and ushered me in.

Lydia was there, waiting for me.

I stopped dead in my tracks and stared at her, my mouth slightly agape. I looked back at Brad, and he shrugged.

"Traitor," I muttered at him.

He rolled his eyes and shut the door.

Lydia stood up from the sofa and slowly walked towards me.

"Don't slap me again," I said. "That bit's getting old."

"You ungrateful bastard," she said through clenched teeth. "What the fuck did you think you were doing?"

I sighed and went to run a hand through my hair, but discovered that the fedora was still atop my head. I removed it and dropped my hands to my sides again.

She looked me up and down. "What, were you at some kind of a costume party you couldn't tell anyone about?"

"He was at the sci-fi convention down at the Holiday Inn," Brad chimed in.

I looked back at him again. "Try not to help, Brad," I said.

He shook his head and headed towards the kitchen. "Whatever, man. Just whatever."

I looked at Lydia again. She reminded me of a kettle that was just about to boil.

"I wasn't at the convention," I said. "I was at the hotel where they're holding the convention."

She looked at the ceiling. "And how much sense was that supposed to make?" she asked.

"Look," I said. "You're never going to believe me, no matter what I tell you, so why don't we just skip this whole thing, and you give me your copy of my apartment key, and we can all get back to our lives."

I heard a snorting chuckle come from the direction of the kitchen. "Nice try, dude," Brad said.

I turned away from Lydia for a moment and sat down in one of Brad's wicker chairs. When I looked up at Lydia, she was eyeing my getup again.

"I thought you hated those bloody things," she said.

"What bloody things?"

"The conventions, you arse. I thought you hated them."

"I do. They're a haven for social misfits."

"Well then, what the fuck were you doing there in a costume, for Christ's sake?"

I hung my head. "I told you. You're not going to believe me."

She turned with a huff and sat back down on the sofa. "Well, then, why don't you just tell me your sad fiction so we can get that part over with and I can go back to telling you what a shit you are."

"Oh. Lovely. I look forward to that."

Her face turned red, suddenly and violently. "Will you tell me where in fucking hell you've been for the last day-and-a-half? I was worried sick about you."

I put my head on the back of the chair and tried to breathe normally. "It starts with that woman I saw in the hospital."

"What woman?"

"The one in the 1940s coat. The one that nobody else seemed to be able to see."

"Oh, this should be good."

I proceeded to tell her about the reappearance of the cobblestone path, my conversation with Irene in the parking lot, the man taking measurements behind the building in the middle of the night, my abduction, my rescue, and the many and varied details of the world Irene and Greaves inhabited.

"You going to write all that down?" Lydia asked. "'Cause it'll make one helluva lot better novel than it does an explanation."

I nodded weakly. "Yeah. I know. Didn't I already say you wouldn't believe it?"

"Yeah. And I don't. So now tell me the real story."

Brad reentered the room with three beers. He had blond hair, so I immediately thought of him as Goldilocks and the three beers. I refrained from saying it out loud, however. I was in enough trouble.

"Here, dude," he said, handing me one of the frosty cans. "You look like you could use it."

"Thanks, man," I said. "I appreciate it."

Brad settled himself in the remaining wicker chair. "That was one helluva story. Lydia's right. You should jot it down before you forget it."

"Yeah. Okay," I said. "I will. Just as soon as I'm able to get back into my apartment and grab some paper."

I glanced at Lydia. She was scowling at me, her arms crossed over her breasts. I always hated it when she did that. It blocked my view of her breasts.

"Well," she said. "If you were kidnapped by some shadowy organization, then you're not safe going back to your apartment, are you?"

I pursed my lips and furrowed my brow. That particular line of thinking had not occurred to me.

151

"You know," I said, "for someone who doesn't believe my story, you're actually being quite helpful. You make an excellent point."

She rolled her eyes and hissed. "Good God, Jack. You can't even tell when your lies have inconsistencies in them. What kind of writer are you, anyway?"

"I'm the kind of writer who is fucking exhausted from a full day of extraordinary experiences and unimaginable stress." I glared at her. "Okay?"

Lydia looked at Brad. "What are we going to do with him?"

"We?" Brad put his hands up. "Listen, I don't care what *you* do with him, but you can leave me out of it."

"Thanks loads," Lydia said. "Big help you are."

"Hey, I got him here, didn't I?" Brad said. "I hand him off to you at this point. He's your problem."

"I'm still here," I said. "Stop talking about me like I'm not."

Lydia curled her lip at me. "Yes, I know you're still there, you prat. I almost wish you weren't. Your level of self-absorption seems to have jumped up a few notches whilst you've been gone, and I'm not sure I can deal with it anymore."

"Oooh," I said. "'Whilst.' You don't hear that one much anymore. Kudos."

Lydia stood up, stepped over to me, slapped me across the face, and returned to her seat. It took all of a second and a half.

"Ow," I said, my eyes watering, "That's not a skill I want to see you developing."

She crossed her arms and glared at me.

It slowly began to dawn on me that I was now in a position not much more enviable than that of The Boy Who Cried Wolf. My best friend and my best female friend were both sitting there, looking down upon me in judgement, and I suddenly knew that I deserved it.

It was true that I was often preoccupied with my own problems. It was also true that I sometimes trivialized other people's problems. It was further true that I had occasionally told untruths to avert potential disastrous consequence after I'd done something questionable.

This was now catching up with me. The fact that I was a creative writer didn't help matters at all.

"So, where does that leave us?" I asked. "You don't believe my story, and I don't have another one to tell you."

"Except for the one where you hook up with some bimbo at this stupid convention and lose your clothes and wallet."

I half-closed my eyelids and half-opened my mouth. "Well, sure. If you want to be completely unoriginal. Not to mention tasteless. You can go ahead and believe that if you want. There's nothing I can do about it."

Brad gave Lydia a look. "He's not protesting. That's kind of a new thing, isn't it?"

Lydia looked at me through narrowed eyes. "What are you up to?"

"Oh, God," I said. "Now I'm up to something. That's just great. Just bloody brilliant." I put my head back on the chair again.

Lydia sat forward and scrutinized me. "You don't really expect us to believe that story, do you?"

"I expect nothing. I just want to sleep. That's all. You can both go fuck yourselves, or each other if that would help any, and let me wallow in my misery. That wouldn't be all that different from any other day, really. Except for the suit."

I closed my eyes and crossed my arms.

"Do you want me to take you home?" Brad asked.

"No, actually," I said. "Now that you mention it, I don't. Lydia made a very good point in the midst of all that sarcastic ranting. If I go home, I'm just setting myself up to be nabbed by the men in black again."

"Men in black," Lydia scoffed. "Of all the ridiculous—"

"They wore dark suits," I said, "so I shall henceforth refer to them as the men in black. I don't know if they're good guys or bad guys. They might be government spooks, or they might be evil corporate goons, or they might be criminals. I have no fucking clue. I just know that they're very unlikely to be cheerful about my disappearance from their detention area."

Brad raised his eyebrows. "Man, he sounds pretty convincing."

Lydia turned her scowl upon him now, giving me a short break from its intense heat. "Don't you dare," she said to him. "He's giving a load of bollocks, and you'd better not forget that. You know how smug he can be."

"Still here," I said, raising my hand into the air.

"And you can shut up now," she said, swinging the scowl back towards me again. "I'm not hearing another word of this. You've done enough, and you've said enough. If I can't get a straight story out of you, then I'm out of it. You can go whine and moan to someone else."

She stood up and grabbed her purse. "Here," she said, digging into one of the compartments and pulling out a set of keys. "You can have these back." She tossed them in my lap and stormed to the door.

She turned for a moment as she hauled the door open. "I'm handing him back to you, Brad. It sounds like you're starting to believe him, so the two of you can just go roll around in your little fantasy. I'm done."

She stomped out into the hall and slammed the door behind her.

I sank further into the chair. "That was not completely unexpected," I said.

Brad crossed his legs and shook his head. "Jesus, man. Do you have any idea what you do to her? Did you even see her face just now?"

"No," I said. "I was leaning back with my eyes closed." I opened my lids slightly for a moment and glanced at him, just to drive the point home.

"You hate everybody, don't you?"

"No. I don't. I simply have a very low threshold for tolerating stupidity. That's all."

"Lydia is not stupid, man. She's fucking out of her mind worried about you."

"Lydia can be *very* stupid at times. She's overly emotional, and she doesn't think things through."

Brad stood up and took a swig of his beer. "You're a piece of work, man. A real piece of work."

"So I've been told."

He returned to the kitchen, leaving me to my turmoil, anxiety, and confusion.

The truth was, I was scared. I hadn't the first clue what I should be doing. I didn't know how to protect myself, and any plans I might come up with in that regard would be rendered exponentially difficult by the simple fact that nobody would believe my story. If two of my closest friends didn't believe it, then nobody would. Nobody who would be able to help me, at any rate.

I had no proof of anything I'd told them. I didn't know how to find the agency that wanted to interrogate me, and I had no means of returning to the alternate world, so that left me with a highly implausible tale of unexpected adventure and a whopping headache.

Brad returned and resumed his seat. My eyes were still closed, but I could feel him staring at me.

"What?" I asked. "What now?"

"Listen, dude," he said. "Did you ever think that maybe…"

He spoke much more quietly now, more tentatively. This got my attention. I opened my eyes and raised my head.

"That maybe I'm losing my mind?" I asked.

He looked at the floor.

"Don't you think I've asked myself that question at least three times a day ever since I got out of that fucking hospital?" I hadn't intended to raise my voice, but the volume came unbidden. "Don't you think I wondered the same thing every single goddamned time I saw that woman? I still can't believe the things I saw over there. I don't know what's happening to me. But I don't have any other memories except for being kidnapped and going over to another world. So what does that make me? Delusional? Psychotic? Schizophrenic? Insane?"

I was breathing rapidly now. Brad's gaze remained fixed on the carpet.

"I don't know what I did to myself with those stupid drugs," I continued. "I don't know if I damaged myself in some way, or made my problems worse. I didn't think it worked that way, with fucking over-the-counter medication, but maybe it does. Maybe it flipped some kind of switch in my head, and now I'm some kind of fucking maniac. Or lunatic. Or worse. I'm scared half to death that I've done some kind of permanent damage to myself. Do you understand that?"

He looked up at me again. "I'm sorry, man. I didn't mean to stress you out more. But you do seem different since you got out of the hospital."

"Exactly," I said. "And that's what scares the shit out of me."

"Then you need to get yourself checked out. I mean really checked out. Cat scans, or whatever it is they do now. Find out if there's something screwed up."

"That scares me even more. If there really is something wrong, then they'll probably institutionalize me. And that'll be pretty much the end of life as I know it."

"Yeah." Brad stared past me at the wall for a moment. "So you don't want to go back to your place."

"I'd rather not," I said.

"Yeah." He got up again. "I'll grab some blankets."

At that moment, I could have kissed him.

"I'll say it again, Brad. You're a prince."

"Save, it, man," he called from the hallway. "Just return the favor some time, all right?"

"Sure," I said. "I owe you yet again."

Brad stepped back into the room and tossed a blanket and pillow at me.

"Who else is going to take care of your sorry ass?" he asked.

I thought he made a good point.

Chapter Twelve

(Saturday, 7:12 A.M.)

I awoke the next morning to a shaft of sunlight across my eyes. I wasn't quite sure how Brad had arranged for that to happen, but for a moment I felt like I was in a movie, and that the lighting had been set up specifically for the "early morning awakened by a shaft of sunlight" shot. I blinked a few times and sat up to get out of the harsh glare.

I ran my hands up my face and back through my hair, breathing noisily through my dry, clogged nose. I didn't remember any dreams, fortunately, so I must have slept solidly through the night. I didn't *want* to remember any dreams. My real life was surreal enough at the moment, thank you very much, and I didn't need any more weird-ass imagery to complement it.

I stood and stretched, then stepped towards the front window with a mind to adjusting the curtain and eliminating the pesky shaft of sunlight. My angle of approach was such that, through the gap in the curtains, I could see the building across the street and the car sitting at the curb in front of it.

Without my even fully realizing what was happening, my pulse quickened and my knees bent. Within a second I was on the floor, crawling towards the window instead of walking.

I took a steadying breath and raised myself just enough to peer out the window. The car was fairly innocuous, a simple grey sedan that looked to be of the Ford or Mercury persuasion, but the fact that two men sat in the front seat made me swallow hard. They both wore dark suits and ties.

I marvelled at my instincts. I hadn't even thought I was fully awake yet, but here I was, acting like Harrison Ford in *The Fugitive*. Evidently, my reticular activating system was in high gear and on full alert.

Great. So I could now add paranoia to my list of complaints.

I scuttled on hands and knees back to the sofa, grabbed my trousers and shirt—my *otherwordly* trousers and shirt, I reminded myself—and continued my crawl towards Brad's room. There were no windows in the hallway, so I stood when I reached it, pulled on the pants and shirt, and moved quietly towards the bedroom. The door was partially open, so I rolled my head around the doorframe to see where the window was situated. It looked like my position would be unseen from outside, but I didn't want to take any chances.

"Brad," I said, trying to be heard without raising my voice.

Brad was a sound sleeper. I would have to be more assertive than that.

"Brad," I repeated, louder this time. Still no response.

I crouched, crept a couple of feet into the room, grabbed one of Brad's sneakers, and backed out again. I stood again, just outside the doorway, and hurled the sneaker at Brad's head.

The projectile struck its mark, and Brad sat up straight, arms whirling about his head like he'd been attacked by a swarm of bees.

"What the fuck?" he shouted.

"Shhhhh…" I hissed at him. "Be quiet."

He finally regained his sense of place and looked at me. "Jesus, Jack. What the fuck are you doing?"

"Shhhhh…" I repeated. "Come out to the living room. I need to show you something."

"Go away," he replied, and slumped back down on the bed.

"Brad, this is important."

"It's always important with you, isn't it?"

His voice was muffled by the bedclothes he'd pulled over his head.

"They're back," I said.

"Who's back?"

"The guys in the suits."

He rolled over and glared at me. "Are you kidding me? Are we back on this bullshit again?"

I clenched my jaw. "I want you to see this for yourself. You're never going to believe me if you don't see it for yourself."

He let out a long sigh through his nose and threw off the bedclothes. "Fine. Show me, so I can go back to bed."

I led him down the hall towards the living room, gesturing for him to stay behind me. When I reached the end of the hall, I poked my head around the corner and looked towards the window.

"You can't see them from this angle, so you're going to have to crouch down and—"

Brad pushed past me and walked towards the living room window.

"Brad," I said, panicked. "Don't let them see you."

I put my hands to my face as Brad pulled the curtains open and looked out into the street. He cut a stunning figure, bathed in sunlight, his blond hair sticking up on one side, stubble across his chin, and his underwear bunched up into the crack of his ass. I would have laughed if I hadn't been so terrified.

After a moment, Brad pulled the curtains closed and turned around. "Couple of dudes in a grey car. Big fucking deal. I'm going back to bed."

"They've seen you now," I said as he passed me and headed back to the bedroom.

"I live here. Anybody who looks up is going to see me if they time it right."

I followed him back to his room. "Yeah, but they're not just anybody."

He flopped back down on his bed and looked at me. "Couple of dudes in a grey car. That's all. Stop being so fucking paranoid." He pulled the covers back over his head and rolled away from me.

I stood there for a moment breathing heavily, my fists in tight balls. I'd already thought of the paranoid thing, but it's one thing to think it yourself, and quite another to have it stated so bluntly by someone else.

"I'm not into guys, Jack," Brad said in his sheet muffled voice. "If you get your jollies from watching guys sleep, I don't want to know about it. Just go jack off in the other room."

"You're not taking this seriously," I said.

"Fucking right, I'm not," he replied.

I turned away from him and closed my eyes for a moment. I couldn't believe what was happening to me. Part of me knew that Brad was right not to accept what I was telling him. My story was ludicrous. It made no sense. Why would he believe me?

But another part of me, a quite prominent part of my mental landscape, in fact, was absolutely terrified, absolutely convinced that everything that had transpired in the last forty-eight hours was completely real, and absolutely without a clue as to what I should do next.

For the moment, I simply clung to the hope that the men in the car hadn't spotted me. They were probably staking out all my family, friends, and acquaintances. I realized now that it had been stupid of me to stay here last night. I was putting Brad in danger.

I turned back to the bedroom.

"Jesus, will you get out of the doorway?" Brad said.

"Brad, I'm sorry."

"Well, then, show it. Get out of the doorway."

"No, I'm not talking about that."

He turned over and pulled the covers off his face. "What?"

"I'm sorry for getting you into this. I shouldn't have stayed here last night. I should have taken a hotel room or something."

"Don't be stupid. You don't have money for a hotel. You work in a fucking bookstore. What am I going to do, turn you out on the street?"

"I appreciate that. I really do. You have no idea. But I've put your life in danger by staying here. I have to find a way to get out of here without them seeing me. So they'll stop watching you."

He sat up and rubbed his eyes. "First off, that's really touching. I had no idea you were concerned about anybody's welfare except your own."

"That's not funny, Brad. I'm trying to be serious here."

"Yeah. Whatever. Secondly, let's say for a minute that you're not just talking out of your ass. Personally, I think you're full of shit, but let's say for the sake of argument that there's really a bunch of guys in suits after you. If they were, and if they were watching all your friends' places, and all your family's, they wouldn't just do it for, like, one night or one day, and then say, 'Okay, we're done here. Let's go on to the next one.' If they know that you and I hang out, then they're going to watch my place until you show up."

He was right. They weren't watching Brad's apartment thinking I was here. They were watching thinking that at some point or other I would come here.

My knees wobbled for a second, and I sank to the floor. My head began to spin anew. Without even knowing what I'd done or how I'd done it, I'd put the lives of everyone I knew and cared about in danger. My coworkers, my uncle, my bandmates—

"Oh, my God. Lydia."

I struggled to my feet. "Brad, you have to call Lydia. I need to know she's okay."

"What, are your fingers broken? Call her yourself." He pulled the covers over his head again.

160

"I can't. They probably have your phone line tapped. If I call, they'll know I'm here."

"Jesus Murphy," Brad mumbled from within his cocoon.

I watched the shape of his stomach rise and fall under the sheets a few time. After a minute or so, he stirred. The sheets flew to the side, and he sat up again.

"You're seriously pissing me off, my man," he said as he swung his legs off the bed and stood again.

He marched down the hall to the living room, sat down on the sofa, and picked up the phone. "If she rags at me for waking her up, I'm going to kick you in the balls," he muttered.

He dialled Lydia's number and put the receiver to his ear. I stood in the hall, trying to keep out of the living room window's line of sight, and watched him. His eyes roamed the room as he waited for someone on the other end to answer. I couldn't hear anything, but it must have rung five or six times since he'd dialled.

"She's not there," he said.

"Give it another few rings," I said.

He rolled his eyes and sat back on the sofa. We waited for another thirty seconds or so, and then he hung up the phone.

"She's not there."

"That's really weird. She's not normally an early riser."

"Well, maybe she unplugged it."

"Why would she do that?"

Brad gave me an odd look. "Why would *anyone* unplug the phone?"

"What?"

He rolled his head back. "Jesus, you're dense, man. You've been treating her like shit. Would you really be surprised if she hooked up with someone else?"

I nearly stepped full into the room, but managed to remember at the last second that I was trying to hide.

"First of all, Lydia and I are not in a relationship. We're friends. Okay? End of story. Second of all, Lydia's not like that. She doesn't just hook up with random guys. She has standards."

Brad raised his head and looked at me. "Well then why the fuck did she hook up with you?"

"This is not the discussion I want to have right now. I want to find Lydia. She's in danger. Just like you are."

161

"Where is this coming from, all of a sudden? This concern for your fellow human? Did you get a visit from the Christmas ghosts or something last night?"

"Look, I may be a selfish prick sometimes—"

"Sometimes?"

"Will you let me finish? I may be like that sometimes, but that doesn't mean I don't care about my friends. I'm not a heartless bastard, you know. I'm not made of granite."

"You do a damn fine impersonation."

I balled my fists and raised them to my shoulders. "Will you stop it? I'm trying to be serious here."

"Well, there's a first time for everything."

I let my hands drop to my sides. "Try her cell number, will you?"

"I don't know her cell number."

I reached into my mental address book, but when I came to Lydia's page, I found the cell number entry to be blurry.

"Ah, Jesus," I said. "I can't remember it."

"Well, there's not much we can do, then, is there? I mean, since you left your cell phone in an alternate universe and all."

"Don't you have a phone book?"

"They don't list people's cell numbers in the phone book, dude. It's just home numbers and business numbers."

I was suddenly struck with an idea. I turned to look at Brad again. "Then call my place. Maybe she's gone there to grab some stuff for me."

Brad laughed. "Are you serious, dude? After the way she barrelled out of here last night? You'll be lucky if you ever catch sight of the back of one of her boots again."

My whole body sagged. He was right.

"Besides, she gave you back her keys. Remember?"

Again he was right.

"Damn it. I'm worried about her."

"Too little, too late, man. That ship has left the station."

I scrunched up my face. "You're a writer's worst nightmare, you know that?"

"What are you talking about?"

"I'm talking about your unfortunate tendency to mix metaphors. And awkwardly, too, I might add."

He stood up and took a step towards me. "One second you tell me you're worried about Lydia, and the next you're complaining about me mixing my fucking metaphors? How screwed are you, man? How seriously gone in the head are you?"

"Well, you figure it out, Doctor Freud. You think I'm hallucinating. You also think I'm an uncaring, selfish prick. You also think I'm an anal-retentive language Nazi. So you do the math. How fucked up am I?"

Brad moved past me again, shoving me with his shoulder this time. "I'm taking a shower," he said.

I watched him step into the bathroom. Slowly, I turned to face the living room again. The window was still there, wide, glowing, impertinent. It laughed at me, knowing it held something I dreaded to see, but needed to see. I had to know if they were still watching.

I dropped to a crouch and began crawling towards the section of wall to the right of the window. When I reached it, I rose up again and flattened myself against it. I inched towards the window and peered around the frame.

The car was gone.

I had a bad feeling about this, for some reason. I'd have thought that seeing the grey car gone would have been a relief. It should have allowed me some room for doubt that the men were actually agents of the organization that had taken me before. But it didn't do any such thing. All it did was fill me with an odd sense of panic. My tiny measure of control was gone. With them sitting out there, in front of the building, I knew they weren't doing anything to any of my friends. Now that they were gone, I had no idea what the hell they were doing.

I walked to the bathroom. I could hear the shower spray over the atonal mumblings of a man who couldn't sing to save his life. Strangely, I recognized what Brad was trying to sing. It was the aborted fetus of Bruce Springsteen's "Born to Run". Ignoring the unpleasant sounds, I stepped into the bathroom, waving my hand back and forth amidst the dense fog the shower was putting forth. Brad liked his showers hot.

"Brad," I said.

I was greeted with a thump as something fell to the tub floor.

"Jesus," Brad said. "Give me some kind of warning, will you? You scared the living shit out of me."

"Sorry," I said. "Listen, Brad. The grey car is gone."

"Hallelujah! Now get the fuck out of my bathroom before I start thinking you really do like watching guys."

163

"Brad, I don't feel good about this."

"Neither do I. I'm trying to take a shower, here, and you're out there practically gawking at me."

"That's not what I'm talking about. Besides, you have an opaque shower curtain."

"What does the friggin' design pattern have to do with anything?"

I rolled my eyes. "Opaque means you can't see through it."

"Whatever. You're still standing there while I'm showering. You're creeping me out."

"I meant that I have a bad feeling about the car being gone."

"Oh, Jesus. First you're freaked out because it's there, and now you're freaked out because it's gone. Make up your fucking mind, will you?"

"Will you listen to me?"

"No. No, I will not listen to you. Not until I am clean and dry and with no goddamned fucking audience. *Capice?*"

I turned towards the door. "Yeah. All right." I moved back down the hall and sat on the living room couch.

Brad took easily another fifteen minutes in the shower. Evidently he liked his showers long and hot. I was sure that if I were to say that to him, he would make some kind of inappropriate comment about his manly equipment, so I tried very hard to erase the phrase from my mind and move on to other things.

I was beginning to panic. I didn't know how many agents the shadowy organization had watching my friends and family, but I knew now that two of them were no longer watching Brad. What that meant was, at the moment, a mystery, but it brought all kinds of unsavory scenarios into my already overworked brain.

I just wanted some peace and quiet. Some rest and relaxation. I didn't envision that happening any time soon.

Brad sauntered down the hall in his bathrobe, rubbing his head with a towel, and stepped into the room.

"All right," he said, sitting down in one of the wicker chairs. "What was so all fired important that you had to interrupt my shower time."

"I told you," I said. "The car's gone, and I have a bad feeling about it."

"It just means it wasn't what you thought it was."

"What it means is that it most definitely *was* what I thought it was, and they've changed their tactics. It bodes ill."

Brad stopped his head rubbing and pulled the towel aside. "It bodes ill? What the fuck kind of sentence is that? Are you going to start talking in Icelandic Pento Meter now?"

I hung my head. "It's not Icelandic. It's iambic. And it's not Pento Meter. It's pentameter."

Brad tugged the towel off his head and plunked it in his lap. "See? There you go again. Being all snotty and superior. I can't say a goddamned word around you without getting a lecture about proper grammar or pronounciation or something."

I sighed. "It's not pro-noun-ciation. It's pro-nun-ciation."

Brad threw the towel at me. It fell short, landing on my feet. "Why can't you just have a conversation like a normal person? Why do you have to go all English professor on my ass every time I say anything?"

I threw up my hands. "I'm sorry. I can't help it."

"Jesus. You really are a fucking grammar Nazi. You're not a lot of fun to be around at the best of times, dude, and this language thing just makes it ten times worse. You're lucky I don't kick your ass down the stairs."

"I said I was sorry, okay? Geez."

"Yeah. Whatever." He stepped out of the chair to retrieve his errant towel, and then reseated himself. "So, what were you saying before you started getting all Shakespearean?"

"I was saying that these people—the guys in the suits—have changed their tactics. I don't know what they're doing now, but they're not watching your place anymore, and it's making me antsy."

"I still say you're imagining things."

"And I say I'm not. There's something going on, and I'm almost afraid to find out what it is."

Brad finished drying his hair and hung the towel around his neck. "Man, we need to get you some drugs. Or get you laid or something. You're wound up way to tight."

I leaned forward and put my head in my hands, my elbows on my knees. "It was drugs that got me into this in the first place."

"What? What are you talking about?"

I raised my head and looked at him. "The drugs I took. You know. To try and 'off' myself, as you so colorfully put it."

"Oh. I actually didn't know what you did. I just knew you tried to, well, you know…"

"It was Gravol, Sleep-Eze-D, and Captain Morgan."

Brad rolled his eyes back and gargled a hiss in the back of this throat. "Fuck, man, what are you, some kind of pussy? That'd never kill anyone. Just give you a nice, long sleep, that's all. Jesus. You can't do anything right, can you?"

"That was pretty much the reason I was trying to do it. You know? Major failure in all areas of life?"

Brad straightened up and furrowed his brows slightly. "Uh, sorry, man. I… I didn't realize that was…"

I waved the comment away. "No, you didn't realize. So, let's forget about it. I did what I did, and I think it affected my brain in an unexpected way."

"You mean you started hallucinating."

"No, I mean I started seeing things that no one else could see."

"Right. Hallucinating."

"No. Not hallucinating. I was seeing this woman, Irene. I told you about her. No one else could see her, but she was actually there. Well, she was kind of there. But she was real, and I was the only one who could see her."

"That sounds a lot like hallucinating to me."

"No. It's not. It's this other world thing I was talking about."

Brad put his hands to his forehead. "Yeah, and I don't want to fucking hear about it again. Okay? It's crazy talk, dude. And the more you talk about it, the more I think you ought to be locked up in a padded room somewhere."

"Oh, thanks a lot. You're such a big help."

"I think I'd be a help if I took you back to the hospital."

I put my head back and breathed out. Part of me agreed with him.

"And what's this shit?"

I looked up again to find Brad brandishing my suit jacket, waving it back and forth.

"It's a suit. I told you?"

He eyed it warily. "Yeah, but where did you get it? You can't afford shit like this."

I sat forward. "You're right. I couldn't possibly afford a suit like that."

"Well then…?"

Wheels were starting to turn in my head.

"Feel it," I said.

"It's in my hand, dumbass."

"No, I mean, really feel it. And really look at it."

Brad rolled his eyes, but he did as I asked. "Okay. So…?"

"Have you ever seen a suit like that before?"

He looked at it again, frowning and cocking his head. "Not since last time I watched *The Maltese Falcon*."

"Exactly. It's an old style. But it's brand new. It's like it was made yesterday."

He dropped the jacket onto the arm of the sofa. "So what? You hooked up with a rich chick who digs retro, and she gave you a nice present. That supposed to impress me?"

I put my hands up in front of me and slumped back. "No. I guess not."

Brad stood up and tightened the belt on his robe. "I still think we need to get you checked out."

He turned towards the hall, but stopped short as the phone started to ring.

"Pick it up," he said. "Maybe it's Lydia."

I waved my hands in protest. "No, I told you. They might have the line bugged."

Brad shook his head and turned back into the room. He stepped to the phone and picked it up.

I watched his face as he listened. His expression slowly changed from annoyance to perplexity, then to confusion, then to apprehension, and finally to anger.

"Who the fuck is this?" he demanded.

His frown deepened as he listened again. After a moment, he pulled the receiver away from his ear and stared at it. Then he slammed it down on the cradle and stepped back like it was about to explode.

"What?" I said. I could feel the panic rising in my chest again.

Brad glared at me. "You fucking bastard," he said. "How could you let this happen?"

"What are you talking about?"

"They've got Lydia, you fuck. That was your friend from the spooky agency, saying that if I saw Mister Richmond, would I please tell him that if he ever wants to see his girlfriend again, he'll be in the tunnel that runs between Barrington Street and Marginal Road at nine P.M. sharp."

I could feel the blood draining from my face. "Oh, my God," I said as I stood up.

"What is all this, man?" Brad was nearly shaking now.

"So you believe me now, do you?" I asked, sarcasm dripping off my every syllable.

Brad's mouth quivered as he fought back whatever new harsh retort he'd come up with. "Yeah," he said at length. "About the guys in the suits, anyway." His voice was raspy, quiet. "I don't know what sort of shit you're caught up in, man, but if I find out you've gotten involved with drug dealers or some other bullshit like that, God help me, I'll tear your balls off and feed them to the neighbor's dog. You understand me?"

I swallowed. "Yeah. I get it. But believe me, it's nothing remotely like what you're thinking. If you caught even a glimpse of what I've seen, it would blow your mind right out of your skull."

"I hope you're right, Jack. Because I'm this close…" he put his thumb and forefinger close together and held them up. "…to giving up on you for good."

I knew he meant it. I'd never before heard him speak in such a tone, and, frankly, it scared the shit out of me.

"I'm getting dressed," Brad said. "You start figuring out what to do about this."

"I think it's pretty obvious what we're going to do," I said. "We're going to go down to that tunnel at nine o'clock."

"No. *You're* going to the tunnel at nine o'clock. I'll drive you part way, but I'm not going anywhere near the place. If you've got business to settle with these people, then you do it, you get Lydia out of there, and you leave me the fuck out of it."

He turned on his heel and stomped down the hall to the bedroom. I reached up to touch my forehead. I was sweating profusely. I stared blankly at the space Brad had just occupied. Then, after a moment, I sank back onto the sofa.

This was all my fault, I knew. Everything. All of it. Every last bit of it. All my fault. There was no way I could have known any of this would happen, no way I could have predicted even a tenth of it. But it had happened, and all because I'd been a stupid, selfish, idiot.

And now Lydia was in danger. I doubted I could ever forgive myself for that.

Brad came back into the living room, now fully dressed. He grabbed his jacket from the back of the door, and walked out into the hall without a word. I surmised from these actions that he wanted me out of his apartment. Since it was now evident that the agency men knew where I was, and since I now had a set of keys to my place, there was no reason for me to stay with him any longer. I picked up my old-fashioned jacket, trench coat, and fedora, and followed him.

"Are you going to lock up?" I called after him as I pulled the apartment door closed behind me.

There was no answer, so I just trotted down the stairs and out the main door.

His car was already running when I got there. I swung myself into the passenger seat and pulled the door closed. Before I'd even had a chance to grab my seat belt, he hit the accelerator, and we were launched down the driveway.

I glanced at him several times during the trip, but he acted as if he were the only one in the car. I could almost see the steam rising from his head, his anger was so fully manifested. I swallowed hard and decided it would be best if I stayed quiet. I didn't know what would happen if I spoke to him.

He pulled up in front of my building, put the car in park, and stared out the windshield. I took this as my cue to get the hell out of his car.

"Thanks for the lift," I said, unbuckling my seat belt and opening the door.

"I'll pick you up at twenty to nine," he said. "Don't make me wait for you."

I swallowed again. "Yeah. Okay. I'll be standing right in front of the building."

He didn't respond, so I got out of the car and closed the door. The "thunk" sound hadn't even faded when Brad hit the gas and zoomed away, leaving me standing in a cloud of dust like a cartoon character.

I closed my eyes for a moment and tried to breathe evenly. If I hadn't already been painfully aware of how serious this situation was, Brad's demeanour would certainly have clued me in. He was generally a pretty laid-back fellow, unless he was getting on my case about correcting his grammar, and I could count on the fingers of one hand the times I'd seen him really angry. And this—what I was seeing in him now—was beyond mere anger. It was sheer, unadulterated fury. It sent a chill through my bloodstream.

I pulled out the set of keys that Lydia had given back to me and turned to my apartment building. All I wanted to do at this moment was get out of my ridiculous suit and take a long, hot shower.

As I unlocked the door and headed for the stairs, I thought about the clothes that I was wearing. If all went as I intended, I'd hang them up in my closet and never look at the damned things again. Knowing how the human mind worked, once I got this situation with Lydia resolved, I'd start doubting that my trip to Irene's world had ever happened at all.

I was pretty sure my brain would try and bring order back to its corridors in whatever manner it could.

Oddly, that thought sent a short pang of grief through me.

I reached my apartment door and unlocked it. I had no luggage to deposit anywhere, despite having just been on the most unbelievable trip of my life, so I wandered into the bedroom to undress. I needed a shower in the worst possible way.

I put the trench coat and the fedora on the bed, then removed the jacket and the shirt and tossed them on top of the growing pile. I was about to unbuckle my belt, but I paused, feeling compelled to stare at the jacket for a moment. I stepped closer to the bed, moved the shirt, and pulled the jacket towards me.

I reached for the right-hand pocket, slid my hand under the flap, and put my fingers inside.

Sure enough, it was still there.

I pulled the crystal out of the jacket and held it in the palm of my hand. It was as clear and bright as when I'd first looked at it. It was so luminous that it nearly glowed.

It was as green as Irene's eyes.

I sat down on the edge of the bed and stared at the crystal, looking deep into its center. A calmness descended upon me, and I closed my eyes. I recalled Irene's face, her lovely smile, her beautiful deep eyes, the way the light had touched her cheekbone as we'd sat on the train. I could almost see her sitting across from me, could almost feel the rumbling and rocking of the wheels on the rails.

I opened my eyes and stared down at the crystal. The images I'd just conjured up had been much more than just images. They'd brought sounds, smells, and sensations with them. They'd been incredibly real.

I suddenly realized why I'd felt a pang of grief a few moments before. If my mind was going to eventually convince me that my journey was not real, then it would mean that Irene was not real either.

And that was something I was unwilling to accept.

I stood up and tucked the crystal back into the jacket pocket, where it belonged. I took off the retro shoes, undid the retro belt, and removed the retro trousers. I carefully hung the garments up in my closet, the shirt and suit on one hanger, the trench coat on another, and the fedora on the shelf above. I pushed the rest of my clothes back in place to hide the suit, then I turned and headed for the shower.

I felt somewhat calmer, but I still had no idea how I was going to endure the next ten hours.

♦

Brad pulled up in front of my building at precisely eight-forty. I quickly got in the car and buckled my seat belt. He actually paused a moment before roaring away from the curb this time. The rest of the drive, however, was identical to the previous trip. He looked straight ahead and said absolutely nothing.

For my part, however, ten hours pacing the apartment floors had left me disinclined to remain silent.

"Thanks for at least letting me buckle my belt before you burned rubber," I said, just a hint of sarcasm coming through.

He gaze didn't waver from the road. It was as if I had never spoken.

"Well, this is certainly one way to keep me from correcting your grammar."

"Shut up."

He didn't so much as incline his head in my direction. And his tone left little room for interpretation. I decided my two barbs were sufficient for the moment.

We drove the rest of the way downtown in uncompanionable silence. I'd never felt so uncomfortable around Brad in all the time I'd known him. I didn't begrudge him his anger. I just wanted to talk. About anything. My mind was in overdrive, and I desperately needed a distraction.

It took about ten minutes to reach the south end of the city. Brad pulled into the Tim Horton's at the far end of Barrington Street and swooped into an empty parking space. The car rocked sharply as he hit the brake, and I lurched forward. Had it not been for my seatbelt, my forehead would have slammed into the dashboard. When I glanced at Brad, he appeared unruffled. It was as if he hadn't budged a millimeter during his abrupt physics lesson.

"I'm getting a coffee," he said, looking straight ahead. "You're on your own from here. You go and fix this. I want to see Lydia alive and well. You got that?"

I unbuckled my seat belt and glowered at him. "Thanks a lot. You're a big help."

He turned his head to look at me. His eyes were empty, emotionless. "You fix this."

"And what if I can't?"

"Then if they don't kill you, I will."

"I didn't even think you *liked* Lydia that much."

He paused, his eyes narrowing nearly to slits. He took a long, slow breath.

"Get out. Now. Before I make sure you can't."

I swallowed hard and unbuckled my seatbelt. I hauled myself up and out of the car, closing the door behind me, and took a couple of steps away. I bent slightly to peer in through the back window, but Brad was not moving. I took a few more steps and looked back again. Still no movement. I sighed and walked the rest of the way to the sidewalk. As I turned left to walk further south on Barrington, I let my gaze travel to the car yet again. This time, I saw Brad get out, slam his door, and storm into the coffee shop without so much as a backwards glance.

I checked my watch as I headed up the remainder of Barrington Street. It was ten minutes to nine, and I figured it would take me about five minutes or so to walk to the tunnel. It had been years since I'd visited this part of town, so I hoped I was leaving myself enough time. I quickened my pace, just to be on the safe side.

I walked to the intersection of Barrington and Inglis Streets, which had been nicely curved to encourage drivers to veer right rather than go straight through to the dead-end stub of Barrington. I stopped for a moment and looked around. The area was quiet, quieter than I'd thought it would be. I was both glad and disappointed, glad because I really didn't want anyone seeing me approach the tunnel, and disappointed because if anything did go wrong, well, there'd be no one around to provide help.

Not that I expected to be able to call out for any.

I walked past the intersection and towards the tunnel, which turned out to be not much more than a hundred yards further. I slowed my pace and checked my watch. It had taken me a mere two minutes to walk the distance from the Tim Horton's. Brad had chosen a good launching point for me.

I approached the entrance to the tunnel and stopped. I quickly surveyed the area, just to make sure no one was watching me. Gingerly, I stepped closer. I glanced at my watch again. I was more than five minutes early, but something told me that it really wasn't going to matter. The agency men would already be here. Of that much I was certain. And since I could see no vehicles or persons in the immediate vicinity, I presumed I was to go through the tunnel to the other side.

I steeled myself and stepped across the threshold.

The tunnel was well lit, but that didn't stop it from looking creepy and foreboding. It ran about fifty or sixty yards under the railroad tracks and emerged next to Marginal Road, near the grain elevators. At least I didn't have much further to go.

My footsteps echoed as I slowly proceeded along the concrete floor.

I couldn't see anything at the other end of the tunnel, which didn't surprise me, as it was now completely dark outside. I didn't know what was going to happen next, and my terror by this point was so intense I could nearly chew on it, so I did the only things I *could* do: swallow hard, point my eyes straight ahead and keep my feet moving.

When I got to about the midpoint of the tunnel, the lights went out.

This did nothing to help with the terror.

I stopped moving and put my right hand out to the side. The tunnel wall was still there, so I figured I hadn't taken another trip to a different world. The bastards had simply cut the power to make me sweat even more. Well, if they wanted my sweat, they could have it. There was evidently lots to go around.

I waited to see what would happen next. It was obvious that the agency men were here, and it was their agenda, so I stood still. I didn't dare move. I didn't dare do anything. I didn't want to piss them off, and I sure as hell didn't want to endanger Lydia any further. So I waited.

After what seemed like an eternity, light returned to the tunnel, but from a different direction. I squinted and put my hand in front of my face to cut down on the harsh glare that was shining directly into my eyes. After I'd blinked a few times to clear the moisture and my pupils had narrowed somewhat, I could see that there were, in fact, two light sources, side by side and coming at me from a low angle.

Headlights.

And they thought *I* was melodramatic.

I stood there for another small eternity, bathed in the tungsten glow.

Eventually I heard the sound of a car door opening, followed by shoes on gravel, then the car door closing again.

"Mister Richmond," came a voice from beyond the light. There was no mistaking the infuriating tone of bemusement, even with only two words. It was the man who had been in the interrogation room. "I'm glad you've finally come to your senses."

"What do you mean 'finally'?" I asked. "I didn't know you were looking for me."

"Oh, come, now," he said, his tone almost conversational. "After your disappearance from the accommodations we provided for you—a neat trick, by the way—you didn't imagine we'd just let the matter drop, did you?"

"A man lives in hope," I said, sounding braver than I felt.

He chuckled. "You're a gutsy one, Mister Richmond. I'm growing rather fond of you."

"You have a funny way of showing it."

"Oh, I'm just doing my job. This is nothing personal."

"You made it personal when you took my friend," I said.

"Oh. Is that all she is to you? Just a friend?"

"She's a dear friend, if you want to be ridiculously specific about it."

"Oh, I assure you, Mister Richmond, there's nothing remotely ridiculous about anything I do. I'm deadly serious about my work."

"I don't like the way you phrased that."

"I didn't imagine you would. Now let's get down to business, shall we?"

"Fine. Where's Lydia?"

"Oh, she's in the back seat. She's fine. We've been taking good care of her."

"Yes. I'm sure you gave her a lovely room. Just like mine."

"Such bravado. You're either a brave man, or a very foolish one. I suppose time will tell which it is."

"I want to see her."

"Of course you do."

I paused, thinking he was going to say something further. He didn't. "Well?" I asked.

"You can come the rest of way through the tunnel, Mister Richmond. But move slowly, and keep your arms away from your sides."

I almost laughed. "What, you think I'm carrying a weapon?"

"I don't know one way or the other, which is why I want you to keep your hands in plain sight."

I put my light-shielding hand down, necessitating further squinting, and resumed my deliberate pace through the tunnel. I probably looked like a gunslinger from a Clint Eastwood movie with my hands out from my sides like that, but it didn't matter. There was no one but this man—and probably his partner—to see me.

I moved out of the direct glare of the headlights as soon as I was clear of the tunnel exit. With a few more steps, I could actually see my surroundings again. Marginal Road curved away to my left, and I could just make out the massive silhouettes of the grain elevators to my right. The car was situated on a patch of gravel between the curb and the tunnel. I could make out a vague person-shape in the driver's seat.

"That's far enough," the agency man said.

He put his hands in his trouser pockets and took a step towards me. "Now, Mister Richmond. I need to explain something to you." He looked down and absently kicked a piece of gravel. "You're in no position to make demands." He looked up at me again, his expression harder. "I'm running the show here. I call the shots. Do you understand that? Because if you don't, then we have a serious problem."

"You mean *I* have a serious problem."

He nodded slightly and looked off into space for a moment. "Yes, I think you've got the picture."

"So, what now?"

He pulled his hands out of his pockets and dusted them off. "Good. Back to business." He turned around and stepped back to the car. "What happens is this: You go to the opposite side of the car. I open the back door on this side and bring your friend out. I will not allow her to say anything, but you will be able to see that she is unharmed. You will have a maximum of five seconds to observe her condition, at which point you will get into the back seat from your side and close the door. I will tell your friend to start walking away without looking back, and I will close the back door on this side. I will then get into the passenger seat, and we will be on our way."

"To where?"

"Ah, yes. I forgot one part. Once you are in the back seat, you will put on the blindfold that is there waiting for you."

I snorted. "Yeah. I thought so."

"Are you clear on the proceedings, Mister Richmond? Is there any part that you don't understand?"

"Yeah. Where's the part where I get to kick your face in?"

He chuckled. "Now, now, Mister Richmond. Let's not get carried away. I have nothing against you personally, and I'm attempting to treat you with all the respect the situation allows. I only ask that you cooperate and treat me similarly."

"That's asking a lot, considering," I said.

"Yes, well, be that as it may. I've explained what's going to happen here, and I suggest you go along with it. It's in everyone's best interests. I think you know that."

I glanced at the car's windshield again, but I still could not make out any details, just the vague shape of someone behind the wheel. I could see nothing of Lydia. I wiped my brow again and gave the man my best glare.

"Fine," I said. "Let's do this."

I moved slowly to my right, towards the driver's side of the car, never taking my eyes off the smug agency man. He was also keeping a close eye on me, a slightly amused look on his face. When I reached the driver's door, I quickly glanced down at the window. Even in the dim light, I recognized him. It was the same fellow who had been outside my apartment building with the measuring device and had sat silently in the interrogation room while his boss had talked my ear off. He, too, was looking at me, but with nothing even close to amusement on his face.

I stepped to the back door and stopped. A glance at this window got me nothing. Lydia was seated on the other side.

"Good," the man said. "Now you can see your friend." He reached down towards the door handle, but paused before touching it. "Are you sure that's all she is to you? A friend?"

I clenched my fists and my jaw. "That's none of your goddamned business," I said through my teeth.

He shrugged. "It's not that important to me. I was just curious. However, you did answer the question, even if you hadn't intended to."

He smiled slightly and opened the back door on his side. "Come on out, my dear. Your part in this is over."

He reached inside the car and took Lydia by the arm. I could see her shape through the window as she slid towards her captor and put her feet on the ground. The man helped her out, but she twisted away from him the moment she was standing.

"Not a word," the man said. "From either of you."

I wanted to glare at him again, but I couldn't take my eyes off Lydia. She appeared unharmed, but when she turned around to look at me over the roof of the car, my heart nearly stopped. I had never seen such rage, such pain, such helplessness, etched across a human face. And I knew it wasn't because she'd been tortured, manhandled, or even mistreated. The full weight of her wrath was directed squarely at me.

In those few seconds of looking at her tortured face, everything I had ever done came hurtling back towards me. I nearly fell over with the force of the realization. Lydia would never see me the same way again.

Not ever.

Blood rushed into my face. My fists tightened. I had to do something. I had to break the cycle of helplessness. Everything was my fault, even though I had no control over what these agents and the denizens of the other world had done. But I had to take control of myself. Take responsibility for the things I had done and somehow try to make all this right.

I turned my attention to the man standing beside Lydia. I focused all my energy, my anger, my rage, my frustration, at him. He represented everything I hated in this world. Power without conscience, subjugation without compunction. He had to be stopped. I had no idea exactly how to stop him, but it had to be done. If I'd had the power, I would have sent a bolt of lightning from the center of my forehead straight into his heart.

I tried to control my breathing. I tried to slow time. I tried to see every detail around me. I tried to find some small thing that I could use to my advantage. The situation was intolerable. I had to change it.

The man looked up suddenly and frowned. "What the hell…?"

I followed his gaze, as did Lydia. Above us, the air was rippling and sparkling. It reminded me of the ripples I had seen in the hospital and outside the coffee shop. I couldn't tell how far above us this phenomenon was, but it *seemed* large.

It also seemed to be descending towards us.

"Anthony," the man snapped.

The driver immediately stepped out of the car and closed his door. He looked up at the wavering anomaly and immediately pulled his weapon out of its holster. Without so much as a beat, he began firing bullets at the pulsating artifact.

There was no effect. No holes appeared. The ripples were not disturbed in the slightest. The oddity continued its descent.

The man looked at me hard. "This is your doing, isn't it?"

I continued staring at the thing as it moved ever closer. It reminded me so much of the phenomena I'd seen before, that I actually considered for a moment that it might be tied to me.

"If I had powers like that, I'd have used them to get rid of you a long time ago."

He narrowed his eyes at me. "I told you to come alone."

"I did. My friend dropped me off at the Tim Horton's on Barrington Street. He's long gone."

I looked up again. The ripples were much closer now.

The man reached up as if to grab the edge of the anomaly as it neared the roof of the car, but he was unable to grasp anything. His hand just passed through it. I squinted hard, unable to quite believe what I was seeing.

And then the thing landed, and everything changed.

Chapter Thirteen

A rushing sound filled my ears, but a moment later everything was quiet again. I looked around. I was still standing beside the car. Lydia and her captor were still on the other side. Anthony and his gun were still to my left at the driver's door.

But everything else around us was a different story. I could still see the harbour, but there were no longer any stacks of containers or idle loading cranes. There was no chain-link fence across the road. To my right I could see warehouses, but they were not the same warehouses I had seen when I exited the tunnel.

I glanced to my left. The tunnel itself was still there, as were the railroad tracks above it and the gravel below, but everything was either subtly or dramatically different.

The ripples were nowhere to be seen.

I knew it was still Halifax, but I also knew instinctively that it was a different Halifax.

"What the hell just happened?" the man in charge asked.

Anthony shook his head. Lydia was turning around, taking in her surroundings, her eyes and mouth open wide. I suddenly realized that I was chuckling.

"You did this," the man spat. "You're in cahoots with them, aren't you?"

"Cahoots?" I said. "Do people still use that word?"

I turned to my left, suddenly feeling that something wasn't quite right. I was greeted by the barrel of Anthony's Glock 17 semi-automatic pistol.

"Now," Anthony's superior said, the smugness returning to his voice, "tell me what you did."

I tore my gaze away from the barrel of the pistol and returned my attention to the man on the other side of the car.

"I didn't do anything," I said. "Not that I didn't want to, mind you. I was having all kinds of wonderful fantasies—one in particular involved leaping over the car and dismembering you—but big rippling chunks of atmosphere did not factor into any of them."

"Then where did it come from? And what did it do to us?"

I smiled. "How does it feel, being on the other side of things?"

The man frowned. "Keep that up, and I may allow Anthony free reign with that lovely weapon of his."

"What good would that do you?" I asked. "Have you looked around? We've crossed over the rainbow, pal. You're out of your element, and out of your depth. If we're where I suspect we are, you'd better think about hiding this car and finding some new clothes."

I had a sudden mental image of Michael J. Fox hiding his DeLorean in the bushes.

My tormentor stared at me for a moment. It looked like he was evaluating me, but I couldn't be certain.

"You've been here before," he said quietly.

"I think so," I said.

"What do you mean, you think so?" he demanded. "Either you have or you haven't."

I whirled on him. "I don't know if it's the same world," I snapped. "I don't see anything I recognize yet."

I sensed Anthony stepping closer to me. I glanced to my left, confirming my suspicion that his handgun was, indeed, mere inches from my face.

I turned back to the other man. "Will you tell him to get his fucking gun out of my face?"

The man seemed calmer now, all of a sudden. "No, Mister Richmond. Not until you tell me what I need to know."

"What? You mean where we are? I just told you, I have no idea."

"And, of course, you don't know how we got here."

"No. I don't."

He rubbed his chin. "Why don't I believe you, Mister Richmond? Hmmm? Why do I get the feeling that you're standing there, looking me in the eye, and telling me bald-faced lies."

I let my shoulders drop. I glanced at Lydia. Her eyes were wet, and she was biting her lower lip.

"Lydia," I said.

"No," the man said. "No conversation between you two. Understood? I want you to keep your attention on me, Mister Richmond, and I want you to tell me everything you know about this place."

I kept my eyes on Lydia. Her demeanour had changed dramatically in the last few minutes. She was staring at me now, holding my gaze, tears streaming down her face. Her lips were drawn into a tight straight line. She nodded, ever so slightly.

I could feel the tears welling up in my own eyes.

She understood now. She believed.

That knowledge gave me the strength to turn my attention back to the man standing beside her.

"Why should I tell you anything?" I asked him.

I heard a click to my left.

"Oh," I said. "Right. That."

The man across from me smiled. I still wanted to call him Cigarette Smoking Man, but he didn't smoke, or hadn't yet in my presence, so the name just didn't work. It was probably copyrighted anyway.

"I'm waiting…" he said, all charm and patience.

I hated him with every fiber of my being.

"All right." I glanced to my left again. The Glock was no further away from me. "Like I said, I don't know if this is the same world I was in before, but if it is, it's geographically similar to our own world. At least the parts I saw were."

The man nodded thoughtfully. "You were in an alternate version of Halifax, then?"

I nodded. "Yes. It was remarkably similar. But different."

His eyes were practically glistening with interest. "In what ways was it diff—?"

He didn't finish his question. Something about the size of a shoebox struck him in the head, and he went to the ground. I turned to my left, the direction from which the projectile had come, but I could see nothing. Anthony had whirled to face the same direction the instant his boss had fallen. He was pointing his gun at nothing, scrutinizing the surroundings, a panicked twitch in his stance.

I took that opportunity to launch myself at him. I didn't know if he was so highly trained that he would sense my movement and spin back on me, but at that moment I didn't care. I just hoped that the sudden change of locale and the even more sudden attack on his boss would have left him just confused enough that I could catch him off guard.

I hit him full force with my body, and he went down. He didn't lose his grip on the gun, but he hit the ground hard, and I leapt on top of him.

"Jack. No," Lydia cried out, but it was too late for that. My guilt, horror, and adrenaline had taken over, and I was acting on instinct alone.

Anthony tried to turn over, but I squeezed hard with my legs and kept him where he was. I grabbed his gun arm by the wrist with both hands and twisted. He made a grunting noise, but his grip on the weapon did not loosen in the slightest. I knew I had to disarm him now; I couldn't hold him down for long, and once he managed to change his position, he'd be all over me. I had only seconds.

I slammed his arm to the ground and began pounding on his hand with my fist. He grunted again, but otherwise gave no indication that I was hurting him. He flailed at me with his other hand, but I kept moving my upper body around and avoiding it.

I suddenly felt a sharp pain in my lower back. He had managed to bend his left knee quickly and sharply, resulting in a blow to my left kidney with the heel of his shoe. I cried out in pain, but the injury only served to increase my anger and frustration. I pounded even harder on his gun hand.

A moment later, I was on my feet. Anthony pulled himself to a crouch and looked up at me. The sheer loathing in his eyes was nearly palpable. I stepped towards him, the Glock firmly in both my hands, its barrel pointing directly at his forehead.

"Get up," I said.

He stood slowly, never taking his eyes off me.

"Now," I said, "back towards the car."

He glanced behind him, then started stepping backwards, slowly, carefully. When he was a few steps away from the car, he glanced backwards again, adjusted his position slightly, and stopped.

"All the way back to the car," I said.

He stood his ground and glared at me.

"This is your gun," I said. "I'm pretty sure you know what it can do."

He smiled.

It occurred to me that perhaps I had forgotten something. I remembered hearing the click of the weapon near my head as he had readied it to fire, so I was fairly certain the safety was off.

But I had to be sure. I repositioned the gun, aiming slightly to the right of Anthony and angling down a bit. I pulled the trigger.

The gun went off. Lydia screamed. The left rear tire began to hiss. The safety was definitely off.

I aimed at Anthony's forehead. He was still smiling. He was either trying to intimidate me, or there was something else I was missing.

He must have sensed my confusion, because he chose that moment to launch himself at me. I fired again, a fraction of a second before his full weight hit me at about waist level.

I gasped, the wind knocked out of me as I hit the ground. My arms went up, and the gun flew out of my hands, landing with a clunk somewhere behind me. Anthony, for his part, appeared to be uninjured, as he now reared up above me and connected his fist to my face with a tremendous amount of vigor.

The world seemed to vibrate for a moment, and then it melted into blackness.

◆

When I next refocused my eyes, Anthony was standing beside the car. His boss was sitting on the ground next to him, leaning back against the driver door and holding a handkerchief on a large bleeding wound on the right side of his head.

"Get him up," the older man said.

Anthony stepped over to me and hauled me to my feet. I winced, both from the roughness of my ascent and from the unpleasant sensation emanating from the vicinity of my left cheekbone. I raised a hand to my face, wincing again as I touched the tender area. Anthony had a very strong right arm.

The older man sighed. "This little stunt of yours has accomplished very little," he said to me.

I looked at him, breathing rapidly and heavily. "I managed to get your boy's gun away from him, didn't I?"

He shook his head and drew his mouth into a line. "Yes, but at what cost, Mister Richmond? At what cost?"

I didn't know what he was talking about. But there was something about the way he was looking at me…

I suddenly turned my head to the right. I could see the car, but there was no sign of—

"Lydia," I cried, tearing my arm out of Anthony's grip and dashing for the vehicle.

Anthony made a move to stop me, but his boss waved him down.

"Let him go," he said.

I rounded the front of the car and stopped dead in my tracks.

"Oh my God…" I whispered.

Lydia was lying on the ground, motionless. I dashed over to her, tears forming in my eyes.

"Lydia," I rasped.

I knelt beside her, looking through the film of clear liquid in my eyes. I blinked, and the scene became clearer. Her left shoulder was red. Completely red. Her right hand was positioned just below her left clavicle, futilely attempting to staunch the flow of blood.

Only two bullets had been fired since we had arrived here, and I had fired both of them. The first had punctured the car's tire, and the second…

I had missed Anthony and hit Lydia.

"Lydia," I said, dropping my head and squeezing my eyes shut.

"Jack."

My eyes flew open. Lydia was looking up at me. Her eyelids were fluttering slightly, but she was looking at me.

She was still alive. She'd been so still, I hadn't even been able to tell she was breathing. Her breath was shallow and hoarse, but it was breath nonetheless.

Her right hand came away from her shoulder and moved towards me. It faltered, but it finally slipped off her ribcage and onto the ground. With whatever strength she had left, she lifted it again and reached out to take my hand.

"Lydia," I said, my voice barely a whisper. "It's going to be okay."

She closed her eyes and gave her head the tiniest of shakes. "No," she said. "No."

I tightened my grip on her hand. "Don't say that," I said. "You're going to make it through this."

Again she gave her head a miniscule shake. "Jack. Listen to me."

I leaned closer. Her voice was so weak I could barely hear her.

She looked directly into my eyes. "You're not crazy," she said.

I dared not ponder the implications of what she had just said. There were too many layers, and now was not the time. Still, a slight jolt of energy burst through me at her words.

She held my gaze for a long moment. "Now start believing in yourself, will you?"

I swallowed hard and stared into her eyes for as long as I could. I dared not say anything to her; my track record for profundity was sorry at best. I knew what was happening, and I wanted to be with her, truly *be* with her, at this agonizingly intimate moment.

She smiled at me. "Lost for words at last," she said.

She closed her eyes then, and she was still.

My tears flowed more freely now. I reached out and put my hand on the side of her face. I pushed her hair out of her eyes. I stroked her forehead. Finally, I reached under her, lifted her by the shoulders, and pulled her to me.

I was covered in her blood almost immediately. It didn't matter. I needed to hold her in my arms, to feel the physical solidity of her, to know that she was at least real.

I became aware of a strange movement. My body appeared to be jerking for some reason. It was only as I opened my eyes for a moment that I realized I was sobbing uncontrollably, my arms and torso jumping in spasms as my lungs ejected burst after burst of toxic, accusing, loathing air.

I held her for long minutes, my eyes closed, my body trembling. I finally pulled back and looked at her face. It was peaceful. It was restful. There was no trace of the hatred or torment I had seen sprayed across it when she'd gotten out of the car. She was asleep. She was dreaming beautiful dreams. She was free of fear, sadness, and anger.

"Get up, Mister Richmond," my nemesis said from behind me. "That's enough indulgence."

I stood slowly and turned around. He stood there, a smug half-smile on his face.

"That seems like a pretty high price to me," he said.

I strode towards him. He cocked a curious eyebrow, but I paid no attention. I shoved him aside and stepped back around the front of the car.

"I don't know what you hope to accomplish, Mister Richmond," he said. "The gun is still there. It's only a matter of moments before Anthony finds it."

I frowned. What the hell was he talking about? The gun hadn't gone that far. I'd heard it land, just a second or so after it had flown out of my hands. It couldn't have been more than six feet away from the top of my head when I hit the ground. Anthony probably already had it in his hands.

I didn't care. I strode past the car and headed directly for the place where Anthony crouched, looking for the gun.

It didn't seem possible. He couldn't still be looking for it. It had to be right there.

He heard me coming and stood, spinning around to face me. The hatred and loathing were still etched into his features. I was sure they held no match for what must have been near to rippling across mine.

His hands were empty. Evidently he still hadn't found the gun. I didn't have time to puzzle that one out. If he was unarmed, then so much the better for me. If he had the gun hidden on him somewhere, I didn't care.

He crouched slightly, feet apart, hands raised. It looked like a martial arts stance, but I didn't know for sure, and I didn't care. His whole body could have been a finely tuned weapon, for all I knew, and I still didn't care.

All I cared about was the black hatred that soared across the battered and barren landscape of my mind. The red hot fury that coursed beneath it. The white-hot dagger-point of vengeance that threatened to cut through everything else.

Anthony had put Lydia in harm's way. It was because of him that she was dead.

The rage took me, and I threw myself at him. My entire body tingled with the black hatred, the red fury, and the white vengeance. I flew through the air towards him. The air seemed to crackle as his form became larger and larger in my field of view.

Our bodies connected, and the blackness consumed me.

Chapter Fourteen

Once again I had to go through the ordeal of regaining consciousness. First the hospital, then the injection into my neck, then Anthony's fist to my face, and now this.

My brain being what it was, it conjured up the image of James Garner, who, in his role as Jim Rockford in *The Rockford Files*, was whacked on the back of the head every other week. Any normal human would have had brain damage halfway into the first season.

This time I didn't know where I was. I was no longer outdoors, and I was lying on my back. The room was dimly lit, and the ceiling was unadorned. I was on a firm but yielding surface. A blanket or sheet was draped over my torso and legs.

I raised my head. Bad idea. It was throbbing, and lifting it off the—cot? bed?—just made the throbbing worse, so I put it back down again and tried to relax.

I tried moving my arms and legs. They were unfettered, it appeared, and fully functional. I was able to blink, open and close my mouth, and wiggle my toes and fingers. My breathing seemed unimpeded and unaided.

I was apparently undamaged. Except for the sore spot on my face from Anthony's punch.

I lay there a while longer, then tried lifting my head again. The throbbing had lessened enough that it didn't cause me to feel nauseated, so I took the next step and tried to sit up.

This met with limited success. The throbbing worsened again, so I sat forward and brought my knees up, resting my head in the little valley of blanket that formed between them. This helped a bit, but I had to breathe deeply for some minutes before the throbbing began to subside. I knew I wouldn't be moving quickly anytime soon.

I slowly raised my head and looked around. The room was small, clean, and spare. Near the door was a small table with a lit candle set upon it, the room's only light source. In the corner next to the table was a wooden chair. Beyond that, the bed on which I now sat was the only other object in the room.

I removed the blanket—I saw now that it was woven from something like wool—and swung my legs off the bed. I sat on the edge, heart racing, head beginning to resume its throbbing, and tried once again to be still.

I looked down at myself. My shirt and jeans were nowhere to be seen. Instead, I was sporting a simple tunic and pants, both off-white. My feet were bare.

I wondered what had happened. I remembered lunging at Anthony. I remembered getting closer and closer to him as I hurtled through the air, but after that, nothing. I couldn't remember a damned thing.

Just the emotion. The sheer blackness of the hatred I felt for him. The boiling heat of my anger. The white-hot desire for vengeance. Beyond the feelings, I recalled nothing at all. Not even the moment of contact with Anthony's body.

I must have blacked out again.

But what was I doing here? And where were Anthony and his boss? And where was—?

A sob shook my throat as I recalled what had happened to Lydia. My fists balled into tight, dense cudgels, and the hot, black feelings rose up in me again. The sob tasted like bile.

I tried to damp it down, but the effort was futile. The feelings of guilt, shame, anger, hatred, vengeance—they all battled for dominance and attention. They would not be denied.

I bent my head down as far as it would go. My fists came up into the air of their own accord and then down upon the bed frame with the force of sledgehammers. The bed shook as I screamed out in pain.

The room seemed to vibrate for a moment. I looked up to see ripples in the air, spreading out from my position. I stared hard at them, willing them to explain what they were. My confusion was draped atop crystal clear memory, however. The ripples were strange but familiar. I'd seen them in the hospital, and I'd seen them outside the coffee shop. But the memory gave me no further clue as to what the phenomenon meant or represented.

The ripples reached the bare walls around me, and for a moment it seemed as if I were in a different room altogether. I could see guitars hanging on the walls, and I could hear music coming from down a corridor. It sounded like someone trying to play "Smells Like Teen Spirit" by Nirvana.

I squinted and stared, but the ripples faded and vanished. The walls returned to their previous state of simplicity. The sound faded and was gone.

I sighed and looked at my hands. The right one was bleeding along the "karate chop" area. The left was going to have a killer bruise in the same region. But at least I was now fully awake.

The door opened. A man in a black cloak entered. The deep hood effectively hid his face in shadow.

"I think I've seen this movie," I said.

His head cocked slightly to the side. "You speak oddly, stranger," he replied. His voice was deep and smooth, like a good radio announcer's.

"Oh, great," I said. "Now we're into trite fantasy dialogue. This day just keeps getting better and better."

"I have no idea what you're talking about," he said.

"I didn't really think you would," I replied. "But since you're here, maybe you'd be so kind as to tell me where I am."

He appeared to think about this for a moment. "You're in a safe place," he said finally.

"Hmmm…" I said. "Do you think you might narrow that down just a little bit?"

"Not at this time," he replied.

I nodded. "Not at this time."

I stood and stepped over to him. With a suddenness and force I didn't know I had in me, I grabbed him by the neck of his hood and hauled him towards me.

"Now, you listen to me," I said through clenched teeth. "I've had a really fucking lousy day. I've been through the worst kind of hell I can imagine, and I'm not going to sit here and take this kind of wishy washy bullshit from you. Do you understand me?"

He nodded slightly.

"Good. Now, I want you to tell me where I am, how I got here, and what happened to the other people who were with me."

"I can't tell you anything," he said.

I shook him. "You'd better tell me something," I said. "You really don't want to upset me any more than I already am."

I could see only his chin, and that gave me no indication at all if I was getting through to him. I couldn't see his eyes, but I could feel him staring at me, evaluating.

"The other men are quartered just as you are," he said after a time. "The dead woman—"

I slammed him against the wall, hitting the table with his calf as I did so. The candle tipped over and went out.

"Lydia," I screamed. "Her name is Lydia."

I caught a faint movement out of the corner of my eye. It could have been one of his arms, but I didn't really have time to think about it. Before I knew it, I was flat on my back, staring at the ceiling. My head was throbbing again, and my lungs were gasping for air.

His head came into my field of vision, the features still masked by shadow.

"Lydia," he said, "is in a place where she will not be disturbed."

The burning in my throat subsided as my lungs began to make use of the air they were sucking in.

"What the hell was that?" I asked.

"Self defense."

A moment later, footsteps sounded in the hallway outside.

"Thomas?" a voice said as the footsteps entered the room. "We heard a disturbance."

I heard a slight swishing of cloth that I assumed was Thomas turning toward the new arrivals.

"This one," he said, "is most passionate. I believe the dead woman was of some importance to him."

I let out a growl from the back of my throat. "You sanctimonious son of a bitch," I whispered.

I suddenly felt two pairs of hands, one on each of my upper arms. I was unceremoniously hauled to my feet and plunked down on the edge of the bed.

As I once again caught my breath and tried to still the throbbing in my head, I looked at the new arrivals. There were two of them, and they were both clad in the same robes as Thomas, the one I'd tried to rough up.

As they stepped away from me, they revealed a third newcomer standing in the doorway. He, too, was clad in a black robe, but this one had a deep purple trim around the edge of the hood and sleeves.

I took him to be a leader of some sort.

"You will watch your language while you're among us," he said. His voice was deep and authoritative.

I let my head drop forward. "I just want to know where I am." My whole body was trembling now.

"We'll tell you everything you need to know," the leader said. "In time. We don't know anything about you, friend. We don't know if we can trust you. I hope you understand."

I looked back up at him. "I don't know anything about you, either. So I don't know if I can trust *you*."

"You can trust that we'll keep you safe as long as you're here."

I shook my head in an attempt to refocus. Bad idea.

"Who *are* you people?" I asked, returning my gaze to the leader.

"My name is Daniel," he said. "Thomas, you've met. These…" He gestured at the two who had hoisted me. "…are Quentin and Frederick. That's all we can tell you for the moment."

"Why do you keep your heads covered like that?"

"We have good reasons for keeping our faces from view. Again, that's all I can tell you for now."

I glanced back and forth amongst the four of them. I couldn't see much of their forms with the loose robes covering them, but something about the way they were standing—not to mention the way in which Thomas had taken me from vertical to horizontal in an instant—told me that these men were not just physically fit, but downright dangerous.

"What are you, ninja monks?" I asked.

I thought I heard a slight chuckle issue from inside Daniel's hood. "I'm not familiar with that phrase," he said, "but it sounds intriguing."

He gestured to the other three, and they filed silently out of the room.

"You need your rest," Daniel said as he stepped back into the corridor and closed the door.

He was right about that. I was spent. I lay back on the bed, lifted my legs up onto the mattress, and pulled the blanket back over me.

It took a while for me to calm myself, but I did eventually fall back into the arms of Morpheus.

◆

When I awoke again, the candle was upright and lit. My head felt slightly clearer and my body a bit stronger. I tested the waters by sitting up, but no wave of nausea hit me, no throbbing of the temples this time. I nodded in satisfaction and swung my feet off the bed. No adverse effects from that, either.

So far, so good.

I stood and tested my legs for a moment. Finding them reasonably stable, I stepped to the door and tried the knob. To my surprise, it was unlocked. Slowly, cautiously, I pulled the door open a crack and listened. There was no sound.

I opened the door further and stepped out into the hallway. It was as plain and unadorned as my room. Between the austerity and the robes, I had a hard time thinking that this was anything but a monastery.

I took a closer look at the walls. They appeared to be made of plaster, and they did not look old. If it was a monastery, it was certainly a modern one. Or as modern as a Victorian 1940s monastery could get, I supposed.

For the hundredth time, I wondered if I actually *was* in the same world I'd visited before. My encounter with Irene and Councillor Greaves seemed to have occurred a lifetime ago. I'd been to my own world and back again since that time.

I started to think about what I'd seen in Irene's world, and what I'd seen here so far. There was very little overlap. I'd seen ships in the harbour when I'd arrived here, but I hadn't seen any ships during my visit with Irene. I'd seen vehicles and buildings in Irene's world, but I'd seen no vehicles here other than the sedan that had arrived here with us, and the only buildings I'd seen were warehouses.

It felt like the same world, but that was nothing even close to hard evidence. I needed to be sure.

The only things I'd seen that were common to both worlds were the black cloaks. As soon as Thomas had entered the room, I'd recognized his attire. The man who had so unceremoniously booted me off the train had worn the exact same garment.

Again, it was nothing that would be admitted in court. After all, one might see cloaks like that on any number of worlds. But it was a start, and if this *was* the same world, then that meant Thomas and his people had some kind of power. The power to open doorways between worlds.

Like Irene.

Good. I was beginning to get somewhere. I didn't have a firm grasp on things yet, but bits and pieces were starting to come together. I knew I'd have to rely on my wits and my powers of observation, because it seemed that Thomas and Daniel were close-mouthed sorts. I was unlikely to get much in the way of useful information from them.

At least not yet.

As I stepped further out into the hallway, I heard footsteps in the distance. Quickly, I darted back into my room and closed the door behind me. I resumed my seated position on the edge of the bed and waited.

The door opened a moment later, and one of the black cloaks walked in. From the height and the gait, I assumed it was Thomas.

"Thomas?" I asked.

His body language indicated surprise. "Yes," he said. "How did you know?"

"Your build," I said. "The way you walk."

"You're observant," he said.

"I'm a writer."

He nodded. "Are you hungry?" he asked.

I nodded. "Very astute. Most unpublished writers are hungry. Hell, most writers period are hungry. That's why I work in a bookstore. So I can feed myself."

He stared at me for a long moment. At least I assumed he was staring, as I couldn't see his face for the hood.

"You weren't talking about that at all, were you?" I asked.

"No. I didn't even understand what you just said. I was talking about your stomach and its condition at this moment."

I looked at the floor, once again disappointed at the absence of anyone nearby to appreciate my tremendous grasp of things sarcastic and sardonic.

"Now that you mention it," I said, "I'm famished."

"Then come with me," he said, stepping back to the doorway. "The morning meal is being served as we speak." He gestured towards my feet. "There are sandals beneath the bed."

I slid off the bed and looked under it. Sure enough, a pair of simple leather sandals sat there waiting for me. I slid them out from under the bed, put my feet into them, and followed Thomas out into the hall.

"You didn't lock me in the room," I said.

"No. We didn't feel it necessary." He turned his head back towards me for a moment. "The other two, however..."

I snorted a chuckle. "Yeah. I imagine you would have had a whole lot more trouble with them."

"They are... " He appeared to think for a moment. "... violent men."

We turned left at the end of the corridor and proceeded down an even longer one. Eventually, we came to a double door, and Thomas opened it and stood aside.

I entered a large dining hall. Men in black cloaks were seated around a long burnished wood table. Again, the walls were unadorned, though this time there was natural light coming in through a set of large windows on the opposite side of the room.

As I looked around, I noticed a jarring incongruity. At the end of the table farthest from me sat two uncloaked men. One appeared to be in his sixties, the other much younger. Both wore simple off-white tunics like the one I was wearing.

I suppressed a laugh. My nemesis and his lackey were no longer in control of their situation, and the fact of it tickled me no end.

God knew I needed *something* to cheer me up.

"Please take the unoccupied seat," Thomas said, gesturing towards the very place I'd been looking.

I looked again and finally clued in that there was an empty space next to the older man. He was sitting at the end of the table, and Anthony was sitting perpendicular to him, his back partially towards me. The seat across from Anthony was the vacant one.

My mirth swiftly abandoned me.

"You've got to be kidding," I said. "I'm not sitting next to them."

Thomas gestured again. "That is where guests sit," he said.

I sighed and walked to the far side of the table. Boss Agent noticed me immediately and watched with interest as I moved towards the empty seat. Anthony's head turned towards me as he noticed where his boss was looking.

I stopped behind the chair and immediately froze. I looked in disbelief at Anthony. He wore a makeshift patch over his right eye, and the right side of his face was raked and pitted with scars. The uncovered eye stared at me with enough hatred for both, ten times over.

I looked at Boss Agent, only now noticing the bandage on the right side of his head. With all that had transpired, I'd forgotten about the mysterious projectile that had knocked him to the ground. His injury didn't seem to be bothering him, however. In fact, he was regarding me with an expression I could only describe as mirth.

"Well," he said, "this should provide some delightful breakfast conversation."

My entire body sagged as I pulled out the chair and sat down. I didn't know how I was even going to be able to eat with these two sitting this close to me.

I looked at Anthony's shattered face again. "What the hell happened to you?" I asked.

Anthony looked up from his breakfast, fixed me with a baleful glare, and immediately returned to eating.

"I don't think anyone's really sure what happened to him," Anthony's boss said. "Something happened when you hurled yourself at him, but I have no idea what that was."

I frowned at him. "When I jumped him?"

He nodded.

"That doesn't make any sense," I said.

"No, it doesn't," he replied.

A hooded figure placed a plate of what looked like potato pancakes in front of me.

"Thank you," I said, glancing up at the hidden face.

I picked up the fork at my place and began eating. The pancakes were quite tasty, but they weren't made from potatoes. I couldn't quite place the flavor, but it was pleasant.

The older man put a hand to the bandage on the side of his head.

"No permanent damage, I take it?" I said.

He shook his head. "I'll recover," he said.

I gave my head a quick shake. "Damn," I said. "Not my day."

His eyes darted sharply in my direction, but he recovered with a slight smile. "Never one to pass up an opportunity for a witticism, eh, Mister Richmond? Well, such as it was, anyway. They can't all be prize winners."

"You're a real piece of work, you know that?"

He took a bite of his breakfast and chuckled. "You know," he said, "that is one of the most ambiguous, noncommittal phrases I've ever come across. I wish people would just say what's on their minds."

"Would you rather I called you a selfish, lying bastard?"

He dabbed the corners of his mouth with his napkin. "Well, it's a more honest response, but let me think about it for a moment. My parentage is not in question, so you can scratch that last part. I do lie from time to time, but that's usually in the interests of my work. And selfish? Well, no, I don't think so. And I don't see how my interactions with you so far could even lead you to that conclusion." He looked at me with a smug smile. "So you can call me a liar if you want, but I have to take exception to the other two."

"Nothing ruffles you, does it?" I asked.

"Very little ruffles me. You don't do the kind of work I do without developing a thick skin with an undercoat of cynicism."

"You're not even concerned about where we are, are you?"

He pursed his lips and shrugged. "Something got us here. Something else will get us back. It's just a matter of patience. In the meantime, this little eventuality might just further my research."

"Research?"

"Mmmm." He nodded.

"You're a scientist?"

"No," he said with a laugh. "No, not a scientist. More like a…" He trailed off for moment, thinking. "…a gardener."

"A gardener?"

"Yes. I arrange certain elements, give them the right environment, and then step back to observe the results. If I don't like what I see, I make changes."

"And you thought *my* statement was ambiguous."

"Yes, but there's a difference. You were using a clumsy phrase because it was convenient. I'm ambiguous because I have to be."

I took another bite of my potato-like pancakes. "I don't understand why you're even talking to me."

"Oh, now, Mister Richmond, I can be as civilized as the next man. Like I said to you before, none of this is personal. I'm just doing my job. That's all."

A presence at my elbow aborted any retort I might have made. I looked up to find another cloaked figure standing next to my chair.

"There will be a brief morning ceremony in a moment," he said. I recognized Thomas' voice. "I will have to ask you to finish your breakfast and your conversation, if you would."

I nodded and took the last couple of bites of my meal. My partner in conversation did the same. Anthony had finished his minutes before us and was now staring at me again. It was as if he wanted to memorize every detail of my face so that he would be able to find me and kill me at some unspecified later date.

The notion was as uncomfortable to me as the stare.

Another cloaked individual took our plates away, and a moment later the figure at the head of the table stood up. I presumed it was Daniel, as the cloak was edged with purple.

"Brothers," he said, "our morning begins differently today. The same sun has risen, the same walls surround us, and the same nourishment fills our stomachs. But we are joined today by three men who are strangers to us. Strangers to our world. We know not whence they come, but we are truly honored that they have come to us."

The voice was Daniel's. As I had suspected, he was the leader of this gang.

"Please join me in greeting them," he added.

The two dozen or so men in cloaks turned as one to face us, and they bowed their heads forward. That part I liked. No fuss. Just a nice nod to say hello.

Neither Daniel nor Thomas had said anything to us yet that smacked of religion or mysticism, but I was still getting seriously creeped out by the solemnity of it all. None of them took their hoods down, not even to eat, and the simple meal and the uniform dress code made me think of nothing other than an order of austere monks, living as simple a life as possible in order to honor their god.

Without warning, my brain treated me to an image of these men, walking single file, chanting in Latin, and hitting themselves on their foreheads with wooden boards. It afforded me a moment of pleasure in an otherwise bizarre and confusing situation.

"We know, brothers," Daniel continued, "that the ruling council of our government seeks to travel to other worlds, to other dimensions of reality. To that end, they have harnessed the power of innocents. They have recruited, and continue to recruit, unwitting individuals with lavish promises."

My eyebrows began to move towards each other. This was beginning to sound a little too familiar.

"These people," Daniel continued, "these recruits, are extremely gifted. There is no doubt of that. They possess the ability to do things with their minds that most people cannot. But the ruling council is pushing them, and pushing them hard. They are getting these people to explore the edges of reality with their minds. They are forcing them to attempt breaching the barriers between worlds."

He paused for a moment to let his words sink in.

"The men sitting here with us," he said, gesturing to us again, "are evidence that these barriers have been breached. An insidious plan has been put into motion by our rulers, a plan that would not only ruin the minds of their trusting recruits, not only allow them to steal resources from other worlds, but also cause instability in the very fabric of reality itself."

A murmur of concern rose up from the assembled brothers.

The self-proclaimed gardener leaned towards me. "This was worth the price of admission," he whispered.

♦

When Daniel was finished speaking, he sat down. Almost immediately three of the brothers got up from their chairs and came towards my end of the table. They stopped, one to my right, one to Anthony's right, and one to the older man's right. They gestured in unison, indicating that we should rise and accompany them.

I pushed my chair back and stepped away from the table. The brother who had stopped beside me began moving towards the door at the far end of the room, so I figured I'd better do the same. He led me out of the dining room and back down the corridor, taking the reverse of the route I had followed earlier. He stopped at the room I'd been in, opened the door, and ushered me inside.

I turned to ask him a question, but he pulled the door closed as soon as I'd cleared the threshold. He hadn't spoken a word or so much as glanced back at me as we'd walked, but I'd had the feeling that he would have known immediately if I had tried to sneak away from him.

There was something odd about these hooded brothers, something I couldn't quite put my finger on yet…

After the door closed, I heard a click. It was very much like the sound of a lock being turned. I frowned and stepped to the door. Sure enough, they'd locked me in this time.

This was a poor development.

I began to pace the room, wondering about so many things at once. Why would they leave the door unlocked earlier but lock it now? Why had they decided to tell us the things they'd told us at the breakfast cere-mony? Why did they hide their faces? What had happened to Anthony's face? And where had the object come from that had struck Anthony's boss on the head?

After a few minutes of pacing and ruminating, I stopped and sat down on the bed. I put my head between my knees and breathed deeply. My mind was spinning like an overloaded washing machine, and my nerves were just about tattered to ruin, but I had latched onto something in the last half-hour. Despite all the questions and mysteries, I was becoming more and more convinced that this was the same world I had visited before.

Irene's world.

I had more to go on now than just the similarity of the cloaks to the one I'd seen on the train. Daniel had spoken of a ruling council and its efforts to cross between worlds. Greaves was a councillor, and Irene was an adept who could most definitely travel in such a manner.

The parallels were numerous.

As I tried to collate and process the few facts I had, I heard footsteps down the corridor beyond my door. A moment later the lock turned, and the door opened. The brother who entered moved like Thomas, so I assumed it was Thomas.

"Thomas," I said.

He stiffened slightly, then shook his head. "I'm still not accustomed to people being able to read my body language so well," he said.

I skipped the pleasantries and got straight to the point. "That was quite the speech," I said. "It raised some questions, but I think it also answered at least one."

He folded his hands in front of him. "And that would be…?"

I snorted slightly, one corner of my mouth jerking up just a touch.

"I'm pretty sure," I said, "that this is the same world I visited a couple of days ago. And I'm equally sure that you people knew I'd been here before."

He nodded slowly. "You're correct," he said. "On both counts."

"So the guy on the train…"

"…was one of our brothers, yes."

I stood and took a step towards him. "He sent me back to my own world," I said. "Which means—"

"Which means nothing," Thomas said firmly, "unless you understand the entirety of the situation. Which you don't. So I would advise you to reserve any judgements until your understanding is fuller and clearer."

I folded my arms. "Well, then. Why don't you enlighten me?"

"That's precisely what I'm here to do."

"Really. You're going to answer my questions."

"I'll tell you what I can."

I sat back down and furrowed my brow slightly. "Well, I find that really interesting. You've decided to lock my door all of a sudden, but for some reason you're also suddenly willing to answer my questions. That doesn't add up."

He regarded me for a moment before answering.

"The timing is unfortunate," he said.

"What do you mean?"

"The brothers are performing some routine maintenance of the enclave right now. We didn't want you stepping outside your room during this activity."

"Why? Because I might see something you don't want me seeing? Like your faces, for example?"

"You might have seen... something, yes."

"So you're obviously not going to answer all of my questions, then."

"I'll give you as much information as I feel you're ready to hear."

"Again with the coddling," I muttered.

"I beg your pardon?" Thomas asked.

"Nothing. It's just an old song I've heard before."

"I don't understand."

"Good," I said with a satisfied nod. "Now you know how I feel. Can I start asking some questions now?"

He nodded. "Go ahead."

There were large questions, questions of vast breadth and depth, questions of politics, society, religion, and science with which my mind had been grappling for some time, but I began with none of them. Instead, I found myself focusing on the minutiae of the situation, and on one pesky detail in particular.

"Did you throw the object that hit the older man in the head?"

He paused before answering. "Yes," he said. "Well, not me personally, but one of the brothers who was with me."

I nodded and lifted my eyebrows slightly. I'd actually gotten a straight answer. Things were looking up.

As thought about the injury to the older agency man, something else popped into my head. Something that had been bothering me.

"Did you also take the younger man's gun?" I asked.

"We did."

That explained why Anthony was unable to find it after our first altercation. Pretty slick, these hooded brothers. Ninja monks, indeed.

Unfortunately, these answers only raised more questions.

"So you were watching us," I said.

"Yes," he said. His voice was quiet with reluctance and discomfort.

"Which means you knew we were here?"

"Yes."

"Which leads me to believe that you must have brought us here."

"No."

I couldn't see his expression, but his voice was filled with alarm. The suggestion appeared to shock him.

"Hmmm…" I rubbed my chin and narrowed my eyes at him. "So the anomalous ripples in the air remain a mystery."

"The… the what?"

I smiled. I was happy to know stuff that he didn't.

"Back in my world, this great big patch of ripples appeared in the air above us. Out of nowhere. It was just suddenly there. And it slowly descended upon us, undulating and pulsating like a lake made out of nothing. And when it reached us, we were suddenly here. In your world."

Thomas said nothing.

"How do you like them apples?" I asked.

I could almost sense him frowning.

"So I guess it's a mystery to you, too, huh?"

"It is most puzzling."

His tone was less than convincing. He knew more than he was saying. But I decided to let it go for the moment.

"But getting back to my original line of questioning: Why did you throw the… what the hell was it that you threw, anyway?"

"It was a block of wood."

"A block of wood? Is that what ninja monks carry for self-defense in this world?"

"I still don't know that word—ninja—but no, it was simply lying nearby."

"And what made you toss it at him rather than me?"

201

He paused before answering. "We decided to help you."

"Again, why me?"

"We…" he trailed off, but then got his footing back. "It appeared to us that you were more trustworthy than the other men. More… honorable, if you will."

I chortled. "Honorable? I don't think that word has ever been applied to me. As a matter of fact, if you were to ask some of the people back home who know me, they'd probably tell you that I'm one giant, puckered asshole."

"A what?"

I sighed. "This vocabulary thing is starting to get me down. What I'm trying to get at here is that you chose to help me without knowing anything about me. You observed us for, what, ten minutes, maybe? And I'm really not all that nice a person. Like I said, you can ask anyone. And even with all of that—in addition to the fact that you don't know anything about my world or its customs or cultures—you still decided to help me rather than them. I just don't get it."

Again he fell silent. Again I sensed he was carefully couching everything he said to me. And again, I had only body language to go on.

I pushed ahead. "Okay, next question: How did you even know we were here? And don't tell me that you just happened to be in the area, because that won't wash even a little bit."

His pauses before answering questions were becoming downright annoying.

"That would be… difficult to explain," he said.

"Difficult?" I asked. "Or inconvenient?"

"Perhaps both."

I cocked my head and stared at him. "Who are you people?"

"That's a many-headed question," Thomas said.

I put a hand to my forehead and tried to keep my breathing slow and even. I was becoming more exasperated by the second.

"Well, then," I said, "just pick a head and go with it."

Thomas looked at me for a moment—at least I assumed he was looking at me—then turned away and stepped towards the chair. He sat down, carefully arranging his robes as he did so.

Evidently this was going to be a long answer.

"You could say," he began, "that we're the castoffs of this society."

"Castoffs?"

He nodded. "The unwanted. The rejected. The ones who remind the ruling council of its arrogance and its mistakes. We're not to be seen."

"But why?"

He gave a snorting, derisive laugh. "Because we are incomplete. Damaged. Maimed. Or otherwise disfigured."

I closed my eyes. I almost didn't want to know this. But I had asked the question.

"Are you serious?" I asked. "You're shunned because you have serious injuries?"

He nodded again. "I don't know if you got a sense of this on your first visit," he said, "but there is a great divide in this society."

I frowned. "A divide? What do you mean?"

"A great schism. A division between those who rule and those who serve."

I immediately flashed back to one of my conversations with Charlotte. She'd been almost mortified when I suggested she might have mental abilities like Irene. She'd said her lack of such abilities was the reason she was a servant.

"I did get a hint of that, yes."

"You were with Greaves and the woman Irene when you were here before."

I nodded. "Yes."

"Then you know how well those with mental powers are treated."

"But I thought those powers were extremely rare. How can you have an elite class with such a miniscule percentage of the population?"

"Mental powers aren't rare," Thomas said. "Close to a quarter of the population has them, and they manifest in many different ways. Those like Irene are the elite, the most powerful. They get all the attention. The rest, well, you might not even know they had a mental power unless you saw them using it."

"Does Greaves have powers?"

"Of course. Otherwise he wouldn't be on the ruling council."

Thomas paused, apparently to let me take that in, which I did, in fact, need a moment to do. I'd had no clue that Greaves had mental powers, and had thought that Irene and the other adepts were the only ones who possessed them.

"So, you and your brethren, here. You're all injured, and you're all shunned. I don't get that."

"We were once builders, farmers, soldiers… the foundation of society. When the physical dangers of our trades caught up with us, we were no longer of any use. Those with mental powers take care of their own. There's no medical system for the underprivileged. We're left to our own devices."

"So the government didn't build this place?"

"The government has no interest in this place. And that works to our great advantage."

"I see."

Thomas was almost motionless on the chair. He appeared to be lost in thought.

"Are you all right?" I asked.

He nodded. "Yes. But I think that's perhaps enough questions for now."

"What, you're just cutting me off? I'm just getting started."

"I have questions of my own," he said. "It's only fair."

I supposed I couldn't deny him his own queries after he'd obligingly answered some of mine.

"All right," I said. "Fire away."

"I need to know how you arrived in this world the first time."

"Irene brought me," I said. I told him the story of my hospitalization, my Irene sightings, my incarceration, and my rescue. It took a few minutes, but I wanted to make sure I covered everything important.

My tale was met with another round of silence.

"God damn it." I stood, raking a hand through my hair. "Don't you have anything to say about any of that?"

He said nothing.

"Silence, spoon-feeding, and more silence. That's all I'm getting from you people. And it's starting to piss me off."

Again, I received no response.

"You probably think you're protecting me. Maybe even from myself. Is that it? If I know too much, I'll become some kind of danger? Well, if so, then spare me. Because if this has anything to do with me being some kind of chosen prophet guy, then I just don't want to hear about it."

Thomas stiffened at this. How could he not know how readable his body language was?

"See? There you go. I can tell by your reaction that I'm right on the money here."

I paced towards the door and back to the bed again. "How many times do I have to tell people that there's nothing special about me? I'm just a normal human being with a skewed sense of himself and a penchant for the dramatic. That's all."

Thomas remained still. "I've been instructed not to discuss this with you."

"Of course you have." I put my head in my hands. "Fuck. This is like something out of a bad fantasy novel." I looked up at him again. "What could they possibly want with me?"

He remained motionless. And irritatingly silent.

"Will you throw me a bone, here? Give me something to go on."

Thomas let his shoulders slump. "If I were to speculate," he said, "then I might say it's possible you have some sort of ability you don't yet know about."

I plunked myself onto the bed and hung my head. "That's ludicrous."

Thomas stood and moved towards the door. "It might not be so ludicrous as you think. And it may be up to such men as those two who travelled here with you to protect your world from the threat Daniel spoke of."

My head snapped back up. "What? The old guy and his goon? Protecting my world? That's a laugh."

"They may be trying to protect you as well."

I was instantly on my feet again, glaring at him. "If you're even trying to suggest that those two are the good guys…"

Thomas shook his head. "I know nothing about them. All I mean to say is that I doubt they're the danger you believe them to be."

I pointed in the general direction of the dining hall. "Those bastards kidnapped me. They locked me up. They were going to interrogate me and run tests on me. It was Irene who got me out of that. She made an archway into my cell. And Councillor Greaves took me in, fed me, gave me a place to sleep. And then your guy shoved me back into my own world, which to me means that you people have some mental powers of your own. But no, you say it doesn't mean anything, because I don't know the whole story yet. But never mind, because the secret agent guys kidnapped Lydia and threatened to kill her if I didn't go with them, but we didn't get that far, because the big transparent ripples came down out of nowhere, and then we were here again, and now Lydia's dead!"

Somewhere in my ranting I had grabbed him by the collar again and was now shaking him, the tears running down my face once more. I refused to believe that Anthony and his boss were anything but pure evil. They had killed Lydia. No, worse. They had caused me to kill Lydia. I would never forget that as long as I lived, and no amount of scarring or lost eyeballs would ever be sufficient punishment for what Anthony did to me. He manipulated me into brutally killing someone I loved, and I would see him in Hell itself before I would ever look at him in any other light but that of pure evil.

Thomas grabbed my right wrist. His grip was unbelievably strong. I looked down at his left hand. It was covered by a black glove, which I'd not noticed before because of the voluminous sleeves.

"Stop this," he said. "You're overwrought. You're not thinking clearly. I only tell you what I know. Nothing else."

I kept staring at the glove, trying to figure out why it was unnerving me so. It took me a moment to fully grasp what I was seeing. It wasn't the glove, but what lay beyond it.

The sleeve had slipped back off his wrist, revealing an arm that glinted in the room's candlelight. I thought I must have been imagining things, but even blinking a few times didn't change what I was seeing.

His arm looked like it was made of metal.

He saw what I was looking at and immediately pushed me back towards the bed, dropping his arms to let the sleeves fall back to their normal positions.

The backs of my calves hit the bed, and I crumpled onto it. I stared at him through watery eyes. The shape of his hood seemed to undulate as I blinked. He looked like the Spectre of Death itself.

"What are you?" I asked.

For a moment he appeared not to know what to say. Finally, he straightened himself and took a step towards me.

"I am a brother of the Order of the Electron," he said.

I blinked more tears out of my eyes. I couldn't look upon a man who had just said something so patently ridiculous with tears in my eyes.

"Is that your final answer?" I asked.

"Yes. It's my only answer."

I squinted at him. "The Order of the Electron? Are you serious? You're just saying that to throw me off, aren't you? Deflect attention from what I just saw. Right?"

"No. That's the name of our order."

My logic circuits suddenly started to kick in again. "Waaaait a minute. Electron? That sounds like science to me. Can you guys talk about stuff like that? I thought it was *verboten* in this world."

"Not here in the enclave."

"You can talk about electricity? About technology?"

"Not only can we talk about it," Thomas replied, pulling back his hood. "We have it," he said.

I looked at him. He had close-cropped fair hair, blue eyes, and a craggy but handsome face, which was near-flawless except for his left cheekbone and the left side of his jaw, both of which were made of metal.

Chapter Fifteen

I stared at Thomas for what seemed like minutes before I finally gathered the presence of mind to speak again.

"What are you… I mean… why are you letting me see this?" I asked.

He let his arms fall to his sides and looked at the floor for a moment.

"I panicked when you noticed my arm, but after a moment I realized there was no point in hiding the truth from you any longer. The damage had already been done."

My breathing was shallow and ragged. I was experiencing every kind of emotion I could imagine, except for the good ones, and now my confusion was returning to blur everything.

"Are you…?" I began.

"Human?" Thomas asked. "Mostly, yes."

He pushed his left sleeve back to reveal a metallic forearm that was almost seamlessly attached to his upper arm at the elbow. The elbow itself was mechanical, and the joint moved almost silently.

"I was a soldier," Thomas said. "I lost this arm and the left side of my face in an explosion. Without the enclave, I would have been reduced to begging on the streets. Or worse."

I stepped closer to him and leaned in to examine the forearm more closely. I could hardly believe what I was seeing.

"Wow," I said. "You obviously have something a lot better than a medical system."

Thomas nodded. "The enclave was founded many years ago by a man who believed all human life was precious, mental abilities or not, and that technology could be used not only to improve life, but also to mend it."

I stood up again and looked at him. "You mean this is all done here?"

He nodded. "Here, and in similar enclaves in other locations. We have laboratories, operating rooms, and a research facility. All underground. If anything happens to the enclave here on the surface, they'll all be well protected."

I looked around. The stark simplicity of my accommodations belied the technical ingenuity Thomas was describing.

"So all this…" I said, gesturing around with my arm.

"All this is a ruse. We maintain the appearance of a religious order to hide our true purpose and abilities. So far it has worked extremely well."

I stepped back to the bed and sat down again.

"Well, that explains the robes and the hoods."

"Yes, whenever we leave the facilities below, we don the robes. We maintain strict vigilance at all times."

I put my hand to my head. I could feel the pressure building again. I wouldn't be able to keep taking in new information for much longer. There was a breaking point in there somewhere, and felt like I was rapidly closing on it.

"And your guy on the train?" I asked, suddenly flashing back to my unceremonious departure from this world. "Isn't it risky, having someone out and about like that, what with metal bits ready to be uncovered?"

Thomas nodded again. "There are a few brothers and sisters who venture out into the general population. Only the least injured of us can be out there, due to the risk of discovery, but we're not alone. A large number of ordinary, uninjured citizens have come to our aid. They don the robes as well, and they help us find those who need us. Out there, we're known as the Order of Isidore, and we minister to the sick and injured. We have enclaves in cities throughout the world."

I looked blankly up at him. I'd suddenly run out of words.

"I can see you're overwhelmed," he said. "Perhaps I should stop now, and let you take it all in."

I looked at the floor and ran my hand over the back of my head. "I know I wanted answers," I said, "but, frankly, I'm a little mystified. Why have you told me so much?"

He smiled. Well, the right side of his face smiled, anyway. "I believe you can be trusted," he said.

"Trusted with what?"

"It's not a matter of specifics," he said. "It's a matter of your heart."

I closed my eyes. This was becoming too much for me. "I don't understand what you're telling me," I said. "You're not making any sense."

He smiled again. "It's enough to know that you're on the right path," he said.

More riddles. More vagueness. I needed something specific to get me to the next moment. My world was falling apart, and I had no glue, or thread, or twine, or even spit and chewing gum. I didn't know how to move ahead from here.

"I need something specific," I said. "I need a fact, a piece of information, something logical that I can take hold of. Because nothing that's happened over the last few days makes any sense at all. Nothing."

"Stay the course, friend. You will prevail."

I grunted and stood up. "That still doesn't help. I don't even know what course I'm on, let alone how to stay it."

I stepped away from the bed and moved towards the table and chair. "I'm out of my element here. Everything is foreign to me, and I can't keep a coherent grasp on anything I start to think about."

Thomas stepped up behind me. "Tell me your name," he said.

I turned around to look at him. It hadn't even occurred to me that I hadn't yet told these people who I was.

"My name's Jack," I said. "Jack Richmond."

He nodded and looked at me, his jaw set, his eyes narrower. "Jack," he said. "You've been through a lot in a very short time."

I furrowed my brow slightly. "Yes. You could say that," I said.

"You must be experiencing great turmoil."

I squinted and frowned more deeply. I had no idea where he was going with this. "That would be another affirmative."

"We can teach you some very effective meditation techniques."

"Meditation?" I gave my head a slight shake. "Not really my thing. My mind isn't inclined to shut up for any length of time. But thanks for the offer."

He nodded slowly, gravely. "It's important to stay calm. Especially when stress abounds."

I shrugged. "Yeah. Sure. That seems a reasonable thing to say. Even classy, what with your excellent use of the word 'abounds', which, by the way, you just don't hear very often anymore. At least on my world."

He looked at me with that enigmatic half-smile. "It's especially important, I think, for you."

"What? Staying calm?"

He nodded.

I felt my frown coming back. "And why, exactly, would that be? Am I going to explode or something? Am I going to rip the fabric of the universe if I get angry again? What are you trying to get at?"

"Observe your own reaction. You're becoming agitated by my mere suggestion that you need calm. This, to me, indicates, that I'm correct."

I allowed a growling breath to escape through my nose. "Is that supposed to be some weird kind of logic? Maybe I just find you generally annoying."

He laughed. "You use a lot of words, Jack Richmond. And you're skilled at putting them together. But do you listen when others speak to you?"

"What? Of course I listen. How could I carry on a conversation if I didn't listen?"

"Have you been listening to me?"

I rolled my eyes. "Yes. Duh."

"You've heard my words with your ears," Thomas said, "but do you hear them with your heart?"

I closed my eyes and sighed. "What the hell does that mean?"

"Jack," he said. "We trust you now. Will you not also trust us?"

I opened my eyes again. "I don't know who to trust," I said.

"Then trust yourself."

I looked intently at him for a moment. There was a familiar ring to what he'd just said. Someone else had said something similar to me, not that long ago—

I took in a shuddering breath as it came back to me. Lydia's face appeared in my mind's eye, her last breaths escaping her, the blood draining from her body. "Start believing in yourself, will you?" she'd said.

And now I heard "trust yourself" from the mouth of this strange half-monk, half-cyborg, in this bizarre alternate world, with my chaotic circumstances swirling about me like a sea funnel, and it made more sense to me than it ever had at any other time in my life.

"Trust myself," I said, allowing myself a slight smile. "That's good advice."

He must have sensed a change in me, because his smile returned. "I'm relieved," he said.

We looked at each other for a moment, and I thought I could feel a sort of bond develop between us. Neither of us said another word, but I began to realize that, in listening to what he'd said, and realizing that I needed to trust myself, I was also beginning to trust him.

This was an unusual occurrence for me.

The moment was broken by hurried footsteps in the hallway outside. Thomas turned to face the doorway just as two of his brethren entered. They paused for a moment, evidently surprised that he had taken his hood down, but they recovered almost instantly.

"What's the meaning of this commotion?" Thomas asked sharply.

"Brother Thomas," the man in front said. "We are discovered."

Thomas turned his body to face the man. "What? Explain yourself."

The man stiffened slightly, but did not falter. "The enclave is no longer a safe haven. Men are approaching. Armed men. They are heading directly for us."

"This is impossible," Thomas said, moving towards them. "We have taken every precaution. There is no way—" He stopped suddenly, then turned towards me. "Perhaps I was wrong to trust you so quickly, Jack Richmond."

"What? You think *I* have something to do with this?" I asked, incredulous.

Thomas stared at me a moment, his breathing both audible and visible. He turned his head to look at his two brethren, and then he turned back to me again. His mouth was drawn into a tight, straight line, and his jaw was clenched. Finally, after what seemed an eternity, he turned his whole body back towards the men.

"Gather weapons from below," he said. "Fortify the entrances and cover the windows. We cannot let these men inside the enclave."

"Yes, Brother Thomas," the first man said. He and his companion turned and sped out of the room.

But it was already too late. More noises reached us from the corridor beyond, distant but unmistakable. Crashing sounds, shouting sounds, and the occasional sound of a weapon being discharged.

I knew immediately that the Order of the Electron was not the only group that possessed technology.

I closed my eyes, suddenly realizing that these men didn't stand a chance.

Thomas turned to me, his eyes wet with incipient tears. "You must come with me," he said. "I'll take you to the safest place in the enclave."

I sighed. "I really don't think there's any time left for that," I said.

He frowned and cocked his head. "Why do you say that?"

"Just listen to it out there. They'll have this whole place locked down in a matter of minutes."

I could see the desperation creeping into Thomas' expression. In a moment, I knew, his entire face would crumble, and so would any hopes of saving the brotherhood or the enclave.

The sounds drew closer. The shouting became less chaotic and more organized. The crashes and gunshots became less frequent. The sounds of boot-heels on hard floors became louder.

And then they were upon us. The boot-steps rounded the corner and proceeded towards us down the corridor. I couldn't see it from my angle, but I could see the side of Thomas' face as he looked out through the doorway, and from his expression, I knew what was happening.

Mere seconds later, a man in uniform entered, rifle raised and aimed at Thomas' chest. A second man entered, his firearm pointed at me.

"Bring them," a voice shouted in the corridor.

The soldiers waved their weapons towards the door. Without a word, Thomas moved towards the corridor. I followed, my heart slowly sinking into my abdomen.

Chapter Sixteen

(Sunday, 8:27 A.M.)

We were herded down to the dining hall, which was rapidly filling with brothers of the order, all being similarly herded by well-armed soldiers. All their hoods were down now, no doubt yanked back by their chaperones, and bits of hardware were visible here and there in the throng.

Near the front of the room stood Daniel, his purple-trimmed robe an almost defiant contrast to the drab green of the uniforms and the solid black of the brothers' robes. I could only imagine what he was feeling as he watched his charges all being poked, prodded, and manhandled into the huge room.

Our escorts steered Thomas and me towards Daniel, and it was only when we were mere feet away from him that I noticed who else was standing at the front of the room.

Councillor Greaves was surveying the proceedings. To his left stood the lovely Irene DiFalco. My heart sped up slightly as I took in the sight of her. I was inordinately happy to see her, but I was confused by her presence here. It smacked of something sinister.

Greaves' eyes found me as I approached his position. "Jack," he said. "I'm relieved to see that you're all right."

His face and voice were both sincere. I glanced at Irene. She, too, appeared relieved. I gave her a quick smile, which she returned almost surreptitiously.

I looked at Thomas. "I don't understand any of this," I said. Thomas, for his part, seemed unmoved by my confusion.

Greaves stepped towards me, one corner of his mouth twitching upwards. "Of course you don't," he said. "This is not your world. Our ways are strange to you. But everything will make sense once we've cleaned up this mess and taken you to a safe place."

"I thought *this* was a safe place," I said.

Greaves shook his head. "Oh, I don't think so, Jack. I don't know what these men would have done to you. I'm sure they've tried to gain your trust, but once they accomplished that, I shudder to think—"

"He's lying," Thomas said. "He's a member of the Council. He can't be trusted."

One of the soldiers who had come in with us stepped forward and jammed the butt of his rifle into Thomas' solar plexus. Thomas gasped and crumpled to the floor in a ball, hands over his abdomen.

I glared at Greaves. "Was that really necessary?" I asked him.

Greaves shook his head and made the universally annoying *tsk-tsk* sound. "These men have poisoned your mind long enough," he said. "I can't let their words affect you any further."

"Poisoned my mind?" I said. "These men have been taking care of me since I arrived back in this world. They've shown me nothing but kindness."

Greaves' half grin turned into a sneer. "Yes, that's how they do things here. Lull you into a false sense of security. Then they'll take all your secrets and use them to whatever advantage they can come up with. Probably towards their ultimate goal of bringing down the government."

"And what if that government deserves to be brought down?" I asked.

Greaves face hardened. "Hmmm… I see we're going to have to do some serious deprogramming here, Jack. Your mind has been warped much more severely than I thought would be possible in such a short time. I'm truly sorry that this has happened to you."

I was beginning to feel a niggling in the back of my mind. Something here was not right. Greaves seemed—different. He wasn't quite the same man I had met during my first visit. It was subtle, but it was there. I decided to test the waters.

"Councillor," I said, "I don't even know what to think anymore. And I don't know who to trust. I still hardly understand anything about your world. I just want to do the right thing. And I want to get back to my own world."

I hoped that my vague but earnest statement would prompt him to give me a bit more information. I needed to know if he was truly trustworthy. I was beginning to doubt it, but I also couldn't forget how kind he'd been to me during my previous visit. The change I was seeing in him might simply be due to his assuming a command position in this current situation. But I had to be sure.

He actually smiled at me now. "Your confusion is understandable," he said. "And I don't wish to add to it. But I really must get you out of here and back to civilization. I want to see you well and whole and ready to travel back to your world."

I took that moment to glance at Irene. Her face was pale, drawn. A veil of worry lay across her exquisite features. Our eyes met, and she shook her head, almost imperceptibly.

That was all I needed. Irene knew something was wrong, and I trusted Irene above all other persons in this messed up, cockamamie world.

I returned my gaze to the councillor. He was still smiling, but his eyes held something else. Concern? Worry? Or was it fear?

"Thank you, Councillor," I said. "You've taken good care of me before, and I have no doubt that you'll do so again. I appreciate it."

I thought I saw confusion ripple across Greaves' face for a moment, but it vanished almost as soon as it appeared. I wanted to smile, but I refrained. I had to convince him that I was confused, weary, and grateful. It wasn't a difficult act. I'd been confused for days, I was weary of the bizarre events that kept surprising me at every turn, and I was grateful at that moment for Irene and her quiet confirmation of my suspicions.

Greaves smiled again. "I owe you a debt of gratitude as well, my boy," he said.

"Really," I replied. "I don't see how that's possible."

"Oh, good Heavens," he said. "I would never have found this place without you."

I saw Daniel stiffen at that. I glanced at him, then looked back at Greaves. "I'm afraid I don't follow you," I said.

Greaves' smile seemed to broaden even further. "Why, it's because of you that we're here," he said. "Isn't it, Irene?" He turned to look at her.

Irene looked even paler and more distraught than before. She threw her shoulders back, however, when Greaves turned to look at her.

"Yes," she said. "I'm attuned to you, it would appear. There's something about you, Jack, something that adepts like myself are able to sense. I don't yet understand what it is, but it reaches my mind nonetheless."

A little marble that had been rolling around the edges of an indentation in the back of my mind suddenly plunked into place. My mouth became dry, my hands cold and clammy. I tried to process what I'd just heard.

I looked at Irene. "You can track me with your abilities."

Irene swallowed hard and nodded. Her shoulders were no longer thrown back, and her eyes were moist with incipient tears.

Greaves looked at me with a twinkle in his eye. "Irene is one of the finest adepts we have. She can sense variations in energy like no one else. She is our most valuable asset. And now we have another reason to treasure her. We can not only track people like yourself, Jack. We can distinguish them from the rest of the population. You can't begin to imagine how elated I was to learn that."

My brain began to spin again. This was all my fault. I'd brought this down upon Daniel, Thomas, and the rest of the brethren. I was a danger to them, and I hadn't even known it. I still didn't understand how it was possible, but the fact that Greaves and Irene were standing in the room was testament to the fact that it was. What made it all the worse was the fact that I didn't even know what type of energy they were talking about. It was maddening.

"Now, I'll admit," Greaves continued, "that you're the first person we've encountered who gives off this signature, but I seriously doubt that you'll be the last. After all, there are a lot of worlds out there."

A lot of worlds.

My stomach and jaw began to tighten. Of course there were more than just two worlds. I recalled the ripples in the air that had descended from on high, and my uncertainty as to whether they had transported me to the same world as before. Without even fully realizing it, I'd already been open to the notion of multiple universes.

And now that notion was anchoring itself solidly in my mind.

Thomas and Daniel were right. Greaves and his compatriots were planning to invade other worlds. For what purpose, I did not know. But that didn't matter. It was wrong. Plain and simple. It was just wrong.

"Starting to get the picture now, Mister Richmond?"

I turned to look behind me. The older man from the shadowy agency was standing not five feet away, his trusty sidekick next to him. He wore his patented smile as he gazed back at me.

"Nothing's ever straightforward, is it?" he said.

Greaves narrowed his eyes and pointed at the agency men. "Bring those two over here," he snapped.

The uniformed men took Anthony and his boss by their arms and led them to my position.

"You two are from Jack's world," Greaves said. It was not a question.

The older man chuckled. "So it's Jack now, is it? First name basis. All great friends, are we?"

Greaves narrowed his eyes. "I am led to believe that you are not a friend to Jack."

"Oh, I'm more of a friend to him than he can possibly imagine. While he's been blindly wandering around the cosmos, banging into walls, I've been gathering every fragment of information I could get my hands on. And I have a much more complete picture of this situation than your dear friend Jack here could ever hope to cobble together. So, you might say, I've been looking out for him."

"Looking out for me?" I gaped at him. "You've done everything in your power to ruin my life. I don't know what the hell you planned to do with me back at your concrete bunker, but I have these people to thank for my escape. If anyone's looking out for me, it's them."

I hadn't meant to defend Greaves so assiduously, but my feelings for the grey-haired man and his disfigured lackey won out. When I thought about it, though, it didn't hurt my position at all. Greaves would be even more likely now to believe that I trusted him.

I had no idea whom to trust, however. The three groups in the room would all have me believe that it was they and only they who had my best interests—not to mention the interests of both worlds—at heart. With a clearer head, I might have been able to deduce if any of them was telling the truth, but the fact was that I was too tired and confused to even sort out the choices on a fast food menu. I was certainly in no position to figure out the intricacies of inter-world politics. That would have been a massive feat even with all my wits and a full tank of energy.

"You still don't get it, do you," the agency man said. "I'm sure they've told you that my people are trying to breach the barrier between worlds in order to invade their world, but in fact it's quite the reverse that's true. We're developing technologies to ward off an invasion from *them*."

Councillor Greaves crossed his arms and made a *tsk-tsk* sound. He seemed amused by the proceedings.

The agency man held my gaze for a moment. For once in the time that I'd known him, he actually seemed sincere. His smile was gone, and his eyes were steady and focused.

I squinted at him. "Jesus Christ! Are you trying to tell me that you wanted to—?"

"Yes. We knew there was something different about you, Mister Richmond, and we needed to find out what that was. We weren't going to dissect you or count your rings, for God's sake. We needed you."

"So why all the cloak and dagger?"

He let out a dark chuckle. "Would you have come with us willingly?"

I shook my head.

"Well, then. There you have it."

He was still too smooth and slick for my liking, but he was at least making some sense. I glanced at Anthony, whose half-scarred visage still radiated hatred and loathing in my direction. I knew that if we ever made it back to our own world, I'd have to watch my back, probably for the rest of my life.

"Well, this is all fascinating," Greaves said, "but I think we've had enough chit chat for one day, don't you, Jack?"

I turned to him. "Yes. Yes I do."

His face quivered for a moment. I wasn't sure what emotion was trying to come to the fore, but I could tell he saw something different in my expression.

"I don't believe any of you," I said. "As far as I can tell, you're all a bunch of self-serving pricks who'll do whatever it takes to move your own agendas forward. I don't have a clue how things work in your nutty-ass world, and I don't care to learn any more about it. You people are going to send me home. I don't care how you do it." I looked at Greaves. "Get Irene to do it." I looked at Daniel. "Or get that rail-riding brother of yours back here and have him do it. I personally don't care. Just get it done. Or so help me God, I'm going to start breaking limbs."

Greaves' eyes widened slightly. "And how long do you think you would last? Have you noticed how many firearms are in this room?"

My stomach was churning now. I swallowed hard to keep down the bile that was trying to creep into my mouth. My breathing began to speed up.

"Do I look like I care?" I said. "Do I look like a man who's giving any consideration to his own safety right now?"

I glanced at Daniel. His eyes had widened slightly as well.

"You're a fool, Mister Richmond," agency guy said. "You have no idea what you're dealing with here."

I whirled on him. "I'm starting to get a pretty clear picture," I snarled.

He grunted and smirked. "Oh, yes. Of course you are."

"Save your smug sarcasm," I snapped at him. "I've had it up to my eyeballs with you." I turned to Greaves. "And with you." I looked back at Daniel. "And I don't even want to *know* about you people. Your Order of the Erection, or whatever you call it. And your shiny bits and pieces. What the hell kind of place is this, anyway?"

They were all looking at me now, the councillor, the brothers, the soldiers, the agency men. And not a one of them was looking anything even remotely resembling comfortable.

Thomas struggled to his feet, his hands still clutching his abdomen. "Jack," he groaned. "You really must try to keep yourself calm."

"Oh, that again!" I cried. "What the fuck is that all about? Why is it so all-fired important for me to keep calm? What am I, a walking time bomb or something? Am I going to spontaneously combust? What?"

"We just want you to be safe, Jack," Greaves said. "That's all."

"Bullshit!" I screamed. "None of you gives a good goddamn about my welfare. You all just think I'm some sort of resource to be tapped. And I don't even know why. I don't even know what's different about me."

"Don't do this, Mister Richmond," agency guy said.

"Don't do what? Yell? Scream? Make a fuss?"

"I think you know what I'm talking about."

"No! I don't! I haven't got a sweet fucking clue what you're talking about. Don't you get it? I'm just a guy from Halifax who doesn't do anything particularly well. There's nothing special about me. I'm not a resource. I'm not a weapon. I'm not even a particularly good guitar player. So why the fuck am I here?"

"Jack, please," Thomas said.

Greaves glanced back at his soldiers and raised a hand. Four rifles came up instantly, all trained on me.

"That's not going to solve anything," agency guy said.

Greaves shook his head. "He's losing control of himself. I need him safe, and I need him healthy."

"Well, filling him with holes isn't exactly going to accomplish that, now, is it?"

Greaves glared at the older man. "It's a precaution."

"Well, if that's your idea of a precaution, I'd be fascinated to see your extreme measures."

"Shut up!" I cried. "All of you. Just shut up."

I saw the soldiers adjust the rifles on their shoulders and tense their trigger fingers. My stomach tightened. My jaw clenched.

But oddly, those sensations were not based in fear. There was anger, of course. And confusion. And a deep longing to get home. But there was no fear. I didn't quite understand it.

But as I looked around the room again, I realized that there *was* fear. It just wasn't coming from me. It was coming from all around me. From everyone else.

These people were afraid of me.

As bizarre a notion as that was, it was also a strangely empowering one. I looked around the room again. Councillor Greaves wore a stricken expression on his wrinkled face. Daniel and Thomas were looking at me with wide eyes.

I glanced behind and to my right. Anthony's face held no surprises. Just the same old hostility and animosity he'd had on since I met him. Tremendously boring. His boss, on the other hand, had a slight crease between his eyebrows and a distinctly concerned look in his eyes. The smugness appeared to have gone into hiding for the moment.

I was liking this. Yes, I was liking this quite a bit.

The notion of my having some sort of mental powers was slowly becoming less and less implausible. If this many people were nervous about my state of mind, if this many people were bound and determined to keep me calm, then there must be something to what Irene and Greaves had said to me on my first visit and what Thomas had said to me only a short time ago.

I wondered… if were I to let go and lose my temper, would I turn into something like the Incredible Hulk?

I had to admit, that would be pretty cool.

Jack smash.

But there was really no time for flights of fancy like that. I had to focus. These people wouldn't stand there staring at me for much longer. I had to do something, and I had to do it quickly.

Unfortunately, I didn't know *what* to do. If I had some sort of powers, I hadn't the first clue how to use them. Just letting my rage fly was unlikely to accomplish anything. I'd probably cause damage, either to property or persons. Or myself.

I turned away from the agency men and faced forward again. This time, my gaze came to rest upon Irene. Her deep green eyes stared right back at me, but unlike the other sets of eyes in the room, hers held not a whit of fear. Her gaze was intense but calm, alert but unruffled.

Of all the people I'd encountered in my tumultuous last few days, Irene was the one, the single solitary one, who didn't seem to want anything from me. She spoke to me as an equal, despite the huge gap between our cultures and experiences.

There was a serenity about her that I found compelling. I'd noticed it immediately upon our first meeting. She just took things in, rarely commenting, never judging. She was an observer who appeared to enjoy the observing. The world seemed to delight her at every turn.

She treated me the same way. With acceptance, kindness, and little bit of wonder. She didn't judge me, or foist expectations upon me, or hold me up to some arbitrary standard. She just accepted me for who and what I was. She let me be myself. And in so doing—in that simple act of allowing—she made me more aware of myself.

And that, I suddenly realized, was the greatest gift one human being could give to another.

Thank you, Irene, I thought, not taking my eyes from her, *You've helped me more than you can know.*

—But I do know. And my help isn't finished yet.—

I looked around, startled. Where that had come from? Was it my own wishful thinking, speaking in Irene's voice inside my head? Or was I really, actually losing my mind this time?

I looked even more intently at her. She was smiling ever so slightly.

Was that you? I thought.

—Yes. It was me.—

Neat trick.

"Jack. Are you all right?"

I looked to my left, startled. It was Greaves who had spoken.

"Uh, yeah. I'm fine. Much calmer now, actually."

Greaves gave Irene a sidelong glance. "That's good to hear." His voice and his expression both contained ninety-nine and forty-four one-hundredths percent pure suspicion.

"Uh, Irene has that effect on me," I said, trying to keep it light. "You know, one look into those gorgeous green eyes of hers…" I let out a small, self-deprecating chuckle. It probably didn't help much, as I was not prone to small, self-deprecating chuckles and was unaccustomed to their use.

—Jack, that's not helping.—

Didn't think so. What am I supposed to do now?

—Open your mind to me.—

What? How do I do that?

Greaves was now looking back and forth between Irene and myself, his frown deepening.

"Irene," he said, "what are you doing?"

Irene turned to him, her serenity now disturbed slightly by ripples of discomfort. Still, she managed to give him one of the best poker faces I'd ever seen.

"Nothing, Councillor."

Greaves narrowed his eyes. "Are you communicating with our friend Jack here?"

"No, Councillor. I'm simply trying to help calm him down."

Her face remained completely neutral. But a telltale bead of sweat was forming at her hairline. I hoped I was the only one who noticed it.

—Jack. Open your mind to me.—

I don't know how to do that.

—Just relax, and allow your senses to take in everything around you.—

That's easier said than done.

"Irene…?" Greaves stepped closer to her.

"Councillor, I don't understand…"

The bead of sweat reached critical mass and began its descent down her forehead.

"Whatever it is you're doing, I want you to stop it right now."

"But, Councillor, I'm not—"

"Enough, Irene." Greaves glanced around for a moment, his eyes coming to rest on two of the soldiers who were currently guarding some of the Electron brethren. He raised a hand and snapped his fingers. "You two. Over here."

The soldiers stepped over to where Greaves and Irene were standing.

"What the hell are you doing?" I asked.

Greaves' eyes darted to my position. "Not another word from you, Jack. You've said quite enough."

"I'll talk if I damn well want to," I said.

"No," Greaves said, turning his body towards me and straightening his narrow shoulders. "You're going to do what I tell you to do."

"Or what?"

The older agency man let out a snort. "I think you can see where this is headed, Mister Richmond."

My head snapped around to look at him. "All I can see is my hands wrapped around your throat."

"I think it's time for you to retire that routine," he replied. "It's getting a bit old."

"Enough of this." Greaves turned back to face Irene. "Take her," he said to the soldiers. "I'll deal with her later."

My blood was pounding in my temples. "Don't you even touch her," I said, stepping towards Greaves.

"And there we have it," the agency man muttered.

Irene's face was now anything but serene. Her eyes were wide, and the drop of sweat on her brow had been joined by a number of its kin.

—*Jack. Now would be a good time.*—

Time is the problem. How can I relax when they're about to take you away?

—*Everyone is being very cautious with you, Jack. They don't know what you're going to do next. Use that to your advantage. Take the time.*—

The profound irony of the situation was not lost on me. I now had to completely relax and open my mind in the midst of armed guards taking away someone I cared about.

I briefly wondered if there was any other way, but one look at Irene's earnest, pleading expression told me there were no more exits off this road.

I had to try.

I straightened my shoulders and closed my eyes. I listened to my breathing for a moment, noticed it slowing slightly, and then turned my attention to the room around me. I could hear the rustle of fabric as people in the room shifted position. I could hear the faint whispers of the brothers as they tried to speak to each other without angering their captors. I heard the creak of a floorboard as someone near me moved their weight from one foot to the other.

"Well, this is certainly an interesting development," the agency man said. "What are you going to do, Mister Richmond? Meditate everyone to death?"

"Jack. What are you doing?" Greaves asked.

"Wouldn't you like to know," I said.

—*Don't speak, Jack. Focus on me.*—

Sorry.

With my eyes closed, her voice was much clearer in my mind. I surmised that it was because there was less sensory stimulation to divide my attention.

Say something else.

—*Just breathe. Keep breathing.*—

I imagined her voice as coming in through a small door in my head. Then I sent imaginary workmen to that spot to make the doorway bigger. As a veritable self-help junkie, I was more than familiar with visualizations. I'd listened to enough tapes to fill a good-sized bedroom.

That's good. Keep it up. Keep talking to me.

—*We can do this, Jack. We can do it together.*—

I told the workmen to make the doorway even bigger.

So they did.

And then a whole lot of white light came flooding in.

Chapter Seventeen

(Sunday, 9:12 A.M.)

I was in whiteness. It was not the sharp, violent white of my blade of vengeance, but a more solid, even white. It surrounded me, suffused me, permeated me.

It was everything.

I saw nothing, heard nothing. I seemed to float. My thoughts drifted through my mind like clouds, puffed and cottony against a blank white sky. I couldn't feel my body. I couldn't feel anything. I just knew I existed, and that I had thoughts.

Cogito, ergo sum, Descartes had said. I hoped the old boy wouldn't let me down at this particular juncture.

I had no sense of time, but I managed to retain some semblance of my sense of self. I knew who I was, and I had an inkling of where I had just been, but I had no idea where I was now or how I had gotten here. I knew I had been feeling strong emotions only a moment before—if moments existed at all in this place—but my mind was now still, the emotions distant ghosts of what they had been.

The peace of the whiteness, the calmness, the serenity—they made everything else seem silly, trivial. What had gone before did not matter. Only *now* mattered.

It occurred to me that I had read that concept in a book somewhere, but I couldn't quite put my finger on the title of it. As a matter of fact, I couldn't even locate my finger.

As I adjusted to being in nothingness (a concept that would likely have given Jean-Paul Sartre heartburn), I began to realize that my senses still worked after all. I could hear a faint humming sound, and I could see a shadow in front of me.

So… this place was not eternal whiteness after all. Maybe it was just a matter of acclimatization.

I squinted, realizing with delight that I could actually feel my eyelids.

The shadow shape in front of me was slowly becoming more defined, more solid. I wondered what it was.

Or perhaps *who* it was.

The shadow was taking on a vaguely person-like shape. There appeared to be a head and arms, though I could not at this point make out legs.

The reason for this quickly became apparent, as the shadow shape began to take on colors, highlights, and sharper edges. It was indeed a person, and that person was wearing a long coat that extended nearly to the ankles, so no lower extremities were visible, save for the feet.

Irene stepped towards me. There was no sound, but she appeared to be walking on something solid.

I looked down. I could see my own feet now, and they were standing on a solid, white floor.

I lifted my head again to regard Irene. "Nice place you've got here."

She smiled. Even in this bizarre location, her smile was exactly the same. Genuine, open, welcoming, amused, and intrigued. All that at once, in a little area of enamel only a couple of inches across.

I looked around again. We were still surrounded by whiteness, though now the whiteness seemed a little more defined. At least there was a floor now.

"Is this real?" I asked her.

She laughed. "Does it matter?"

My shoulders sagged. So it was going to be one of *those* conversations. "I don't really think I was looking at it in those terms."

She cocked her head slightly. "Does it seem real to you?"

I frowned. "I've never actually been in an eternal whiteness before, so it's a little hard to judge."

"What about me? Do I seem real to you?"

"Well, you look exactly the same, but that could just be my mind conjuring you up."

She took another step towards me and extended her arm. "Take my hand."

I reached up and took her gloved hand in mine. I could feel the texture of the dark leather and the pressure from her fingers as she squeezed my hand.

I looked at our hands, then back up at her face. Again her deep green eyes enveloped me. I tightened my grip and pulled her towards me.

"Seems real enough," I said, gently placing my other hand on her face.

"Well then," she said, smiling. "There's your answer."

I leaned forward and kissed her. She put her free arm around my shoulder. Our hands disengaged, and we embraced.

After a long moment, our lips parted, and I leaned my forehead against hers.

"It had better damn well be real."

She slid her chin onto my shoulder and hugged me harder. "It's as real as you want it to be, my love."

I returned the tightening of arms and held her as close as I possibly could.

My emotions were no longer the distant spectres they'd been when I'd first arrived here. They were returning now, swirling through my consciousness like thick liquids in a blender.

There was more than just this moment. I wanted to deny it, but it would not be denied. I wanted to remain here, holding Irene in my arms, and just forget about everything else.

But everything else, for its part, was not about to sit around and be forgotten.

I released my hold and pulled back slightly. Irene did the same, and we looked into each other's eyes for a moment.

"There's something we need to be doing," I said.

She nodded.

I pushed an errant strand of hair off her face. "And I get the feeling we need to hurry."

Images of Irene being taken away by soldiers flashed through my mind. The whiteness had so enfolded me that I'd nearly forgotten what was going on out there, beyond us.

"It's bad out there," I said.

"Yes."

"What do we do?"

"What do you *want* to do?"

I narrowed my eyes at her. "You have a most irritating habit, Miss DeFalco, of answering questions with other questions." Back in my world, she would have made a top-drawer psychiatrist.

"I've been told that before," she said, grinning. "It's my inquisitive nature, I suppose."

I gave her a lopsided smile and shook my head slightly.

"Still," she said. "My question remains: What do you want to do?"

There were so many answers to that question. I wanted to go home. I wanted to stay here with Irene. I wanted to bring Lydia back. I wanted to punish Anthony and his boss. I wanted to go back in time, before my attempt to end my own life. I wanted to go forward in time, past this horrible mess, to a time when Irene and I could be together. I wanted... I wanted so much.

I returned my focus to Irene. "I don't belong here," I said.

She shook her head.

"And you don't belong in my world, either."

Again, she shook her head.

"Where does that leave us, then?" I asked.

She put her hand on my face. "Here. Now."

I nodded. "I guess that's all we ever have."

She gave me a small, brave smile. "You're wiser than you realize, Jack Richmond."

We gazed into each other's eyes for a long moment. I saw moisture building up in hers, and I could feel it building up in mine.

"Say it," she said. "Say it out loud."

Back to the question again: *What did I want to do?*

"What I want to do," I said, "is put everything back where it belongs and close these doorways between our worlds."

A tear escaped the corner of her eye. "Yes," she whispered.

I knew without doubt that she meant not only that she agreed with me, but that she knew it was possible for us to do it. I also knew that it meant I would never see her again.

"What will happen to you?" I asked.

"I'll live a quiet life, as a servant, or something like that. Pretending not to have my powers. Never using them again. Not in the way I have been, at any rate."

"Not in the way you have been?"

"I'll use my powers only to convince others I have none, and to keep watch on the barrier between our worlds."

"You'll be able to do that?"

"Yes, and so will you. We'll be connected, Jack. You and I. Guardians of the barrier. You in your world, I in mine."

"Guardians—?"

She gripped my shoulders. "Trust me, Jack."

Of course I trusted her. She hadn't steered me wrong yet.

"Do you still have the stone I gave you?" she asked.

"Yes, it's back in my apartment. On my world."

"Good. And I have something of yours, too."

"You do?"

"Yes. You left some of your belongings behind, remember? In Councillor Greaves' house?"

I'd nearly forgotten, what with everything that had transpired since.

"Right. My clothes. My wallet."

"Yes, and your wristwatch."

"I left my watch behind?" I didn't even remember taking it off. Obviously I must have, when I went to bed in the councillor's guest room.

"After you disappeared from the train, I told Councillor Greaves that it would be easier for me to get a sense of you if had something that belonged to you."

I nodded again.

"So you see," she said. "We'll be connected. Always."

That was a comfort. A small one, but a comfort nonetheless.

Another tear began to run down her cheek. I wiped it away with my thumb.

"I love you, Irene," I said.

She wiped a tear off my face, a tear I hadn't even realized was there.

"And I love *you*, Jack."

We kissed again, and the whiteness swept through me, scattering me, displacing me.

And I was gone.

♦

I awoke to more whiteness. Bright whiteness. Unbearably bright whiteness. I squinted at it, wondering where I was this time. Part of me hoped it was some kind of afterlife.

"He's conscious," a voice said. I couldn't see who had spoken. The white was too bright.

"Can you hear me?" another voice said.

"Yes," I said. My voice was weak, but it was there.

My eyes began to adjust. I began to see shapes. There was still a lot of white, but I could see other shades now, too. Pink, green, blue. All pale, all soft. But still, colors.

"Where am I?" I managed to ask.

"You're in the hospital," the first voice said.

"Oh," I rasped. "That again."

I squinted and looked around. The brightness was gradually becoming more tolerable, and I could see that I was surrounded by pink walls. A pale green curtain was pulled back and hung in bunches near the head of my bed. A person in a light blue uniform stood to my right. I knew the routine by now. This was probably a nurse.

"What happened to me?" I muttered.

"We're not entirely sure yet. You were found unconscious outside a music school in Windsor Junction. Do you remember why you were there?"

I remembered nothing about a music school. There was a vague memory of music, but beyond that, I had no clue.

"I don't remember anything. Did I get mugged or something?"

"Well, you had no I.D. on you, so that's a possibility. But you weren't injured, either, so we're puzzled as to why you were unconscious. We didn't find any signs of any kind of seizure, either. So we hoped you might remember something."

I looked blankly at her and shook my head again.

"All right," she said. "You need to rest, so just take it easy for a while. Maybe something will come back to you later on."

I nodded. "Okay."

She stepped quietly out of the room, leaving me to my exhaustion. I lay there for a long time, trying to decide whether I should think or not. I wasn't sure I wanted to think just then, but on the other hand, what the hell else was there to do?

So I allowed myself to think. I thought about everything. My suicide attempt, my visits to the other world, my conversations with Lydia—

A sob cracked its way through my chest and out my throat. Tears welled up in the corners of my eyes. Lydia was dead.

I remembered. I remembered it all. Every detail. From the interrogation room to the aborted train ride, from Charlotte's kitchen to the breakfast in the enclave.

Something jostled inside my skull when I thought of the enclave. It had to do with music and what the nurse had said a moment ago. I'd seen ripples in my room in the enclave, and for a moment those ripples had revealed guitars on the walls. And I'd heard music down a corridor. It could have been a music school. Had I been seeing back into my own world?

And if that was the case, did that also mean that the enclave itself was located in the geographical equivalent of Windsor Junction?

I sighed. More questions. I'd hoped I'd have fewer by now.

As I continued to remember all that I'd experienced, another pang of grief shot through me, not for Lydia this time, but for the loss of what I hadn't even realized I'd wanted until it was too late.

Irene.

♦

I relived everything ten times over, and then I relived it again. Nurses came and went, monitors were checked, drugs administered. I lay still through it all, answering what questions I could and ignoring the rest. Somewhere in all of that the light coming through the window began to change, and I sensed that I had been in the room for a very long time.

And then I looked at the doorway, and there was Brad.

He looked sad. His eyes were sunken, his skin sallow. He looked as if he'd been awake for a long time.

"Brad," I said, my voice slightly less raspy.

He stepped into the room. His arms were crossed, his eyes empty.

"Lydia's dead," he said.

I gazed up at him. I assumed he was making a guess, or asking a question to which he already suspected the answer. But his tone of voice suggested that he was telling me something he thought I didn't know. But how could he know? Lydia had died on another world, as far from the day to day life of Brad Williams as she could have gotten.

"They found her in her apartment. She'd been shot."

They found her. It didn't make sense. How could she have been found in her apartment?

"She—" I stammered. "She was where?"

"In her apartment," he said. He was struggling to keep the anger and blame out of his voice. I could see that. I could hear it.

"But—"

He stepped up to my bed. "Lydia's dead, and I can't even have the satisfaction of blaming you for it."

I gaped at him. "What?"

He turned away from me and stepped towards the window. "Some guys from some fucking government agency came to see me," he said. "They told me about the whole mistaken identity thing."

I squinted. "Mistaken what?"

He turned towards me. "Mistaken identity. As in, it was some other Jack Richmond that these—I don't know what the fuck they were—terrorists? gangsters? Whoever they were, they had the wrong guy."

He turned back to the window.

I tried to process what I'd just heard. Some other Jack Richmond? Mistaken identity? What the hell was going on? Who had gone to see Brad? And why?

"I just can't believe that Lydia's dead because of a fucking mistake."

He stepped away from the window and moved towards the bed.

"I still want to beat the crap out of you, even though it's not your fault. But I can't imagine anything I could do to you would be any worse than what you're doing to yourself."

I watched him as he began to pace back and forth, from the window to the door and back again.

Finally he stopped. "Just don't tell me any more fairy tales, okay? No more women from the 1940s. None of that shit."

"No more fairy tales," I said. I knew I'd never be able to speak of any of it again. It was too farfetched, too foreign, too painful. All I'd need now would be to add another element to the tale: The hidden place with the cybernetic monks in the black hoods.

Brad looked earnestly at me. "You'd better mean that."

♦

I heard people saying what a nice service it had been, how wonderfully strong Lydia's mother had been as she spoke from the podium, and how tasteful the music had been, despite it having been played by rock musicians.

I took their word for it. I'd been in a daze the whole time. I heard the odd word, the odd note, but I was mostly reeling from grief, exhaustion, confusion, and guilt.

I was also trying to stay out of the way. I didn't want to miss Lydia's memorial service, but I also didn't particularly want to interact with anyone. If people were looking at me, whispering about me, or otherwise noticing me in any way, I didn't want to know about it.

Brad had driven me to the church, Saint Matthias on Chebucto Road, and he'd sat with me during the service, but we'd positioned ourselves near the back and tried to remain unobtrusive.

Now, as I stepped out of the church, I began to feel the tears welling up in the corners of my eyes. The contrast of the bright fall sunlight with the solemnity of the ceremony just ended caused me to realize, more painfully than ever, what I had lost. What we all, every one of us in that church, had lost.

It was almost too much to bear.

Brad walked with me as we moved down the steps towards the sidewalk.

"You sure you don't want to go to the reception?" Brad asked.

"I don't think so."

"Hey, Jack," came a voice behind us, along with hurried footsteps down the concrete stairs.

I stopped and turned. Winston was trotting down the steps after us. Derek was a couple of steps behind him.

As we reached the sidewalk, Winston stepped up to me and gave me a gigantic bear hug. "How are you doing, man?" he mumbled into my shoulder.

"Okay, I guess," I said. I doubted my tone was convincing.

As Winston disengaged, Derek came up beside me and put a hand on my shoulder.

"Hey, guys," Brad said. "That was nice in there."

"Thanks, man," Derek said. "It was tough, but we wanted to do it."

Derek had switched from drums to guitar for this occasion, and he and Winston had played some beautiful compositions, some of which Lydia had written.

"You're not sticking around?" Winston asked.

"I don't think I can handle it," I said.

Winston nodded. Derek patted me on the shoulder again. "Take care of yourself, man" he said.

"Yeah."

The two of them nodded again, then headed back up the stairs and into the church to dismantle their equipment.

As we turned towards the Maritime Conservatory of Performing Arts, in whose parking lot Brad's car was situated, I had the strangest sensation that I was being watched. A quick glance across the street confirmed my suspicions. A grey sedan was parked in front of a house, a young man with an eyepatch sitting at the wheel.

A knot began to grow in my stomach. I did not need this right now, not right after Lydia's memorial service. I did not want to be reminded of the last few days.

I could taste the bile rising up my gullet as the passenger door opened and a man with short grey hair emerged and stood beside the car. He wore a slightly bemused look and the beginnings of a smirk.

"Go on ahead," I said to Brad. "I'll catch up with you."

"What's going on?"

"Just give me a second. I'll meet you at the car."

I crossed the street, leaving Brad gaping after me, and strode towards the sedan. I noted Anthony's perpetually malevolent glare as I stepped past the back of the car and stood before the older man.

"What do you want?" I asked.

"Now, Mister Richmond, is that any way to greet an old friend?"

"Spare me," I said.

"All right. Fine. If that's how you want it."

"Yeah. That would be perfect. Actually, no. What would be perfect is if you weren't here."

"Mister Richmond, I think you're being just a little bit ungrateful."

"Ungrateful? What have you ever done for me? Except cause me grief, more grief, and, oh yeah, some extra grief on the side?"

"Oh, we've done more for you than you can imagine. Who do you think came up with the story about the mistaken identity?"

I could feel the blood draining from my face.

"You did that?"

"Of course. We can do things like that. Your friend there believes it, doesn't he?"

I frowned. "Yeah. He believes it."

"Well, so does everyone else. You'll have no problems with the police. You'll have no problems with anyone, in fact."

I balled my fists and closed my eyes for a moment.

"Why would you do that?" I asked.

"Well, it's in your best interests. And ours."

"Really."

"Yes. Really."

I gaped at him for a moment.

"I see. And I'm supposed to just lie down, expose my belly to you, and say thanks. Is that it?"

"Well, that's a tad dramatic, but I certainly hoped you'd be a little more appreciative. But I suppose that would be asking a bit much, considering."

"Yeah. A lot much."

"Well, I suppose that's that, then."

He stood there for a moment, his hands in his coat pockets, looking me up and down.

"I repeat," I said. "What do you want?"

"Oh nothing much. Just making sure you're hale and hearty. Oh, and I suppose we owe you a debt of gratitude as well."

"What?"

"Oh, yes, indeed. I don't know exactly what you and that woman—Irene, was it?—I don't know what you did, but I assume we have you to thank for our return to—shall we say—normalcy?"

"Don't you even say her name," I hissed.

"Now, now, Mister Richmond. I just wanted to express—"

"I don't want to hear her name coming out of your foul mouth."

"I don't generally use profanity, if that's what you mean, but I can make an exception in this case, if you'd like."

"You know damn well what I mean."

"Yes. Actually, I do. And I must say, I'm surprised that you'd take up a dalliance with a strange woman from another world so soon after the loss of your dear Lydia."

I didn't think about his words. I didn't contemplate them, or ruminate about them, or even mull them over. I simply acted. The world turned red, and I acted.

I stepped up to him, my fists now tight balls of rage, and I slugged him hard across the jaw. He reeled backwards, lost his balance, and fell on his ass.

His compatriot was out of the car in a flash, and my left arm was suddenly pinned behind my back and tugged upwards at the wrist, but it didn't matter. My right hand throbbed in pain from the collision with the jaw bone, but that didn't matter either.

None of it mattered. Lydia was dead, and Irene was lost to me, and seeing this man sprawled on the ground at my feet was giving me the closest thing to satisfaction I'd felt in a long time.

"Let him go, Anthony," he said, sitting up and rubbing his jaw. "Our friend here is just blowing off a little steam."

He took his sweet time about it, but Anthony did eventually loosen his grip on my arm. As his boss stood up and brushed off his coat, he let go of my wrist, and I gently shook it out, willing the feeling to return.

"You're always full of surprises, Mister Richmond," the boss agent said. "I think that's what I like about you."

My feeling of satisfaction withered. This man was nearly unflappable.

"I did have another reason for tracking you down," he said, reaching into his coat pocket and producing a small card. "Here."

I eyed it suspiciously as he offered it to me, but I reached out and took it. It was a simple, plain white business card with a crisp, professional typeface. It bore the name "Amanda Garlock, M.D." with an address and phone number beneath it.

"She's a psychiatrist," the older man said. "I think she can help you."

I looked up at him in disbelief. "What on earth makes you think that I'd even consider anything you recommend?"

"Oh, I'm sure your obstinance will prevent you from seeing the wisdom of the suggestion, but don't say I didn't at least try."

With that, he got back in the car. He reached for the door, but before closing it, he leaned out and looked back at me.

"We're not the villains you imagine us to be, Mister Richmond. And Doctor Garlock is very skilled at what she does. I suggest you get in touch with her."

He closed the door. Anthony, who was now standing beside the driver door, gave me one final venomous glare for good measure, then stepped into the car and started the engine.

I crossed the street again and started walking towards Brad's car.

"What the fuck was that all about?" Brad asked as I got in.

"Old business," I said. "Business I'd hoped was over and done with."

Brad glanced back towards the spot where the car had been, then muttered under his breath and shook his head.

♦

I said very little during the ride back to my apartment building. I was drifting from grief over Lydia to grief over Irene to anger at the men in the grey car to confusion over what had happened to me over the last few days.

I knew the exhaustion would catch up with me as soon as I entered my apartment, and I welcomed the opportunity to lie down and sleep. I needed to shut out the sensory world for a while and let my brain and body catch up with themselves.

Brad pulled up in front of my building and put the car in park.

"You gonna be okay?" he asked.

I stared out the windshield. "I don't know," I said.

Brad nodded. "Let me know if you need anything, all right?"

I managed a small smile. Despite it all, Brad was still my friend.

I looked at him. "Thanks, man. I really appreciate that."

He managed to turn up one corner of his mouth.

I got out of the car and reached into my pocket for my keys. I was just about to close the passenger door when Brad leaned towards me.

"Listen," he said. "Some day you're gonna have to tell me the whole story about that suit."

I frowned. "Suit?"

He gave me a long-suffering look. "Your zoot-suit. The retro get-up."

"Oh. Right." I gave him a sidelong glance. "But I thought you said no more fairy tales."

He waved the comment away. "Call me when you feel like going for a coffee or a beer or something."

"Okay."

He put the car in gear and rumbled off. I stood on the sidewalk, watching him retreat into the distance.

I sighed and turned towards my building.

As I unlocked the front door and headed for the stairs, I thought about that suit that Brad had just mentioned. If all was as I remembered it, the garment was still hanging in my closet. I was glad I had it, because knowing the way the human mind worked, once I'd been back in my own world for a few days, I'd start doubting that my trips to Irene's world had even happened.

I hoped not, but I was pretty sure my brain would try and bring order back to its corridors in whatever manner it could.

That thought sent another pang of grief through me.

I reached my apartment door and unlocked it. I had no luggage to deposit anywhere, despite having been on the most mind-blowing trip of my entire life, so I simply wandered to the bedroom to undress. I needed a shower in the worst possible way.

I removed my shirt and threw it on the bed. I was about to unbuckle my belt, but I paused, feeling compelled to stare at the closet for a moment. I stepped around the bed, opened the closet door, and shoved some of the clothes to the left.

I sighed. There it was, in full retro splendor, the trench coat on one hanger, the suit on another. The fedora sat on the shelf above them.

I sat down on the bed, suddenly realizing my legs had become wobbly. I bent over, hanging my head between my knees, and just breathed. Relief was washing over me like a salve, and my eyes were watering.

I took a few deep breaths to bring myself back to center, then sat back up and wiped the tears from my eyes with my fingers. To my surprise, I found that when I brushed some of the wetness from beneath my eyes, more wetness emerged to take its place.

I stood up and stepped to the mirror. My eyes were red, and the tears were running down my face like a heavy rain on a windshield. I shook my head in disbelief.

I grabbed a kleenex, blew my nose, and wiped my eyes. As I balled up the tissue and tossed it in the wastebasket, I realized I was trembling.

I sat back down on the bed, trying to sort out the thoughts and emotions that were tumbling through me at the moment. As I gazed at the suit again, I began to realize what was happening. The relief at finding it was just the tip of the iceberg. Ever since this whole bizarre sequence of events had begun, there'd been small part of me that just wanted to forget everything that had happened and get back to life as usual. That part had grown larger with each bizarre experience and had reached colossal proportions by the time the soldiers had rounded everyone up at the enclave.

That part had simply not believed that anything that was happening was real.

There was another part of me, however, that believed just the opposite. Its voice had been weak in comparison to that of the skeptic, but it had been there nonetheless, and it had become stronger each time I'd encountered Irene.

My last conversation with her in the blank whiteness had clinched it. Despite our gossamer surroundings, that moment had been the most real of all.

Lydia had said it to me with her dying breath: I wasn't crazy.

More tears came as I thought of Lydia and the terrible fate that had befallen her. No one would ever know what had really happened. No one except for me and the two men from the agency.

I blinked the new tears away and looked at the suit again.

I stood and stepped towards the closet, reaching for the right-hand pocket of the suit jacket. I slid my hand under the flap, put my fingers inside, and felt around.

Sure enough, it was still there.

I pulled out the crystal and held it in the palm of my hand. It was as clear and bright as when I'd first looked upon it. It was so luminous that it nearly glowed.

It was as green as Irene's eyes.

I sat back down on the edge of the bed and stared at the crystal, looking deep into its center. A calmness descended upon me, and I closed my eyes. I recalled Irene's face, her beautiful smile, her deep pools of eyes. I could see her standing before me, as she had in the white place. I could see her reaching towards me, touching my cheek—

My eyes flew open. My hand went immediately to my cheek. My breathing had become rapid again. I had felt it. I had actually felt her hand on my cheek.

I shook my head. I must have imagined it.

I looked down at the stone again, smiling. It didn't matter. Irene and I were connected. Whatever had happened after our last conversation, I knew she was alive, and I knew that I would feel her presence even more strongly as time went on.

And I knew that we would see each other again.

I stood, still gazing at the stone, and finally tucked it back into the suit pocket, where it belonged. I kicked my shoes off, undid my belt, tossed my trousers on the bed, and headed for the shower.

www.ingramcontent.com/pod-product-compliance
Lightning Source LLC
Chambersburg PA
CBHW071142170626
46809CB00002B/737